NOW LORRAINE
HAS GONE

Jeff Lowder

ROCKHAMPTON
PRESS

Rockhampton Press

Cover design by Scott Perry

ISBN: 978-1-7340799-2-0

"No marriage is perfect," Ash said,
"but the happy couples I know are best friends—
who like to get it on once in a while."

Chapter 1

Thought I'd never see you naked again, Lorraine, and I damn sure didn't expect to find you dead."

With stark white walls and low-wattage floor lamps, the room could be part of a chain hotel anywhere. This one happens to be in St. George, Utah.

It's three in the morning and my wife—I think she's still my wife—is on her back, lifeless in a jumble of bedding and cast-off clothing, augmented breasts on full display.

"What's that, Daniel?" asks a fat guy in a wrinkled suit. The Washington County coroner and I have never crossed professional paths, but we've met.

"Sorry, Jed. I just—"

"Can you affirm this is Lorraine Horvath?"

"Yes." My voice is thick, unfamiliar.

He pulls up the bedsheet and my wife disappears forever. The sobs catch me by surprise. Lorraine, my partner of fifteen years, is gone.

But wasn't she gone the day she filed for divorce?

Maybe I could have saved our marriage, if I'd—

But she was sleeping around, not me.

Lorraine was set to take away my 401(k) and any hope of retirement.

But she died two days before the bitter divorce was final.

"Jed," I say, "what happened?"

He speaks without looking up from his clipboard. "Sudden cardiac arrest. They attempted CPR, but— So sorry, Daniel."

"They?"

"Excuse us, coming through." A couple of Sunday-suited guys maneuver a gurney stenciled Nimitz Brothers Mortuary through the narrow bathroom hall. They wiggle and wedge alongside the bed, then one asks, "You the husband?" I nod, and he hands me a pre-filled form. "Just sign at the bottom."

Still in shock, I make a scribble split by the dotted line.

With practiced efficiency, they zip her lifeless form into a black rubber bag then load it onto the cart. "We're very sorry for your loss, Mr. Horvath," one recites. "Here's a card with the number and address of the mortuary." Then Wiggle and Wedge…and Lorraine make their way out.

The coroner attempts to follow, but I stop him with, "So, Jed, you mentioned CPR. Who called the paramedics?"

He lowers his head, shakes it. "The uh, the attempted resuscitation was administered by, uh, Dr. Silberg."

"Colin Silberg? The plastic surgeon?"

He affirms with a nod.

My jaw goes slack, mouth drops open. "What was…why was my boss in a hotel room with my wife?"

Jed gives me a look I read as, You can't possibly be that slow. You graduated med school, for God's sake.

"That's really all I know, Daniel. Sorry, gotta go." I allow him out of the room with a backhanded wave and the hotel door closes behind him with a heavy thunk.

Sorrow? Relief? Something in between? It feels like I'm being torn apart by rival emotions battling inside me, wrenching my soul in opposite directions. Time ticks by, allowing the conflict its moment in my mind. Ten seconds seems appropriate.

I bury my face in my hands. "Rest in peace, darling Lorraine."

Then I scream into my palms, "Free at last, free at last, free at last."

Chapter 2

My buddy Ash and I coast our full-suspension mountain bikes down a sandy hill east of I-15, then pedal into the corrugated steel culvert that runs under the freeway.

"Watch out for baby heads," he yells.

Likely washed in by a recent flash flood, softball-sized rocks form a slalom course the length of the giant pipe. Visibility is poor—literally a glaring light at the end of a dark tunnel. I pull off sunglasses, clamp the temples in my teeth, and manage to make it through to the other side without tacoing my front rim on a bike-wrecker stone.

Eight minutes later, I'm gasping for my very life. One more crank, next breath...one more crank, next breath...I finally reach the peak of an enormous rock slab that looms west of the interstate and struggle out of the saddle. Once I've laid the bike safely on its side, I bend at the waist, propping myself up with hands on knees.

The slickrock is countless shades of gray, mottled with dark desert lichen. At the bottom of the monolith the Navajo sandstone gives way to endless desert floor, russet dust dotted with pale green Great Basin sage. God, it's beautiful. God, it's taking a long time for my heart rate to drop below the mid-100s.

"You okay, Danny?" Ash asks. "It's only been a day since, you know."

Ashan Bakri is a brilliant gastroenterologist and half owner of the clinic that has employed me for the past two decades. He's almost fifteen years my senior, but no one would guess it. At just over six feet, Ash is lanky and fit, with olive skin that does not seem to age. My late wife called us Mutt and Jeff. I'm barely five-eight with skin so pale I get a mild burn if someone mentions the sun. Where Ash is a graceful aspen, I'm more pine stump, thick muscles hiding under twenty—or so—extra pounds. Point is, in a side-by-side comparison, most people would say I lose. Hell, even his English is a little better than mine. "Not bad for an immigrant," he likes to say. This immigrant was born in Vancouver, BC and came to the US fifty years ago.

Ninety more breathless seconds expire before I'm able to answer him.

"I…really…needed…this."

Ash looks confused. "This?"

"To…clear my head…somewhere…I absolutely can't…have… a single thought but…my next breath."

"So no Lorraine talk?"

"Not today."

"Got it," Ash says. "But on a somewhat related note, I'd steer well clear of Jane if I were you."

I feign indignity. "Jane? We see the same patients, I'm just—"

"Not sure why she keeps coming on to you, but it's sure as hell not because she thinks you're a long lost Hemsworth brother. And now that Lorraine is, you know—" Ash launches himself down the back of the hill, hollering over his shoulder, "Catch me if you can, Mutt."

After the descent and another long climb, I finally do—catch up to him, that is.

We stop for a standing rest, and when my heart approaches normal, I say, "So how are things with you, Ash?"

He shrugs. "Eh."

"Eh what?"

"Got a notice from doppel yesterday."

It takes me a moment to realize he's talking about D-O-P-L, the Utah Division of Occupational and Professional Licensing. "What the fuck?" I blurt.

"Woman claims I molested her."

"Did you?" Probably shouldn't have said that.

Ash shoots me a squinty look. "Don't be a dick."

"Anything happen she might have been confused about?"

"Other than sticking a camera up her hiney? Nah. Says I fondled her seventy-year-old breasts, but I was nowhere in the vicinity."

"Of the room?"

"Of her boobs."

"Some kind of nutcase, then?"

He shrugs. "Don't have much interaction with the talking end of my colonoscopy patients. And I use Propofol for twilight sedation, so most don't remember anything afterwards."

"Nothing?"

"A few hallucinate. Hell, I had one guy come out of it and ask where Jennifer Lawrence was. Wanted to thank her for the hand job."

"Guessing he didn't complain."

"He did, actually. Didn't want to wait five years for his next—air quotes—procedure." My breathing's mostly recovered, and we share a good laugh. "This is going to sound weird," Ash says, "but I feel like somehow Silberg's behind it. Think he'd do anything to squeeze me out." Then Ash pedals off.

§

The setting sun reaches through my west-facing windows, painting stretched orange trapezoids on the kitchen floor beneath me. I'm putting in a ridiculously small load of dishes, singing along with the syncopated vocals of Johnny Nash's "I Can See Clearly Now," freestyling the first line to include "Lorraine."

Our duet is suddenly overlaid with the pulsating chorus of "Another Brick in the Wall"—my ringtone.

"Alexa, pause."

The number on the screen is from area 503. Got to be a robocall, so I decline. But before I can set the phone down, Pink Floyd is back. I answer with, "Leave me the hell alone, or I'll—"

"Danny, don't hang up. It's me, Rhonda." Long silence, then, "Rhonda Horvath, your cousin." The voice is nothing like the tentative, high-pitched tone from our teen years. She sounds calm and confident, almost sultry. Her call is a surprise, a big one. We're first cousins; Bernie, my dad, and her father, Deloy, were brothers. But I haven't spoken to Rhonda since I was seventeen. We're not estranged exactly, our lives just took different trajectories. And we have a, well, a history we've yet to work out. Or even talk about.

"How are you holding up?" she asks.

The hell? "I'm doing okay, I guess. It's, um, it's really good to hear your voice." *After nearly thirty years?* "What's up with you, Rhonda?"

"I saw a post on Facebook. Lorraine Horvath's Untimely Death. I'm so sorry."

Facebook should mind its own damn business. "I'm fine, really."

"Even so, I'm coming down."

She pauses, probably waiting for me to respond. I got nothin'.

"From Tillamook," she says.

"Tilla—?"

"Tillamook. Oregon."

"Appreciate that," I say. "I really do. But you don't need to come all the way from Timmalook."

"Tillamook, like the cheese."

Cheese?

"You need family at your side. I'm at the Salt Lake airport, about to board the commuter to Saint George."

What the hell, Rhonda? "I, er, can I pick you up...or something?"

"Nah. Already scheduled an Uber. Should be at your door by eight o'clock."

My heart rate spikes. "Okay. Can't wait to see you." I'm not being polite. This is totally unexpected, weird actually, but I really can't wait.

§

I whip the door open before she has a chance to ring the bell. Rhonda's six minutes late, but who's counting.

"Danny! Or is it Daniel now? Or Dr. Horvath?"

"Danny'll do."

Her hair is not quite shoulder length, chestnut color streaked with enough gray to confirm it's natural. Faded jeans and a flannel shirt suggest a kind of aging grunge vibe. It's good to see her after all this time. Really good. My last mental picture was of a gangly sixteen-year-old, braces accentuating her wide smile. She's an adult now. Hell, at forty-five she's just one year my junior, and her adult face is even prettier than that too-thin teenager's. Rhonda's irises are still the gold-flecked green I remember. There are wrinkles, of course, but mostly at the corners of her eyes, giving the impression of a permanent smile. Lorraine's description of me as "a pound or twenty past ideal" might apply here, but a little curvier looks just right on Rhonda.

She parks her roller bag and we share an A-frame hug with pats to backs. Then Rhonda pulls a red bandanna from the pocket of her jeans and wipes beading sweat from her eyes and forehead. "God, it's hot. It's September and I feel like I've died and gone to— Oh, shit, Danny. I'm so sorry."

"It's totally all right. Everyone around here complains about the heat."

"That's not what I was apologizing for."

"I know." We exchange cautious smiles. "Don't worry about it," I say. "For me, it's as much relief as it is grief."

Her eyes and mouth register surprise. "That sounds like a tale needs telling."

"Let me show you to the guest room," I say. "Take as long as you need to settle in. If you still want to hear them, I'll tell tales till you nod off from sheer tedium."

I stare at the bedroom door closing behind her. It seems beyond peculiar for Rhonda to show up on my doorstep after all these years. But I am happy to see her.

Thirty minutes later, Rhonda steps into the kitchen-family room, hair wet, wearing red basketball shorts and a gray Gonzaga Law T-shirt.

"How'd you even find me?" I ask.

"Searched for 'Dr. Daniel Horvath,' and your St. George clinic popped up. You should Google yourself sometime."

No thanks.

I glance at the shirt. "You're a lawyer, Rhonda?"

"Since 1998."

"Makes sense, I never could win an argument with you."

Not sure what makes me think I can read her mood— she's a virtual stranger. But somehow Rhonda seems more than just relaxed. Maybe safe is the word.

"Better after the shower?" I ask.

"Yup. I feel like a new woman."

"Me too." I grin. "But more about that later." I must be a little nervous, I mean, that old joke?

"Can I get you anything, iced tea, soda, or—"

"This an alcohol-friendly household?"

"Lorraine made sure we were always well stocked."

"That supply include the makings for a Jack and Coke?"

"Depends," I deadpan. "What's in it?"

§

"Alexa, play 'Reelin' In the Years,'" I order.

Rhonda looks up from her drink, grinning like a kid with candy. "Steely Dan! You still groovin' on our dads' old music?"

Groovin'. There's a word I haven't heard in a few decades. "You like the old stuff?"

"Yup," Rhonda says. "There's a reason they call it classic rock. But we also loved our grunge bands, as I recall. I still listen to Nirvana and Foo Fighters. How about you?"

"Yeah," I say with a lazy shrug.

Thirty seconds of silence ensue, born, perhaps, out of respect for old and really old rock and roll.

"If it's not too painful, Danny, how did your wife die? That was not on Facebook."

"Heart stopped. In bed. In a hotel. With my boss."

"Oh, my God." Rhonda pauses for a moment, then, "Foul play?"

"Nope," I say, with a headshake. "Did Facebook tell you Lorraine filed for divorce shortly before she died?"

"That explain the For Sale sign out front?"

"Yeah, she's taking half the proceeds from the house sale…and my entire 401(k)."

"Was the divorce finalized?"

"Nope.

"She's not getting anything now."

I can't help an irreverent smile. "No, I guess she isn't."

"You do something to drive her away?" An impish grin says she meant it as a joke, but try as I might, I can't ignore a little tingle of self-doubt.

Ten minutes later, Rhonda is still nursing the drink, nodding and uh-huhing convincingly while I vent about my spiteful, serial adulteress of a late wife.

"It didn't matter what I did, what I ordered at a restaurant, which tie I chose, I was always wrong."

"In fairness," she says, "at least fifty percent of the time you probably were."

"Nah. More like sixty-forty in my favor. Anyway, you don't know me well enough to—"

"Danny, here's something that hasn't changed in all these years—I can laugh at almost anything."

"Even my dead wife?"

"That cheater? The hell with her, right?"

Could it be the whiskey that's got me giggling about my two-days-gone Lorraine? In any case, it's astonishing how easily we're sliding back into the pattern of our teenage years, matching each other smartass remark for smartass remark. Maybe matching is not the right word—I've always been a beat or two behind.

Rhonda sips and listens while I recount more memories of my lousy marriage.

Once I'm vented out, I tell Alexa, "Shuffle Doctor Dan's Favs," a playlist that for me bridges time and emotion from The Beachboys to Jane's Addiction. She (it?) randomly selects "Here Comes the Sun," and the two of us listen in a silence as comfortable as too-big jeans. George finally sings the last line and the iconic outro wraps the greatest Beatles song of all time. Don't know about Rhonda, but for me the music is a time machine back to those precious years before puberty fucked everything up.

Barenaked Ladies are next: "Grade Nine." It's been a lot of years since I escaped ninth grade. The lyrics still make me cringe, but I let it play to the end.

"Wow." Rhonda's voice quavers. Is she a little bit choked up? "Hearing that, I'm suddenly at one of those awkward junior high dances, boys against one wall, girls lining the other."

"Still remember when you came over and asked me to dance," I said.

"Thanks a lot, Danny. I've been trying to forget that moment for more than three decades." She allows herself a little giggle, as sweet and innocent as that thirteen-year-old at the fifth-period Valentine's party. "You refused to dance, just left me hanging. The walk back to the girls' side of the gym seemed like five humiliating miles. So, yeah, I remember."

"I'll never forget how lucky I felt that my best friend lived close enough that we went to the same school. But you had to know the other boys teased me mercilessly. I heard 'Danny's got a girlfriend, Danny's got a girlfriend…and she's his cousin,' a whole lot. If I wouldn't dance with you—and I'm not admitting it happened that way—it was out of sheer self-preservation. I'm sorry, Rhonda."

She takes a sip of her drink, then punches me on the shoulder. "Lighten the hell up, Danny. Been a lot of water under a lot of bridges since then. Speaking of back then…" She pauses, as if deciding whether to continue or not. "You ready to talk about…you know."

I avert my eyes and give my head a sad, slow shake. Not now, not ever.

Chapter 3

S ix years ago, when my dad died, I had my first experience with the "memorial industry." It felt like a con game, and I hated every minute in that mortuary, so I'm happy to have a wing woman this time. But where is she?

"I'm so sorry for your loss, Mr. Horvath. Please have a seat." I sink into an aging leather armchair then pull half-frame reading glasses from my shirt pocket and slide them onto my nose.

Elbows on a wide desk, a fifty-something man in a too-tight suit—Roger Nimitz, the nameplate reads—issues a practiced sigh, then steeples his fingers. "I think we share one goal for our visit this afternoon," he says, "that the memory of your loving wife be properly celebrated."

Celebrated? A guilty shudder passes through me.

"Let's just keep this as simple as possible," I say. "Lorraine wouldn't want us making a lot of fuss over her." I'm tempted to reach for my nose, check if it might have grown a bit. Lorraine had craved every ounce of attention she could get, except, it turned out, from me.

Roger rolls on. "As you know, the services are really for the living, a way to pay their respects, your respects. I'm certain you'll want to create the proper atmosphere, show your friends and family how devoted you are. And as a highly respected member of our community, well…"

And there it is, the selling proposition, the real reason I should choose the "'very best of everything." If I go cheap, the community will surely think less of me. I'm probably being played, but he may have a—

"Stop right there, Roger." Rhonda is suddenly at my side.

"Excuse me? Mr. Horvath and I were—"

"It's Dr. Horvath. I'm Rhonda Horvath, his attorney."

"Attorney? Do we really need—"

"And family member. You were saying?"

Nimitz makes a feeble attempt to upsell everything from a copper-clad casket to live doves. It's tempting. I mean, who wants to come off as a cheapskate to friends and colleagues? But per our plan, bad cop Rhonda jumps in.

"Mr. Nimitz," she says, "your instructions were straightforward—keep the whole affair as inexpensive as humanly possible. Stop jerking my client, er, Dr. Horvath around."

Nimitz makes a few notes, then mumbles under his breath while he works the calculator.

"Bottom line?" Rhonda asks.

"The best I can do is $6,608, but I really don't think—"

Rhonda interrupts. "And if Dr. Horvath opts for cremation?"

I raise a halting palm. "No cremation."

"What? Thought you'd be all about sending her to hell precooked."

Roger issues a little gasp. His chin drops and his eyes enlarge.

"It's not me," I say, "it's her mother."

Rhonda looks at me like a puppy whose favorite toy just disappeared behind its person's back. "What the hell does her mom have to do with it?"

"Estelle fervently believes that when someone is cremated, there's nothing left for Jesus to call forth on resurrection day."

"What kind of mumbo-jumbo—?"

"Strictly speaking," I say, "ashes don't contain DNA." I look over Roger's shoulder to a huge painting of a hippie-looking Jesus with outspread arms. "Who knows, maybe Estelle's onto something."

Rhonda drops her head, gives it a waggle and murmurs under her breath, "Christ on a Wheat Thin cracker. You sound as loony as her."

Roger over-clears his throat. "So, Dr. Horvath, the basic package at 6608?"

"Done," I say, with no more emotion than if I'd bought a broken bicycle at a yard sale.

"Let's see it in writing," Rhonda adds.

Nimitz two-fingers the keyboard for a bit, then steps to a nearby printer, retrieves a multi-page invoice, and lays it in front of me on the desk. I poise a pen over the page.

"Hold on," Rhonda says. She picks up the little sheaf and begins reading.

Ten minutes later, Nimitz coughs, an obvious attempt to hurry her along. Rhonda yanks off her tortoiseshell reading glasses and stares down the death merchant.

"Mr. Nimitz, is there some reason you might want Dr. Horvath to sign this document before his attorney has read every word?" When it comes to bad cops, Cousin Rhonda is the best—make that worst—I've seen.

Nimitz goes bright red. Embarrassment? Anger? Both?

Rhonda takes her time with the last two pages, then nods and slides it over for my signature.

From somewhere behind the desk, the funeral director produces a debit card machine, and I swipe my VISA.

DECLINED. What the hell?

Three more tries, three more *DECLINEs.* I give Rhonda a helpless look. "I can't imagine what is…I mean…there should be close to twenty grand in the account, and another five K available credit."

The Amex Gold yields the same result.

I mumble to the desktop, "Lorraine, you conniving little…"

§

Back home, Rhonda is perched on one of four leather-clad bar stools surrounding my kitchen counter, a chunk of Italian marble the color of milk chocolate veined with gold and pale yellow. My late wife wanted an "open concept" design, so the kitchen anchors the north side of a single great room encompassing a square dining table and family/living room well-appointed with furniture in mocha leather. The south wall features a sixty-five-inch TV mounted directly onto a floor-to-ceiling wall of rounded river rock.

In the background, Alexa plays R.E.M.'s "Everybody Hurts." It's a couple of hours since the mortuary, but I'm still pacing the room like a cage-crazy bobcat.

"She cleaned me out, Rhonda. One checking and two savings accounts, plus forty grand in credit card debt. Had to dip into my 401-fucking-(k) for her casket and enough money to get me to the next paycheck." I run frustrated fingers through my hair. "Apparently, taking most of everything I've worked for wasn't enough for her."

"Almost forgot to ask, is there a will?"

"Not that I know of," I say. "Do you think she—?"

"You were legally married at time of death—law says you can't cut a spouse out unless he agrees in writing. Tell me you didn't do that."

I roll my eyes at the question. "So, the money's still mine, we just have to—"

"Find it. Yup."

"And I can just explain the fraud to the credit card companies and they'll—"

"Both names on the card accounts, I assume."

"Yeah, but—"

"No yeah-buts. You're on the hook for the credit card debt unless..."

§

"Got anything?" Rhonda calls.

I walk into the great room and say, "Went through everything I could find. Nothing. I can't imagine where Lorraine might have stashed the money. Guess it could be in a new account without my name on it, but there's no paperwork in the house."

"We'll figure it out," Rhonda says. "How about we give that a rest for now. Is there stuff left to do for the funeral?"

After perching on the neighboring stool, I say, "Not a funeral, a graveside service. Simpler, cheaper, easier."

"How long were you and Lorraine married?"

"January would have been our sixteenth anniversary."

"How much of that time were you miserable?"

"It was never great, but the past three years were hell on earth." Hearing myself say that aloud feels like a quick taser to the chest.

She gives her head a slow side-to-side. Is she sad for me or just stunned at how woefully stupid it all sounds?

"Almost since the day I started work at the clinic, I've admired Ash and Jeri Bakri."

"What? Who?"

"Ash is a colleague, gastroenterologist at the clinic. We're also biking buddies. Sixteen years ago, when Lorraine and I had just become engaged, Ash and I were taking a water break up on Smith Mesa. I asked him what the secret to the perfect marriage was."

"And?"

"'No marriage is perfect,' he told me, 'but most of the happy couples I know are best friends—who like to get it on once in a while.'"

"Best friends who get it on once in a while, huh?" Rhonda says it with a mischievous smile. "I like that."

"What he said shot through me like an arrow. In those few words, Ash had captured the only thing I've ever really wanted in my adult life. Well, that and early retirement."

"So, you didn't marry your best friend?"

"I thought I had. But not long after we said 'I do,' she flipped some kind of switch, suddenly became aloof and entitled."

"Like a doctor's trophy wife?" she asks.

"More like a wannabe trophy wife who decided she hadn't aimed high enough."

"Why did you stay?"

For a few seconds, I stare at Rhonda, confused by her question. "I made a promise."

"Of course, but—"

"And I was—maybe scared is the word." Before Rhonda can ask of what, I say, "Afraid of change, of making a new life, afraid of what people would think, and by people, I mean...mostly Mom."

"Yeah." She says it with what I read as an I-get-it nod. "So, Aunt Martha is still—"

"Never moved from the house on Wilson Avenue."

"I miss our old neighborhood," Rhonda says. "How is she doing?"

My entire body sags under the weight of the question. "Mom has a bad heart valve. I've tried to convince her, but she refuses to have it replaced. Now it's too late for the surgery, and the congestive heart failure is getting worse almost by the day.

"You see her much?"

"As often as I can, but—"

"I'd love to visit your mom while I'm here." Rhonda takes my hand and gives it an empathetic squeeze. "But right now, you need a Jack and Coke. And make me one while you're up."

§

An hour or so later, Rhonda's in my recliner, and I'm draped over the couch. We're not quite drunk, but the Jack has rendered us sufficiently relaxed not to give a single shit about anything.

"Danny," she says, "haven't noticed any photos of kids or grandchildren."

21

"I wanted a couple—grandkids, that is—but Lorraine didn't want children. Did you know it's statistically quite rare to find childless grandparents?"

"Says who?"

"The Internet."

"Thank God for the World Wide Web," she mumbles into her drink. "So you chose to stay in a horrible marriage. How did you manage to remain sane for fifteen long years? Work?"

"Work? Oh, hell no. I mean there are days it feels like I'm maybe making a difference. But most of the time I just hate my boring thing. Not boring thing, that sounds like my penis. I definitely don't hate that." I giggle. "I mean…my, my work."

"Okay, so just quit and—"

"Bust…bus dishes at the Chuck-A-Rama?"

"Chuck-A-Whata?"

"Chuck-A-Rama. It's a local reshta, rest, uh…food place. All-you-can-eat."

She shoots me a disgusted look. "You sure dermatologist or busboy are your only two career options?"

I take a second sip of my third drink. "Well, I got an idea for a screenplay based on a comic book superhero," I say, exaggerating the sarcasm. "That's never been done, sho…so maybe it'll be a big…you know, a hit. And once I quit the clinic, I could hook up with—"

"With whom?"

Whoopsie. In vino veri-something.

"Tell me about your job, Rhonda. What does a lawyer do in Timmalook?" Et voilà! Subject officially changed.

"Same as lawyers everywhere, make people's lives a living hell for money."

My laugh is grossly overmatched to the old joke. Getting closer to drunk perhaps? "Seriously, Rhonda. We haven't seen each other since we were teenagers. I want to know what your life has been like since…I don't even know if you're married. I mean, your name's still Horvath."

"Nice try," she says. "But back to the original question, who would you hook up with?"

I may have been a little quick to declare voilà!

"No one. Anyone," I mumble.

Rhonda's expression says she's not buying it. "This anyone have a name?"

"It's Jane. But she's kind of a co-worker, so—"

"You and this Jane having an affair, Danny?"

"She came on to me a couple of times, but I regifted…resisted because I was—"

"Married?"

I confirm with a nod.

"You remained faithful to the woman you couldn't stand to be with?" she says. "That's kind of shweet."

Shweet?

"But now she's dead," Rhonda continues, "so screw her."

Addled by alcohol, my brain struggles with Rhonda's last sentence. Did she mean just go for it with Jane? Or maybe screw my dead wife, which is a pretty disgusting thing to say, even for someone who's more than half in the bag.

"So are you?" I ask.

"Are I what?" Rhonda asks.

"Married?"

"For thirteen months," she says, "twenty years ago."

It surprises me a little that Rhonda has spent the last two decades alone. I mean, she's smart, easy on the eyes…but there is the little matter of her unisex wardrobe.

As if she'd read my mind, Rhonda says, "Straight as an arrow, if that's what you're ponderin', Daniel-san. Believe me, I've had more than my share of lungerack…lumberjack dick."

She may be drunker than I am.

"Prorty rights."

"Huh?"

"Prorty rights. I'm a prorty…property rights attorney. I sue little farmers." Giggles suddenly overwhelm her. "God, that sounds like rural miglets…midgets. Small dairy farmers. I help big ag rezone or eminent-domain the little guys out of business."

"Rhonda, that sounds   "

"Horrible, right?"

I should be happy to have company in my misery, but mostly I feel drunk-sad for my friend.

"And I raise eggs," she blurts.

"People can't raise eggs, silly."

"'Course not," she titters. "I raise chickens…and they raise the eggs." Heavy sigh. "I'm very tired."

She leaves the recliner and pushes her way onto the couch, forcing me to the floor. Before long, her breathing transitions to the ragged snoring of drunken slumber. But sleep eludes me. My jacked-up mind is racing tight circles around a single thought: What kind of idiot gets bombed a few hours before the craziest day of his life? Make that second craziest—so far.

Chapter 4

Rain is rare in the desert, but when it does fall, it tends to come all at once. Like today.

Lorraine's mother flew down from Salt Lake earlier. At seventy-eight, she's a whip-thin Grande Dame, looming over me by an unstooped four inches. Estelle has to be emotionally devastated, but you'd never read it in that granite face. She, Rhonda, and I shiver shoulder to shoulder in the storm. Other than the wet chill, Rhonda seems mostly okay. I, however, am hungover, maybe even still a little drunk. The back of my head is pounding like there's a tiny auto body guy inside, thrashing a dented fender.

"Your mom's not coming?" Rhonda asks.

"She wanted to, but her doctor insisted she wasn't healthy enough to travel." Might be for the best. Mom would see through my sadness façade in thirty seconds.

Meanwhile, our favorite Nimitz brother tussles with a yellow golf umbrella. Yellow, Roger? Aren't umbrellas, funeral umbrellas, at least, supposed to be black? But black, yellow, or polka-dotted, umbrellas are useless in this wind and sideways rain. I smile to myself; ten to one Roger thinks the miserable weather is God's passive-aggressive revenge on a cheapskate widower.

The ferocious downpour stops as suddenly as it began. The clouds scud their way south, and everyone scrambles for sunglasses. Before long, wisps of steam rise from the grass and the mourners' dark clothing.

I can't really ignore my former mother-in-law any longer. "Hello, Estelle."

"Daniel." She offers an accusing hand, and I shake it. Never hugged the woman, not gonna start now. But I can be polite; I mean, after today, I'll never have to see Dragon Lady for the rest...of...my...life.

"Estelle Anders, this is my cousin, Rhonda Horvath."

A shallow nod. "Ms. Horvath." She turns and stares forward. Estelle was never one for small talk.

"Where's Mr. Estelle?" Rhonda side-whispers.

"In a box in Salt Lake City. Waiting for God to reassemble him."

Rhonda resorts to a fake cough that can't quite conceal her laughter.

From across the abyss, a dozen or so steaming people face us: Ashan and Jeri Bakri, Jane from work, and...Colin Fucking Silberg? How does he have the balls—and epic bad taste—to show up here? I glare across the grave at the adulterous bastard, soaked blue seersucker clinging to him like a pastel dishrag. Ash must see the fury in my face—he mouths *no* accompanied by a tiny headshake.

Between Silberg and me, the casket or coffin or whatever it's called rests on wide nylon straps, part of a contraption that will no doubt be used to lower Lorraine the minute we're out of sight. There's a large pile of reddish dirt, make that mud, not six feet from the hole. Roger had tried hard to convince me to pay an extra hundred to cover it with plastic grass. Instead, I splurged on a vase of white carnations long since blustered away.

A clergyman I've never met from a church I've never entered reads some Bible passages, then invites us to bow our heads and join him in prayer. After the collective "amen," I turn and give Roger the think-we're-about-done-here nod.

"That concludes today's service," he says. "Please be careful when you—"

"No, wait." Colin takes a step closer to the casket. As if it weren't enough that the former blond surfer is five inches taller and nine years younger than me, I'll be damned if that summer-weight suit isn't already dry.

"We can't lay her to rest without somebody saying a few kind words. If no one minds, I'll go ahead and—"

"I mind, asshole." Suddenly in the grip of dizzy rage, I leap-slide across the polished wood lid, narrowly escaping a tumble into the gaping grave. I clamp my hands around Colin's neck, fully intending to choke the life out of him, and scream, "You shit scum." Shit scum? Without the hangover, I probably could have done better. But I think he gets the gist—I really hate him.

"Danny, no!" Ash manages to pry open my death grip. "It's not worth it."

I wrench free and throw a wild punch in Colin's general direction. He catches me by the wrist, yanks my arm behind my back, and leans in from behind, mouth inches from my ear. "Let it go, Horvath," he whispers. "She didn't love you. She never loved you."

"No shit," I yell. Ragged wrath consumes me, and my inhibitions evaporate like the recent rain. "You fucked my wife to death, now you can keep her. But where's...my...money?"

I spin around, grab both his ears and force his face into the mud pile. "Urphunghglog."

Mugging for the horrified onlookers, I say, "What's that, Dr. Silberg? I can't hear you."

In my peripheral vision, two wannabe heroes step forward like they're going to intervene. "One more step and I rip his lyin' ears off!" I give my threat a couple of seconds' thought. "Course that's lying ears, not lion." It makes no sense either way, but they back off.

"Arrgh!" Colin twists himself free, and we slap in each other's direction like kindergarteners at recess.

Then, without the decency of a warning, the shit scum pirouettes and catches my chin with a solid elbow. The world is suddenly out of focus, and I fall backwards, arms flailing, crashing against Lorraine's cheap casket. The box does a shuddering slide, one corner into the swampy grass, the opposite end resting precariously against the tipped aluminum frame.

I see fuzzy Estelle faint dead away and hear Rhonda saying, "Daniel Horvath, you're an idiot—a bona fide, one hundred percent, gold-plated idiot."

Ash grabs my lapels and jerks me upright.

"Let go!" I scream.

Ash releases his grip on my suit jacket, and I stumble backwards, sliding under the tippy contraption. "Nooo!" My arms flap like useless wings, time seems to slow, then I feel a body-slam and hear a sickening plop. It takes a second or two for my brain to catch up. I'm flat on my back in three inches of muddy water—at the bottom of my dead wife's open grave.

Rolling to a slimy sit, I try to take stock of the situation. Broken bones, sprained ankles? Don't think so, however, my brain's so awash in adrenaline, I probably wouldn't feel compound fractures of both femurs. But something registers. I am indeed that gold-plated idiot Rhonda mentioned a few seconds ago. No denying I've deeply disgraced myself. I also assaulted Dr. Colin Silberg, half owner of the Red Rocks Clinic, my boss. Then it hits me with the sudden impact of today's cloudburst—a new squall is surely brewing, the perfect storm of no money and no job. And it's gathering pretty damn fast.

§

The lukewarm shower is beginning to rinse off the mud—but not the humiliation—from this day like no other. "Are you kidding me?" I break into a humorless laugh at the universe's heavy-handed metaphor for my life. Directly at my feet, rinse water darkened by desert dirt is literally circling the stainless-steel drain.

After drip drying for a minute or so, I step out of the stall, peripherally noting a muddy lump that an hour ago was a two-thousand-dollar suit. Who cares? It's not like I'll be attending another funeral anytime soon. But an unbidden image of my ailing mother sparks through my occipital lobe, and I toss the pants and jacket over the shower curtain rod to drip dry.

After a quick toweling, I throw on a terry bathrobe and head for the great room.

"Wanna talk about it?" Rhonda asks. In cargo shorts and a baggy Bulldogs tee, she's commandeered my beloved recliner. I perch on a nearby barstool.

"Talk about what?"

She shakes her head. "And he was so smart as a boy."

I don't reply. And Rhonda doesn't jump in to rescue me from the awkward silence. After about a minute, I say, "Whatever you're thinking about earlier today, it's probably worse. That guy I assaulted? He's my boss. Make that was my boss."

"Think he'll press charges? A lot of people witnessed you initiating the altercation."

Initiating the altercation? There's some lawyer talk. "I doubt he'll want to make this an ongoing story in The Spectrum."

Her left eyebrow rises.

"Local paper."

"Forget him," she says. "You can get a new job in a heartbeat, Danny. Better yet, open your own practice."

"That would take a lot of cash, and I don't—"

"The money's still yours. Probably," she says. "It just might take you a while to track it down."

"Rhonda, I wish you didn't have to get back for work. It'd be great if you had the time to help me see this through. Not sure I even know where to start."

"Actually,"—her expression is suddenly strange, almost sheepish—"I kind of do."

"Do what?"

"Have the time. I'm on a sixty-day leave of absence from work."

The hell, Rhonda? "Sixty days? For what?"

"Bereavement."

Confusion renders me a little dizzy. "You took two months off because my wife died? You never even met her."

"Danny, I owe you an explanation."

"Ya think?"

Rhonda abandons the recliner and kneels by my side. "Maybe even a confession."

"Uh, alright." My confusion now teeters on the edge of anger. "Confess away."

"I'm just coming out of a sort of long-term affair."

"Sort of long-term or sort of affair?"

"Five years...with a partner in my law firm."

"Sorry to hear it, but—"

"I just desperately needed to get out of Tillamook for a while."

"So, my wife's death was just—"

"A convenient coincidence, yes. An excuse for the leave." She averts her eyes. "I am so sorry."

"They let you take leave for a cousin, make that cousin-in-law?"

"The partners were happy for any reason to put some space between me and the adulterous asshole."

"Technically, doesn't it take two to adulter?"

"I didn't cheat on a spouse and lie to a teenage daughter," Rhonda croaks.

"You lied to me." I am now officially pissed. "My wife's death was no more than a convenient coincidence. Weren't those your words?"

"It started out that way. I admit it. My plan was to make an appearance at the funeral, then spend the rest of the month road tripping around the southwest. I was really hurting, Danny, but when I heard your voice on the phone, I...I...something inside me wanted to see you, maybe patch things up after all these years."

"Patch things up?" I say. "I told you there's nothing needs patching." But a sudden heaviness in my stomach says otherwise.

"Sorry. I guess I meant get reacquainted. And now that I'm here—"

"What? Now you're here, what? Hang around a little longer 'cause you feel sorry for me? Don't think I can sort things out for myself?"

She mutters, "You did just say you had no idea where to begin." When I don't respond, she fills the silence. "You miss her just a little, Danny? I mean, fifteen years of marriage, that has to count for something."

"You really want to know, or is this still part of the act?"

Welling tears and a tiny headshake are her only answers.

"In all honesty," I say, "there's a part of me that's sad. Being married to Lorraine was like trying to pass a kidney stone, but I kept thinking I could make it work."

"I knew it," she says. "This screw her, I'm glad she's gone act is an overreaction, a defense mechanism that—"

"And then there's the guilt. I might be dealing with a twinge of that."

"Why? She was the unfaithful one." Rhonda pauses and looks at me a little sideways. "Unless you're telling me you and that Jane—"

"Never. Assuming you're not using the Bible definition."

"The Bible?"

"You know, the part where Jesus said that looking at a woman to lust after her is committing adultery in the heart."

"In my considerable experience," she says, "adultery involves organs quite a bit lower than your heart."

I give up a weak little laugh. "I know I'm supposed to be grieving, but I can't."

"Cut yourself some slack, man," Rhonda says. "Your wife was a cheater who stole your money and died in another man's bed. You're finally free to restart your life exactly the way you want it."

"If we can find that missing money." We fall quiet for a moment, then I break the silence with, "Please stay, Rhonda. Stay as long as you can." Did I just go from throwing her out to begging her to stay in under a minute?

"Where's your phone?" she asks.

"My phone?"

"I'm adding my number to your contacts."

With a shrug, I slide it over to her. She pokes the screen a few times and sets it down. "Now it's official—I'm back in your life."

"For good?"

"Let's call it for better or worse." She hugs me from the side, real breasts against my upper arm. "Poor Danny. You've been as lonely as—"

I stand and face her. "As you, Rhonda?"

"You forgetting something?" she asks with a tiny headshake.

"Like what?"

"Like all that lumberjack dick."

We both laugh like we are still those silly teenagers. Laugh until we cry.

§

I'm just this side of sleep, recliner back all the way, eyelids heavy. Last I looked, Rhonda was on the couch, curled up like a fetus in a sonogram.

Aggressive knocking at the front door jolts me fully awake. "Open up," someone says. The voice is deep, testosterone soaked.

Out of sheer spite, I take my sweet time stepping to the door and opening it.

What the hell? Seems I was wrong about never having to see Estelle again. The witch is at my threshold, backed by a big-bellied man who could fill a Prius-sized hole in Dixie State's defensive line.

I manage to speak. "What are you—"

She steps in. Her huge companion is right behind, enveloped in a smell cloud so strong he might have come directly from a major spill at the Axe Body Spray factory. And yes, I know what Axe smells like—a lot of my patients are teenaged boys.

"I'm here for her things," Estelle says. "For my daughter's possessions."

"What exactly?"

"Her car, to start with. And the jewelry, of course."

"Remember me, Estelle?" Rhonda appears at my side. Her right hand's extended, but the old biddy makes no move to shake it. "I'm Dr. Horvath's cousin. And attorney."

Estelle says, "I'll need the car keys, and of course, the title." The man with the tattooed neck takes a step forward. "Then we'll be looking through the house for anything—"

"The vehicle belongs to Dr. Horvath, Estelle. And as far as I know, he has no plans to gift it to you or anyone else."

"The car belongs to my daughter," my angry ex-mother-in-law snarls.

"Belonged to your daughter," Rhonda corrects. "Sadly, she is deceased. The law is very clear that the surviving spouse automatically inherits—"

"She was trying to divorce him!" Estelle shrieks.

"She was Dr. Horvath's legal spouse at the moment she died. The law is clear on that."

"This isn't about the law, it's about my little girl, my flesh and blood."

"You may not like it, Estelle," Rhonda says, "but this is all about the law."

The old woman turns and gives her hired muscle a nod. He lifts a booted foot to step forward—but sets it back down when Rhonda shows him her palm.

"Would you like Estelle and her friend to leave your home now, Dr. Horvath?"

"I would. Always nice to see you, Estelle, but it's time for you and Mongo to go. And never come back."

Instead of turning for the door, Estelle lets her head and shoulders sag and commences a low whimper. She's pulled this before; it's complete bullshit.

"Daniel," she manages through the sobs, "I miss my girl so much. I just wanted a little something to remember her by."

You need a nearly new Lexus to remind you of your dead daughter? How about a fucking photo album, Estelle?

"Daniel, please."

The waterworks are as phony as the boobs we buried with her "little girl," but the tears are starting to get to me. "Maybe just—"

"She's entitled to nothing," Rhonda reminds.

"I know that. But there is a lot of stuff I'm just going to toss out."

"If that's what you want," Rhonda says, then turns to Estelle. "Just remember Dr. Horvath has the final say on what stays or goes. Every single item, no matter how small."

I nod my okay, and Estelle responds with the tiniest possible dip of her chin.

"But," Rhonda adds, "Hulk. Wait. Outside."

§

"What would make a nice memento, Estelle?" The front door has just closed behind Sammy the Bull, and I figure I can make a small attempt at civility.

"I...I'm not really sure. Maybe if I could just look through the house—"

"Not in your wildest dreams, lady." Rhonda's tone chops off any possibility of negotiation.

"How about her clothing?" I offer. "There's none of that I plan to keep."

She replies with a decidedly unenthusiastic shrug.

I lead the way to our—my—bedroom, retrieve an armload of dresses from the closet, and drop them on the bed, still on hangers.

"You want them all, Estelle? Or maybe just this little number?" I pick one up from the top of the stack, a skimpy black cocktail dress with spaghetti shoulder straps. "Work clothes," I say. "She wore these to show homes or sit at a supposed open house, always at night, for some reason." I peel off another and another and another, all equally slutty.

If Estelle's embarrassed for her daughter, she's not showing it.

"Maybe," she says, "um, just give the dresses to charity."

"I will," I say, sweeping the pile onto the floor.

"Not sure what's in here." When I pull out the top drawer of Lorraine's dresser and dump the contents onto the bed, a gasp escapes Estelle's turkey-wattle throat. And mine.

"Good God," I blurt. It's a jumble of barely-there night gowns, butt-crack panties, and lacy half-bras, none of which I'd ever seen before. I run my hand through the items, hoping to shock Lorraine's mother with the obvious decadence, but my fingers find something solid. I pull the item out of the pile and hold it up for inspection. A second or two tick by before my brain fully registers. A veiny penis. Seven or eight inches long. Rendered in rubber. Black. With an electrical cord.

"Really, Lorraine?" I mumble. "Did Colin know you were cheating on both of us?"

Estelle faints dead away, but I drop the silicone selfie stick in time to catch her. My immediate thought is to lower her to the carpet, but instead, I hoist the bag of bones onto the bed, then pause for a moment to take in the unusual sight— the old woman, eyelids fluttering, surrounded by pale pink and blue filigree like the victim of a terrorist bombing at Victoria's Secret. At first I can't decide if the vision is comical or kind of sad. Screw it, I'm going with comical. Hilarious, actually.

It doesn't take long for Estelle to recover. Once she's able to sit up on her own, she announces, "I, uh, I think I'd like to leave now."

"Of course," I say, pointing to the sex store on the bed. "You're welcome to any of these items."

Still a bit wobbly from the faint, Estelle makes her way out of the bedroom without a backward glance.

Moments later, I hold the front door for her.

Once Estelle is gone, Rhonda says, "She was definitely searching for something specific."

"Yeah," I say. "I get the sense the car thing was no more than misdirection."

Chapter 5

The cellphone jolts me awake with "Help Me Rhonda" by the Beach Boys. What the hell? I don't remember changing my ringtone. "Hello?"

"Coffee's on," Rhonda's voice says.

I throw on a robe and stumble out to the kitchen.

"Morning, Sunshine." She sets a steaming cup next to hers on the counter. "You're surely not going back to work the day after burying your wife."

"Tomorrow. Maybe."

"Perfect. Let's take a road trip."

"Road trip?"

"I haven't seen Aunt Martha in years, and you need to get up there and show your mother you're okay. How about we finish our caffeine and start driving north?"

"Okay. I'll call Mom and tell her to expect us for lunch."

"You sure she's up to cooking?"

"KFC's her favorite. We'll stop at the one nearest the house."

§

The Boss's "My Hometown" is playing on the FM, Springsteen's husky vocals weaving in among subdued organ chords. Every time I turn onto Wilson Avenue, a head rush of nostalgia blasts me. More than a third of my life was spent here learning, loving, and finally leaving.

"So, Rhonda. Is it anything like you remember?"

"Wow. Feels like I'm just walking the few blocks over to play with Danny and Jocelyn. The trees are enormous. The houses seem tiny, and I'm surprised they still look so nice."

"Gentrification."

"Gentrification? This ain't Brooklyn, Danny."

"That may not be the right word, but homes now fill up the entire valley. Well-built houses, even old ones, are at a premium. You wouldn't believe how much a two-bedroom, one-bath fixer in this neighborhood goes for."

"Like this?" she asks.

I pull into the narrow driveway and immediately realize I should have prepared Rhonda. The yard is ankle-deep in dead leaves and the house is barely visible behind an overgrowth of juniper shrubs and firethorn pyracantha thick with orange berries. The little bit of shake shingle siding that shows through is in desperate need of paint. This is sadly, conspicuously, the only place on the block untouched by the HGTV crowd.

My face warms with embarrassment that my childhood home has aged so poorly, but God knows I've tried.

"Rhonda, I know how this looks."

"Yeah," she mumbles. "Horrible."

The truth is, the dereliction is not my fault. I've offered—insisted on—paying for a major reno. But each time Mom refused so vehemently, I had to back off. Not sure I'll ever understand why, but what I do know is, I don't owe Cousin Rhonda an explanation.

We make our way up the crumbling walk to the front door. I reach out, but it swings open before I make contact. Mother has one hand on the inside knob, the other on the handle of a small, wheeled oxygen tank cart. Her tiny frame is bent to the shape of a shepherd's crook, but Mom's clothing is clean, almost stylish for her age. And the silver hair is beauty-parlor perfect.

"Oh, Daniel," Mom says in a low, gravel-gargling voice. "My poor, sweet Daniel. Get in here."

Dated is probably the word the Property Brothers would use to describe the home's interior. Dated, as in dark wool carpet, foil-accented wallpaper and a green linoleum kitchen floor. But the home is well ordered, even spotless. Pretty much the same as the day I moved out, plus thirty years of fade and frazzle.

Mom delivers sweating glasses of iced tea and the three of us take seats on matching chrome and vinyl chairs. KFC boxes rest on a Formica tabletop with half its floral pattern worn to blurred aqua. Time has taken its inescapable toll. On the home and Mom.

Rhonda's eyes are wide, seeming to take in every evocative detail. She seems overwhelmed, perhaps enthralled to have been transported back to her youth, to the place—if not the time—where carefree children were enveloped in love and safety.

"Aunt Martha," Rhonda says, "it's so wonderful to see you, to be back here after all these years."

"It's marvelous to see you, Rhonda dear," Mom says. "I can't thank you enough for coming to Daniel's rescue in his hour of need. I'm sorry I couldn't...*cough*...bear the travel to

St. George for the services. Believe me…*cough*…I know how painful it is to lose a spouse."

Mom stares off for a moment, then continues. "I think we women do okay alone, but these men—" She waggles her head and tsk tsks.

"I'm fine, Mom. Lorraine and I were a toxic combination, you knew that."

"So what? Your father and I had our problems—you don't even know. But we stayed together…*cough cough*…as God intended. You honored yourself and our family by doing the same." She looks to Rhonda, "I've always been so proud of my Daniel."

Not sure if it's anger or embarrassment that heats my cheeks. Inertia and flat-out fear of the unknown, more than some misplaced 'honor,' had held me in a marriage that was wretched for both parties. But I just smile and change the subject. "You seem more frail than last month, Mom. What does your cardiologist say?"

"Doctor Williams is sticking to his story that I'm an old fool for refusing the heart valve replacement. But my life's in God's hands, same as always. Someday, maybe someday soon, I'll just go to sleep and wake up surrounded by all my loved ones who went before. Doesn't that sound glorious?"

Glorious? To me it's a fairytale, but Mom believes it to the core, and I can't help but envy her the solace of her certitude. I offer my mother a feeble nod, then take a bite of KFC biscuit, sticky with the Colonel's honey sauce.

"So, Rhonda," Mom says, "Daniel told me you're a lawyer working in Oregon. Are you married? Kids? Tell me everything."

§

After an hour dining and chatting, Mom's face looks as drained as our tea glasses, her breaths alarmingly shallow. I help her to an overstuffed chair permanently drooped to her shape. The green tank she'd met us with at the door is now tucked back in the bedroom, replaced by an oxygen concentrator the size of a carry-on roller bag. I check the electrical outlet and the machine's green lights, then adjust the soft plastic cannula under her nose.

"Rhonda and I will stay awhile, make sure you're all right."

"Don't be silly. If you two start back now, you can beat commute traffic."

"Aunt Martha," Rhonda says, "we really don't mind staying."

"Get on out of here," Mom says with a wiggle-fingered wave. "You're already disturbing my afternoon beauty rest. But hugs first."

Rhonda bends down and gives Mom a careful embrace, then I kneel next to the chair and take both her hands in mine.

"Love you, Mom. I'll have a contractor here next week to spiff up the landscaping and give the house a fresh coat of paint."

She whispers in my ear, "I'll meet him at the door with your Dad's shotgun. You're a good son, Daniel, but I don't need your money."

Can't help but wonder if Mom's stubbornness is the same genetic defect that kept me in a loveless marriage so damn long. We kiss cheeks and I stand. Had to offer, of course, but right now I couldn't pay to have the leaves raked, let alone for a full makeover.

"Daniel." There is an urgency in Mom's voice that stops me before I cross the threshold to outside. "One more thing? Just you and me?"

"Of course. Rhonda, can you give us a minute? I'll meet you in the car."

I take the few steps back to my mother's chair and kneel next to her. "What is it, Mom?"

"It's Rhonda." She leans around me, perhaps to confirm that her niece has left the building. "I sensed something between you—a kind of chemistry. Don't let it go there, Danny."

"We're cousins. Nothing more, Mom."

"She's a blood relative, son. Don't you forget that. Not for a single minute."

§

I close the car door and stare at the sad old house beyond my windshield.

"You all right, Danny?"

"Oh, uh, fine," I mutter, slowly withdrawing from my reverie. "Thanks for coming along, Rhonda. You've always been Mom's favorite niece."

"She's an amazing woman and a huge part of my childhood."

I turn the ignition key and music pours from the car speakers, Guns N' Roses' version of "Knockin' on Heaven's Door" on 103.5, Utah's Classic Rock. Trembling at the mental image of Mom's tiny hand rapping on a huge golden gate, I click off the radio, then back out and steer the car west down Wilson.

"You okay?" Rhonda asks.

"Fine." But the quaver in my voice betrays me. "I can't help wonder how well I really knew, er, know, my mother. It may not even be real, but I have a sort-of memory of Dad hitting her and—"

Joan Jett's punchy chorus cuts me off. Seems Rhonda's ringtone is "I Hate Myself For Lovin' You," at least for this caller.

"Mark?" she answers tentatively.

Mark. Could this be the guy she came here to hide from?

Except for the occasional "but," "I don't really," and "please stop," she listens in silence for a minute or so, then, "I know. It's been hard for me, too...*long pause*...I can't talk about this right now, Mark. I'm with someone."

Can't help wondering if "with someone" was meant to communicate she couldn't speak freely or "Piss off, I've already moved on."

After a long silence on Rhonda's end, she says, "No, Mark. I can't say it. I won't say it. Goodbye."

She ends the call, and her head slumps forward.

"You okay?"

"Yeah." She sounds anything but.

"Let me guess. Mark's your fuck buddy from the law firm?"

"Fuck buddy?" bursts from Rhonda's mouth. "Screw you, Danny. Just because you're dancing on your wife's grave doesn't mean everybody— You can be a real asshole, you know that?"

My cruel words still hang in the air, and it hits me she's right. In fact, if there's something a notch or two below asshole, that would describe me at this moment.

"Rhonda, I am so sorry."

She offers no response, no indication she had even heard the apology. Her neck goes limp, and she mutters into her lap, "Why do I always fall for the married ones?"

§

We arrive home without Rhonda having spoken another word, so I decide to make margaritas as a sort of peace offering. She accepts hers with a small nod and almost-smile.

When we've nursed our margs down to an inch or so, Rhonda barks, "Alexa, play classic rock from the eighties."

"Playing rock music from the 1980s," the woman in the black cylinder says. The next sounds are shrill, cloying as sweet tea. Goddamn "Winner Takes It All." Goddamn ABBA.

"Alexa!" I shout over the musical equivalent of over chewed taffy, "Skip."

The Swedes shut the hell up, and the powerful little speaker pumps the iconic bass riff recognized across the planet as the intro to "Another One Bites the Dust."

"Queen," Rhonda says. "That's more like it." We flash each other knowing smiles and join the beat with little shoulder dips. Perhaps my cruelty from earlier has been forgiven, or at least forgotten.

"Rest in peace, Freddie," I intone as the final chord fades.

"Amen." Rhonda raises her glass in tribute, and the room suddenly throbs with Chris Stein drumming the beginning of "Call Me."

Back in the junior high years, our favorite of my dad's old CDs was "The Best of Blondie." When no one else was around, we'd crank up "Call Me" and dance ourselves into a frenzy. I'd hop up and down, arms waving, and Rhonda would transform into Debbie Harry, tossing her hair while leaping, crawling, and prowling the family room "stage." This was more than mere music. It was an experience like nothing we'd felt before, a rogue wave of hormones that washed away the feral fear of adolescence—for three minutes and thirty-two seconds.

We sit for a moment, content to bob heads and tap feet, but when Debbie belts the chorus, there's no holding still. We leap to our feet, twelve and thirteen again, flailing about in the overpowering here and now as if possessed by booming bass and those damn sexy vocals. God, it feels wonderful to let loose, just act like a silly kid again—no Lorraine to judge or put me down.

The song fades, and Rhonda pulls us into a hug, as content and sweaty as spent lovers.

We sag back down into our respective seats, and I say, "Alexa, soft rock, volume down."

Sometime later I awake from a dreamless nap. Rhonda is asleep in the fully reclined chair. Low but unmistakable, in time with my barely beating heart, Clapton's "Tears in Heaven" softens the air.

I'm sinking back into slumber when an unformed notion niggles somewhere in my head. Rhonda. Something about Rhonda. Despite the odds, it seems like we're becoming best friends again, as if time and life had never intervened. It feels good to have a pal to keep me grounded with that astonishing wit. And to dance to Blondie till we drop.

Pals. Not to worry, Mom, that's all we'll ever be.

Chapter 6

D idn't you get the message?" Ash asks. "I had the receptionist cancel your patients for—"

"I can be packed up in an hour."

It's 7:30 a.m., two days since the funereal catastrophe, and I'm in Ash's—Dr. Ashan Bakri's—office, focused on the half mug of half-caff I'm holding in my lap.

"Let me finish," he says. "She cleared your schedule for the rest of the week. And take next week off, too, if you need it. Think of it as a stay-the-hell-out-of-the-clinic-until-you-get-your-shit-together leave."

"So...you're not firing me?"

"Colin's pressing for it, but I reminded him you have a contract. Lucky for you, 'employee trashing his own wife's funeral' is not listed as grounds for termination."

"What about punching the boss?" I don't say out loud.

"Also," Ash continues, "he can't just do whatever the hell he wants. I still own half the place. You have every right to hate him, but goddammit, Danny, you better figure out a way to get past this."

"Thanks, bud." I take the tepid coffee and stand. "See you on Monday...maybe."

"And when you do come back, I'd steer well clear of Jane—and Silberg, of course. So, Danny."

"Yeah?"

"We still on for lunch?"

§

"As a physician, I feel it's my duty to tell you that stuff's gonna kill ya." We're in a roomy booth at Crown Burger, an upscale joint oddly furnished to look like an old English mead hall. The air is redolent of deep-fried onion rings, and Ash is holding half a pastrami cheeseburger so juicy I think a glob of grease just dripped off his left elbow.

He mumbles through a mouthful, "So what's with the salad?"

"Gotta get down to fighting weight. You know how it is."

"I know how it is, all right," he chuckles. "But I don't think you meant fighting weight. Maybe a different F-word. Speaking of which, is Jane putting on the full-court press now Lorraine has gone?"

"We haven't spoken since the funeral. And so what if she does? I'm a single guy."

"And she's a clinic employee. Don't hand Silberg an excuse to fire your."

I change the subject with, "What about you, Ash? Anything new in your world?"

He sets down the remains of the death sandwich and wipes hands and mouth with a brown paper napkin. "DOPL's threatening a thirty-day suspension of my license."

"The boob thing you mentioned?"

"Yeah. I think Silberg's behind it."

"You mentioned that. But it doesn't make sense to me. Your gastro patients generate a lot of income for the clinic."

He gives his shoulders a small shrug. "True enough. But there's also the issue of the partnership agreement."

"What does that have to do with—"

"It specifically states that if either of us loses his medical license, that party forfeits his entire ownership share to the other."

"What? That is completely fucked up. Did you understand it when you signed?"

"I knew what I was agreeing to, but who thinks the state is ever going to come around and yank your license?"

"Sorry, man. All of a sudden, the idea that Colin has his prints on this doesn't sound so farfetched."

"Anyway, it's worth four or five mil to him if I go down. So, yeah. And p.s., the first thing he'll do after I'm gone is fire your pasty ass."

"You got an attorney?"

"Yeah. Three fifty an hour." Ash checks his watch. "I have patients in fifteen. Finish your bunny chow, and I'll get the bill."

"Today's lunch is on me," I say, wadding up my napkin and dropping it onto the remains of the salad. "Save a few bucks for the shyster."

"Danny, you suddenly forget the part about your money going missing?"

§

Ash drives us back to the clinic and drops me in the parking lot between my Subaru and a pale blue cotton cover under which rests one of Colin's restored classic Chevrolets. Ash doesn't seem to notice that instead of immediately heading for my car, I follow him inside and stand directly behind him.

"You look wonderful, Marlene." Jane ushers a small woman with perfect silver hair and a heavily bandaged neck out of the salon. "See you next week."

51

Marlene and Ash pass in the hallway, and Jane says, "Oh, hi. Have a nice lunch, Dr. Bakri?"

"Yup," Ash mutters without looking up. "Thanks."

"It's good to see you, Dr. Horvath. Sure hope you're—"

Ash spins around. "The fuck are you doing back here?" Marlene keeps walking, as if she doesn't hear the vulgarity. He raises his eyebrows and glares at me like I just rode in on a unicorn. "You're on leave."

"I apologize for Dr. Bakri's language, Jane." I turn back to Ash and say, "Just need to grab a file of personal stuff, then I'm gone."

"The fuck you doing here?" Colin Silberg just walked into reception. *Ohhh, shiiit!*

"He's about to go," Ash assures.

"Good." Colin slaps his hands together like he's wiping away something unpleasant. "Before you go, is there anything you'd like to say to me, Danny?"

It's clear as vodka he's angling for an apology. No way. You're the one who should be begging forgiveness, you wife fucker.

"I have a lot to say to you," I growl through mostly clenched teeth. "But now's not the time...and certainly not the place."

"Let me know when you decide what is." His tone is low, menacing. "I'll be more than happy to meet you there. Just the two of us, of course."

The shameless prick just challenged me to a fight? Right here in front of Jane? Angry-dizzy hits me like a tree branch to the forehead. Before I realize it, I'm lunging at him, outstretched hands aching to find his throat and choke him until that smug face bursts like an overripe honeydew.

But something stops me midpounce; Ash has a death grip on a fistful of the back of my shirt.

"Goddammit, Danny. Get the hell out of here before I call the police myself."

Chapter 7

You okay? Rhonda asks.

"Of course." But I'm shaking like a Shih Tzu pooping peach pits. The few days off have gone by quickly. My little leave of absence is over, and the truth is I'm dreading going back to work tomorrow.

"You wouldn't be lying to Cousin Rhonda, would you, Danny?"

My ringing phone rescues me from confession. It's Ash. "How you holding, brother? Bet you're worried about coming back to work, huh?"

"I'm...okay."

"You don't sound like it. Anyway, just called to tell you Colin's in surgery at the hospital all day. You won't be running into him, at least not Monday."

"Thanks."

"However..."

"However what, Ash?"

"My strong suggestion is to take a little more time, focus on the money problem."

"I won't do that to my patients." I think about it for a few seconds, then say, "How about a compromise?"

"Compromise?"

"Yeah. Let's have Reception schedule me only on days when Silberg's in surgery."

"Good idea. I know he's out tomorrow, but don't show your face around here on Tuesday."

"Got it. Make sure the coffee's fresh."

"Yeah, yeah. Just remember, Danny, sooner or later, one way or another, you and Silberg are going to cross paths."

"Sooner or later, of course."

"When you do," Ash says, "just say hello and keep moving. Do not look him in the eye."

"I thought the don't-look-'em-in-the-eye thing was for rabid dogs."

"It is."

§

It's a little after seven, my first morning back at work after burying Lorraine. On the way to the community coffee pot, I notice an open door spilling brightness into the unlit corridor. Happy New You: J. Carneely, Medical Aesthetician, the little wall sign reads. Jane rarely sees clients before nine, but there she is, settled into a beauty parlor chair, painting her toenails. The hem of her gauzy dress is hiked up beyond mid-thigh, and I linger on the scene a little too long.

"Come in," Jane says. Busted. "Welcome to my world."

Stepping over the threshold, I enter a modern landscape of black and white punctuated by two styling chairs and a matching sofa in gleaming chrome and pink leather. The only other color comes from four shelves crammed with what look to be jars and tubes of every hair and skin product known to science. I'm instantly overwhelmed by competing smells of incense, perfume, and strong chemicals.

I think Jane is younger than me by a dozen years or so. It's hard to know—she literally earns her living making women look younger. She's also a sort of work subordinate.

Technically, she reports to the clinic owners, but the majority of her clientele are patients I refer, plus a bunch from the cosmetic surgeon, Colin Silberg. Between us two docs, Jane gets a fair amount of business, but not enough, really, to justify Silberg having torn down a wall and sacrificed two exam rooms for this salon.

Jane's medium-length blonde hair is radiant against skin bronzed by the sun, or perhaps out of one of those tubes. She flicks her head in a little lefthanded toss. Jane does the hair flip thing a lot, perhaps an attempt to cover the thin pink scar that runs from just below her left ear to about an inch from the corner of her mouth. Her appearance is otherwise flawless, and I actually find the imperfection kind of endearing.

"Hey, Dr. Horvath. What a nice surprise."

"It's Dr. Horvath to my patients," I say, "Danny to you, remember?" She gets up out of the chair and pads barefoot to the reception counter between us.

"What a nice surprise, Daniel."

Jane leans on the counter. The unscarred cheek is toward me, elbows—and those beyond perfect breasts—resting on the work surface between an iMac screen and a designer mug stuffed with Bic Stic pens. Why does it feel like her pose has been as carefully arranged as the bouquet of white roses on a glass table nearby?

Is she coming on to me? The words are bland as soft serve ice cream, but the tone strikes me as coy. And there's that suggestive stance. I may be reading too much into the situation—it's been more than a year since my late wife and I were intimate, and in my present hormonal state, a woman flipping me off in traffic would feel like an invitation to a one-night stand.

Jane has flirted with me before, but I'd never risen to the bait. If her youth and employment status hadn't been enough to stifle any ideas about office romance, I was married. Those times before.

"I'm worried about you, Daniel." Her voice is sweet as Mexican Coca-Cola.

"I'm fine. Thanks for coming. You know. Back then. At the services, I mean. Sorry if I—"

Jane steps from behind the counter. Before I realize it's happening, she pulls me in to a full-body hug. And holds it. I'm starting to feel a chubby coming on, so I gently try to draw back, but she enfolds me all the tighter and whispers in my ear. "Daniel." Her hair smells like a flower garden in early May, and my knees are rapidly turning to aspic. "If there's anything I can do, you let me know. When you're ready, of course."

She pecks my cheek, then lets go the embrace and takes both my hands.

"You're sweet, Jane. Really. But we sort of work together, and—"

She silences me with a finger to my lips. "You are a kind and wonderful man. That's all that matters." She turns to leave, then looks back over her right shoulder. "Anything."

I stammer a few nonsense syllables, then duck into my office and throw on a lab coat. Thankfully it's long enough to cover the telltale wet spot on the front of my khaki Dockers.

§

Willie (Shakespeare, not Nelson) once wrote, "time and the hour runs through roughest day," and this one is finally at an end, at least the work part. It's tempting, of course, to engage in more flirting, but right now, I'm terrified of looking into her ice-melt eyes. With a clarifying word or three, Jane could issue a call to action that I'd answer so clumsily I could never look in those eyes again. So I sit in my office, stalling, tapping one foot to the punchy rhythm of Jane's Addiction's "Jane Says." There's a hell of a lot of Jane stuff in my head right now.

Anything, Daniel. Anything.

In this moment, I'm unsuccessfully trying not to relive the memory of Jane's body pressed against mine, our eyes just inches apart, that heady fragrance. The sensations charge and feint, then charge again, assailing my crumbling resolve.

Anything, Daniel. Anything.

It's hard—make that difficult—not to mentally surrender, retreat into a little game of let's imagine a few activities that "anything" might include. I keep reminding myself why it would be wrong to act on my current feelings, but a beautiful young woman just made it clear she wants this chunky middle-aged widower. And I haven't felt wanted in a long, long time.

§

From a stone bench in Town Square Park, Rhonda and I watch the sun set while kids play in a fountain that shoots random jets of water from holes in a concrete pad.

"So, Jane said she'd do anything, huh? Get a grip, Cuz. People say that all the time."

"If you had been there, you'd have—"

"I'd have what? Gagged at the old man hugging the help?"

I take a slow breath and just let her comment disappear into the balmy fall evening.

"Rhonda, seriously, I need you to whip me into dating shape."

She leans back and gives me the once-over.

"Will you do it?" I ask. "For old times' sake?"

"Old times' sake, huh?" After a long pause, she continues, "I will, on two conditions."

"Sure, anything."

"There's that word again. I'm pretty sure you didn't really mean *anything*, so maybe ponder on that a sec."

"What are the conditions?"

"Number one." She shakes her head in feigned—I think—repugnance. "When this unsavory endeavor ends badly, and it will, I have no share of the culpability."

"Of course not. What's the second?"

"When Calamity Jane shoots you down like a clay pigeon, you'll come back to your senses and..."

I wait for her to finish, but she doesn't. "And what?"

Her voice goes low and soft, barely audible over the laughter of nearby children. "What was I thinking? There's, uh, there is no number two."

I scoot closer and give her a side hug. "You're the best, Rhonda. By the way, I'm not scheduled to work tomorrow. Got a little surprise for you."

Chapter 8

I'm so wet, and it feels amazing," Rhonda giggles.

Not sure if she intended it as double entendre—it's probably just my gutter-dwelling mind. After all, we are both being misted by a waterfall splashing into a small emerald pool.

She continues, "This is the most beautiful place I've ever been. What's it called, again?"

"Kanarraville Falls."

I'm taking advantage of a day out of the clinic to show Rhonda a perfect slot canyon thirty miles north of town. Autumn is the best time to visit—the waterflow is down, the canyon more accessible. It's also safer, but I stay alert to any sound that might be distant thunder. A cloudburst even ten miles upstream could produce the kind of flash flooding that's killed many a careless canyoneer.

"Follow me," I yell over the sounds of falling water. Years ago, someone had pounded pitons into the orange sandstone to secure a climbing rope. With the help of the fraying line, we climb-scramble up the face of the falls to the next level, another pool and waterfall.

Rhonda spies the only dry spot and soon we're perched on a boulder blessed by an unlikely patch of sun. She turns her head to catch the warmth on her face. "Ever bring Lorraine up here?"

"I offered. Once. She was not very outdoorsy...not remotely outdoorsy."

"Her loss. You've made the hike a lot, I'm guessing."

I give an affirmative nod. "Yeah. When I'm here, it's like nothing else even exists."

Rhonda glances around. "I see what you mean."

"It's just...it's good for the soul."

"Thought you didn't believe in things like souls." Without warning, she grabs my arm and pulls us both into the surrounding water. It's pretty damn cold.

"Oh my God," I squeal. "I literally heard my balls slam back up into—"

"Watch the testes-talk, old man." She backhands a splash of water in my face. "Remember we're related."

§

It's hot inside the closed-up Subaru, at least a hundred. After a couple of hours wading and swimming in the chilly water, the sunbaked interior feels kind of good. The heat is drying our shorts and shirts, fogging up the windows a little bit. Rhonda unscrews the top of her insulated water bottle and takes a few gulps. I'm holding my CamelBak in my lap, sucking on the blue tube connected to my bladder—the CamelBak bladder, to be clear.

"This Jane person," she says. "Why haven't you and she already done the deed?"

Her bluntness catches me off guard. "I...uh...it's not that simple."

She stares me down. "I'm sure you and Lorraine played hide the hotdog a few times. The whole thing is pretty straightforward...or upward." Her face lifts into a sudden smile. "Hold everything! Don't think you ever told me exactly how old this new love of your life is."

"And up until very recently," I say, "I was married, remember?"

"Nice try, Danny. Exactly how old is Jane?"

"She's, um, a few years younger than me."

"A few? As in?"

I start the engine. "Rusty Cage" by Soundgarden resumes play, much too loud. I shut the music off and turn the AC to high. "Well, she's about…I mean…"

"Five years?"

"Maybe ten." I leave out, or it could be fifteen.

"Baby Jane!" Rhonda laughs till she's nearly out of breath. "Buddy…you are about to…poke that joystick of yours…into a great big can of worms."

I know she meant it as a metaphor, but damn if an extremely unpleasant picture isn't already forming in my mind.

"But I've got you, Rhonda, to help me avert disaster."

"I have to be back at work in less than three weeks."

Rhonda arches her back and struggles out of her soggy pants. She traps the waistband between the door frame and rolled up window, and Rhonda's cargo shorts wet-slap against the Subie's outside. "Nature's clothes dryer," she says. "Pretty efficient."

"Efficient, maybe. Also pretty damn annoying." It's tempting to sneak a glance at her damp underwear, but I don't. She's my cousin, for God's sake.

"I'm almost afraid to ask," she says. "But just exactly how do you think I can aid and abet you in this ill-conceived plan to seduce a way-too-young co-worker? Need a quick anatomy review? Are you not sure you can find—"

"Cut it out. This is serious."

She shows me her palms. "Okay, sorry. How can I be of service?"

"Help me figure out what would make me attractive to a younger woman."

"How'm I supposed to know that?" she laughs.

"'Cause you're younger."

"For God's sake, Danny, I'm forty-five. You've only got me by a year."

"Yeah, but—"

"But?"

"You look so much…seem so much younger."

"For me, at least, some guy pretending to be ten years younger would be a major turnoff. You need to play to your strengths, Danny. If she's the knockout you say she is, she's used to guys hitting her up for casual sex. And—"

"And what?"

"I'm guessing most of those dudes are younger and cooler than you."

True though that may be, it's a bit of a stinger. I do a little nervous finger tap on the steering wheel. "So is there any—"

"At her stage of life, she probably wants stability over one-night stands."

"Mr. Stability, that's me."

"Not if you keep doing stuff that puts your job in jeopardy."

"I can't really take back the funeral thing, so—"

"Stability," she says, "is just another word for money. Does this chick know you don't have any?"

"Jane doesn't care about money."

Rhonda's laughter echoes between the closed windows.

"You're such a simple soul," she says. "A woman doesn't have to be a gold-digger to want some security." She releases an exaggerated sigh. "It's becoming painfully clear this is— you are—going to be a major project, starting with finding your missing money."

"So you'll help me, Rhonda?"

She leans her head back and laughs to the headliner. "A little on the nose, don't you think?"

I mentally scratch my head. "What is that supposed to— Oh, The Beach Boys."

Rhonda laughs as she pulls her now-dry shorts into the car, arches her back against the seat, and wriggles into them, both legs at once.

§

I sign my last signature on today's patient paperwork and release an audible sigh. Coming back to work part-time hasn't been too bad—at least I haven't crossed paths with Silberg yet. I'm grateful my partial week is nearly over. But instead of immediately heading for the door, I don the Sennheisers and lean back, feet on the desk, needing to stall long enough to make sure Jane's gone. I'm looking forward to seeing her, but not just yet.

Eventually I figure the coast is clear. Head still clamped between speakers, singing along, likely too loud, I walk down the hall until I'm stopped by a hand waving in front of my face. *Damn.*

I whip off the noise-cancelling phones and say, "Oh, hey, Jane. Sorry about the singing. I didn't realize anyone was still here."

"You were a little pitchy," she giggles. "That was 'Landslide,' right?"

"Stevie at her best, eh?"

She looks baffled. "Stevie?"

"Stevie Nicks. You know, Fleetwood Mac."

"I'm afraid you're wrong, Daniel. That song is by the Dixie Chicks, I mean the Chicks. Anyways, I gotta run, the love of my life worries when I get home late."

"Love of your life?"

"You've met Charles, right?"

Charles? In the little fantasy I had begun to spin, Jane was single, unattached. Why would a married woman lead me on like that? Mr. Stability Danny knows it's actually better this way, but my inner horndog can't help imagining what might have been.

Chapter 9

Rhonda stumbles out of the guest bedroom, arms forward like a B movie zombie. "Must...have...coffee," she says, making a slow-motion lunge in the direction of my half-empty mug.

"Hold on there, Elvira," I say. "If you can survive thirty more seconds, I'll get you your very own." I insert one of those little plastic pods and press the Keurig's BREW button. A half minute later, a steaming stream fills her cup. Cream and sugar are nearby on the counter, and she adds a lot of both.

"Bagels?" she asks.

"Sorry."

"Toast?"

"All I have is hot dog buns."

"With sesame seeds?"

"Do they even make seeded wiener buns?"

"Of course not," is her rather odd reply. "Toast us up a couple."

Rhonda soon finishes the crunchy roll and uses a napkin to wipe butter from her lips. "I've got some ideas about the money, and there are things we need to do," she says. "Right away."

"I'm working today."

"Have the office cancel your patients."

"What's the rush?" I ask. "It's not like Lorraine's going to be making a bunch of large purchases going forward. She's dead, remember?"

"Really?" Rhonda's voice is up a sarcastic octave. "I'd somehow forgotten."

I respond with a wordless grumble.

"Here's the deal, Daniel. Your finances are supremely screwed up. Maybe Lorraine perpetrated the skullduggery all by herself, or maybe—"

"She had help?"

"Entirely possible. So, the first order of business is to get her name off all your accounts. Go shower, then we'll start with a visit to the county clerk's office. Gonna need a stack of original death certificates before we hit the banks."

§

Our server, a tattooed bodybuilder in a too-small Metallica T-shirt, exits the kitchen balancing a sputtering platter, and the tiny El Mariachi Cafe fills with the grease-borne smell of grilled onions and peppers. He sets the chicken fajitas on the table between Rhonda and me.

"Careful," he warns, "the plate might be hot."

Might be hot? My reading glasses are already freckled from the hissing morsels.

"God, that smells good," Rhonda says.

We've had a productive morning, but it's two thirty, and we're a notch or two beyond famished. We each fill a soft tortilla and tuck in. It doesn't take long before we're staring at empty plates and licking spicy goodness off our fingers.

"Would you like a box for that?" We get a good laugh from Big Dude's joke—the loaded plates had hit the table less than ten minutes ago, but there's not a scrap of anything edible left. He nods to a waiting kid and the dishes quickly disappear, spills and spatters wiped from the table.

"Of course, we could have found some of this online," Rhonda says, "but I figured while we were right there, why not just have the bank and the credit union print it out for us. Shall we take a look?" She retrieves a manila folder from her briefcase and lays it on the table. "Let's start with one of those debit cards that got kicked back at the mortuary."

The first two pages are a list of mundane, expected expenses: gas, groceries, country club dues, etc. Page three, however, contains a stunner—$40,350.00 to Medical Marketing Services, Inc. "Holy shit!"

Rhonda's forefinger double taps the line. "What's Medical Marketing Services?"

"I...I don't... You'd have to ask Lorraine."

"I will, next time I see her. Whoever they are, they hacked your account."

"Or," I say, "Lorraine used them to hide forty grand in anticipation of the divorce."

"That's a distinct possibility. Let's just see what other surprises lurk in these pages." Rhonda licks her pointer finger and flips to the next sheet. And the next sheet and the next sheet...

§

"Sorry to disturb you," the world's most jacked waiter says. "Unless you plan to order again, we're going to need this table."

I glance at my watch, then look around the El Mariachi. It's five thirty, and the dinner crowd is already dribbling in.

"Oh," I say. "Uh…sorry."

We scoop up the papers and take them to the car.

§

"Turn off the damn air!" she yells. The fan is on high and loose pages are flying around the car like dollar bills in a cash grab machine at a furniture store grand opening. I'm laughing so hard it takes me a few seconds to find and click off the AC.

"Do I amuse you?" Rhonda asks, her voice dripping with sarcasm.

"Sorry." My giggles taper off.

"So, what do we know so far, Danny?"

"We know that someone calling themselves Medical Marketing Services has bled our—my—accounts and racked up credit card debt for a grand total north of five hundred thousand dollars." I gulp at hearing myself give voice to the amount. "Somewhere out there, some doesn't-deserve-to-live lowlife is walking around with half-a-mil of my hard-earned money. Shiiit!"

"Half-a-mil that we've found so far. What we don't know is if it was Lorraine or some Russian mobster with a computer. And we need to figure out which. Fast."

"Does it really matter? Either way, my money's gone."

"If it's a hacker, the institutions have to take the hit, not you."

"And if it was my darling Lorraine?"

"That…may be a bit more complicated. Either way, the key is finding out if Medical Marketing Services is legit, and who's behind it. So let's get home and jump on the interwebs."

§

We're back home, both perched at the kitchen island. Illuminated by just her MacBook's screen, Rhonda's face glows pale blue. I realize darkness has overtaken the house, so I climb off the barstool and take a step in the direction of the light switches. Rhonda pounds my kitchen island with the edge of a fist, and I freeze midstride.

"The bastards are a real company," she bellows.

"No need to yell, I'm right here."

"And they're registered in Utah," Rhonda yells.

"Okay. Got it. Who's the owner?"

"Utah.gov is moving to a new website. That's all the info I can get, for now, anyway. But we're making progress, Danny. Celebrate with a drink?"

"Think I'll pass tonight," I say. "I'm working tomorrow."

"Working? But I thought—"

"Just till noon. Anyway, it's caffeine-free Diet Pepsi for me."

"No alcohol? No sugar? That's like making love in a canoe."

We toss our heads back and I repeat the old joke Deloy and Bernie, our brother fathers, had told a hundred times. "How is light beer like making love in a canoe?"

We recite the punchline in unison. "They're both fucking close to water!"

There's a pause, a long silence during which I, and perhaps Cousin Rhonda, contemplate the good old days.

"After all these years," Rhonda says, "I can still see the look on Uncle Bernie's face when he found us in the basement family room. Honest to God, I thought your dad was having a stroke."

"I expected him to forgive and forget eventually," I say, "but it felt like things between my father and me were never the same after that. It was like I—"

"We."

"Like we'd committed some unpardonable sin."

"But we were just kids," Rhonda says.

"Teenagers," I correct.

"Like I said, just kids."

I roll my head and feel trapezii muscles relax a little. Maybe after all these years, it really is time to talk it out.

"Dad never would have caught us if you hadn't been moaning like—"

"Couldn't keep quiet that first time," she says, "haven't been able to any time since."

"I'm so sorry, Rhonda." I'm weeping now—pretty embarrassing. "There's no excuse for what I did. You lost your virginity to your cousin, for God's sake. Can you ever forgive me?"

What the hell, Rhonda? She's laughing.

"Lost my virginity? Is that what you thought for all these years?"

"Yeah, well…"

"Remember Bobby Sams down the block? That kid swiped my V-card six months before you and I engaged in…youthful experimentation, shall we say?"

"But you said I was the first to give you a…I mean, an…you know."

"Let's just say Bobby's cocktail frank was no match for your digits down my drawers. And speaking of la petite mort, as I recall, you happy-ended in your 501s like a no-touch faucet. Was that your first time?"

"Oh, hell no."

"So, boys were boys even before the Internet?"

"Boys have been boys since they developed opposable thumbs," I say. "Anyway, I hope the sex talk isn't making you uncomfortable." 'Cause it's got my gut flipping like a just-caught trout.

"Me? Nah. I'm just happy we cleared your conscience. And come on, if you can't have an explicit sex talk with your cousin, who can you have it with?"

My unease settles, giving way to incredible relief to know I didn't do that to Cousin Rhonda. I'm also beginning to feel increased blood flow to my nether regions. Goddammit, Danny Boy, get a hold of yourself. Not literally get a hold of yourself. Maybe think about baseball, as they say.

"Danny."

Rhonda interrupts an internal chorus of *baseball mitten...baseball stick...baseball puck*. I'm more of a football guy.

"You ever think about if we had gone all the way?"

"Never," I lie.

"What if you'd gotten me pregnant?"

"Can we just drop it, Cuz?"

"Cousin. Exactly my point. Can't you just picture a beautiful baby girl named Randy?" she says. "You know, Rhonda and Danny combined."

Careful, Danny Boy. Do not engage. But I can't help myself. "Wouldn't that be Ranny? Or maybe Donda?"

She ignores my glib rejoinder and presses ahead. "What do you think? My green eyes or your baby blues?"

"I don't really want to—"

"Let's say both."

"Both? Like one blue and one green?"

"I can almost see her," Rhonda says. "Two beautiful blue eyes."

"But you said—"

"And one greenish gold...right in the middle of little Randy's inbred forehead." Rhonda erupts into guffaws.

I give my head a disapproving shake. "That's disgusting."

"I warned you, I can laugh at anything."

Rhonda's sense of humor was always at least half-a-bubble off level, but try as I might, I can't resist her infectious glee, and just like that we revert to our smart-ass teenaged selves, anything for a laugh or a gross-out. I'm soon chortling so hard it's difficult to inhale.

When we finally return to normal breathing, Rhonda says, "Wait. There's more."

"No more, please. I just caught my breath."

"And by now our little Randy would be all grown up. In fact, she'd be almost exactly the same age as, uh, as...Jane."

Screw you, Rhonda. Now you've crossed a line. I flop into my recliner, arms folded across my chest, and begin a well-deserved pout.

"Jesus, Danny," she says. "You're as thin-skinned as a new potato." She claims a nearby section of couch.

Without warning, my brain makes a hard left turn. "While we're on the subject," I venture.

"The subject? Potatoes? Incest?"

"Adultery."

"Don't even start with me, Daniel Horvath," she snaps.

Why does Rhonda suddenly sound so damn— Oh, yeah, that Mark thing.

"Sorry, sorry. My question has nothing to do with you. It's my mother."

Rhonda's mouth drops open and her eyebrows arch. "What about your mom?"

I give my throat a nervous little clear and ask, "Did you ever hear rumors that she might, uh, might have been unfaithful to Dad?"

Rhonda jumps up from the couch. "What?" Her volume is half-a-notch below a yell. "Everybody in my house loved—loves—Aunt Martha. And we all agreed your dickhead father didn't deserve her. I never caught a whiff of scandal about your mom." After a thoughtful pause, Rhonda says, "But there must be some reason you're asking."

"I sort of have this vague memory from when I was six or seven. You know how they are, those fuzzy black-and-white images that may or may not be real after all those years."

"Yeah, got a few of my own. Some might even have been dreams."

"Anyway, it's late at night. I'm hiding at the top of the stairs in our old house on Wilson. My parents are arguing but trying to keep it down so's not to wake us kids. He slaps her hard across the face, and—"

"Your father hit your mom? I knew he thrashed you on occasion, but never her."

"I know, right? He was a repulsive verbal abuser, but other than that one time, I never saw him hit her. Guess that's part of why I don't fully trust the recollection. Anyway, he slapped her...and called her a whore. I had no idea what that word meant, but a few days later, I was angry at Mom about something and called her the name in front of Dad. She ran to her room sobbing, and he took the famous belt to my backside."

"The whole thing must have been horribly upsetting. I mean, you've certainly held on to it for a long time."

I rotate my palms up. "Yeah. Or maybe just an unpleasant dream."

Rhonda seems caught in a silent, unfocused stare. Then her eyes wander back to the MacBook and her fingers resume soft-clacking the keys.

"Anything new?" I ask.

She shushes me without taking her eyes off the computer, then a few moments later, says, "Dammit! The info on company owners and officers is still missing." Her tone brightens. "But I stumbled onto a different site with a juicy bit of info."

"Info? Like what?"

"Like the street address for Medical Marketing, and it's right here in good old St. George, Utah."

"Wow!"

"Throw on some clothes, we're about to pay them a visit."

"So where is this place?" I ask.

"I told you, St. George."

"I mean the street address."

"Eight-fifty South River Road."

The room begins to wobble. "Oh...my...God," I stammer.

"What is it?" she asks. "What's wrong?"

"That's the, the, the—"

"The what?"

"The clinic. Where I work."

We share a ten second, gape-mouthed stare, then I break the silence with, "Colin Silberg, you bastard. It wasn't enough to screw my wife, you had to rub it in by stealing my future? May God, or whoever, damn you to hell."

"You said Silberg doesn't own the clinic outright?"

"Just half."

"So, it could be the other partner, or both of them."

"He's been working hard to push his partner out," I say. "Total asshole—Silberg, that is." I'm now pacing like a tweaker in a holding cell. "I'll grab the keys. We're gonna get the whole story if I have to break every—"

"Slow your roll, Tony Soprano. We haven't a speck of evidence beyond the address. Can't even tie Silberg's name to this shadow corporation—yet."

"But there's the affair, right? Seems that's plenty enough."

"There's no prima facie evidence supporting a connection—no evidence at all, actually. Keep those angry eyes on the prize. We're trying to get your money back and threatening to fracture Silberg's legs won't help your case. In fact, I don't want you speaking about this to anyone till I dredge up at least a little more info."

"I'd actually go for his hands," I say, hot anger pulsing in my temples. "How's he gonna do those precious implants with eleven broken fingers, the miserable fuck?"

"Eleven?"

"I'd break the one with that pretentious pinky ring in two places."

Rhonda waggles her head in fake—I think—disgust. "Who's the partner?"

"Huh?"

"Silberg owns fifty percent of the clinic. Who's got the other half?"

"You'll meet Ash tomorrow night."

Chapter 10

Now who's the one with a death wish?" Ash sits across from me at Crown Burger. I'm pounding down a double cheeseburger, an ornamental pair of crossed lances decorating the wall to my left. "Your salad phase was short-lived."

I chew a juicy mouthful and swallow. "Dammit, Ash, why didn't you tell me she was married?"

"What the hell are you talking about?"

"Jane. Can't wait to get home to the love of her life? Some guy named Charles? The stud probably meets her at the door stark naked every night as hard as—"

"Oh, my God." Ash begins laughing so violently he launches a half-chewed chunk of onion ring onto the table. "That's a mental image that's going to be tough to shake."

This guy is my best friend. How could he?

"She's not married, Danny."

"Then she has a live-in boyfriend."

"Not exactly. Charles is a Jack Russell, a cute little brown and white terrier. And I hope he's not."

"Not what?"

"Greeting her at the door with a massive boner."

§

Five hours after the Charles revelation, I hang up the lab coat and open my office door. I can't see the verbal combatants from here, but I'd know the voices anywhere: Drs. Ashan Bakri and Colin Silberg. I have enough problems of my own—I'm not about to step into the middle of whatever the hell's going on.

"The fuck is this?" Ash yells to background sounds of papers being waved in the air.

"Looks kind of like a letter." Colin's voice is smug, deliberate. "If you'll stop waving it like a pom-pom, I'll take a look."

But the rustling sounds continue. "Let me save you the trouble. It's a goddamn notice from the State of Utah. Says my license has been suspended."

"Suspended, huh?" I still can't see his face, but it sounds like Colin's enjoying the interchange.

"You don't seem surprised, Silberg."

"Last I knew, that groping complaint was still unresolved, so…"

"There's no doubt in my mind you're the weasel behind this whole fraud. How'd you do it? Bribe the old lady? Pay off somebody at the state? I'm gonna—"

"You're going to what? Exactly what is it you are going to do, Dr. Bakri?" It sounds like Silberg is laughing.

Ash issues a low growl worthy of a Rottweiler, and I run out and tackle him mid lunge. It all feels vaguely familiar.

"Colin," I shout. "Get the hell out of here. Just walk away."

Ash resumes growling, and Colin Silberg leaves the waiting area, hesitantly, but without further comment.

I release Ash, and he says, "You know you couldn't have held me back for long, right?"

"Just needed to hang on long enough to exorcise the dog demon."

His expression softens. "Thanks, Danny. Don't know how much you heard."

"Enough to know your license is suspended."

"And I've got thirty days to show cause why it shouldn't be permanently revoked."

"Holy shit, Ash. Just toss you out of medicine after all these years? Leave you without a way to earn a living?"

"It's not going to happen, Danny. One fucking way or another, Silberg's going down."

§

After the events of earlier today, I expected Ash to cancel the dinner invitation. But here we are. "Rhonda," I say, "this is Dr. Bakri…Ash."

She smiles. "Nice to meet you."

"And you." The Silberg confrontation is just a few hours behind him, but whether from a deep meditation session or a secret stash of Xanax, Ash appears calm as a twelve-year-old beagle.

Ash's and Jeri's home is a tidy two-bedroom, two-bath southwest adobe. What it lacks in sheer square footage it more than makes up for in style. Rhonda seems instantly enthralled.

"Stepping into your home is like entering an art gallery."

"Thank you, Rhonda," Ash says. "I'd like you to meet my wife. Jeri is a talented interior designer."

Rhonda swivels her head to take it all in. "Talented is an understatement." She extends her hand for a shake, but Jeri draws her into a hug.

"So nice to meet you, Rhonda."

"The pleasure is entirely mine, Jeri. How did you decide on the darker, Santa Fe-style pieces?"

I've always loved the Bakri home. But tonight, I'm paying attention for the first time, enjoying seeing it through Rhonda's eyes. The furniture reminds me of gazing into a steaming cup of espresso, the rich, distressed brown set off perfectly by walls done in the palest blue. Glad no one can read my thoughts just now—a guy could lose his man card. But it really is something special.

"I wanted a kind of earth and sky motif," Jeri says.

"You pulled it off beautifully. Is the furniture your own design?"

"Actually, yes." Jeri's expression seems to be one of artistic pride, tinged with mild embarrassment at the attention. "Built by a small manufacturer in Tonala, just outside Guadalajara. They're the only builders that do the slate inlays."

Rhonda nods. "The little blocks of color are perfect against the—"

Ash interrupts with, "Am I the only one who's hungry?" We follow him through the kitchen and into the shade of a covered patio.

Rhonda issues a spontaneous "Ooh." Before us stretches the Entrada Country Club's fourth fairway, lush grass gilded by the setting sun.

"Please sit," Jeri offers. "It'll take Ash a couple more minutes to sear the tuna, and I'm dying to learn more about Daniel's new girlfriend. Tell me all about yourself, Rhonda."

Girlfriend? My hand involuntarily releases its grip, and the bottle of Corona strikes the concrete patio in a detonation of shattered glass, beer foam, and a flying wedge of lime.

§

"I'm sorry about earlier," Jeri says. "There's so much Ash forgets to tell me, half my life feels like arriving in the middle of a movie."

"Sorry, dear," Ash says. "But they would make a nice couple, wouldn't they?"

Nice couple? For God's sake, Ash, just drop it already.

"It's wonderful of you to fly down to help Daniel through this, Rhonda," Jeri says. "How did you wind up in Oregon, anyway?"

"I did my law school at Gonzaga."

"In Washington?"

"Yes, Spokane. I fell in love with the northwest but wanted to live nearer the coast. Tillamook is in dense forest, along the world's most beautiful bay. It's heaven on earth."

Ash laughs. "Southern Utah must look like the surface of the moon to you."

"It's different, for sure," Rhonda says. "But it might be growing on me."

§

It cools down a bit when the sun goes down and we move from the patio into the Bakris' living room. Something new-agey—Enya?—plays low in the background.

Jeri takes a sip of Chardonnay, then says, "You're an attorney, Rhonda, what do you think? Could the state actually revoke Ash's license to practice medicine?"

Rhonda's brow furrows in thought. "Have you engaged counsel, Ash?"

"I called her today, but Monday is the earliest she could meet." A crack is forming in Ash's calm façade.

Jeri pats his arm and says, "In the meantime, maybe Rhonda could give us her take. If nothing else, it would help you ask the right questions when you meet with Ms. Monaghan."

"I have exactly zero experience with medical licensing issues and don't know Utah law, but…" Rhonda's voice trails off and she stares thoughtfully into her wine glass.

"But what, dear?" Jeri asks.

"From what you've told me about Ash's predicament, I can't imagine it's legal to void a license over an anonymous complaint. And by the way, it's not literally anonymous."

Ash is obviously surprised. "What do you mean?"

"Someone at the state's choosing not to share the complainant's name with you. And there's no way they have that right. How can you defend yourself without knowing who made the allegation?"

"Okay, I'll make sure we discuss that," Ash says.

"The best defense is a vigorous offense." Rhonda is getting more animated as the discussion develops. "Make it clear that this is a clusterfuck—sorry, a big mess—and that someone is going to pay. I think Monaghan will agree that working the word 'lawsuit' into discussions as often as possible sometimes works wonders."

"Thanks, Rhonda," Jeri says, "you're the best." She turns to me. "Isn't she, Daniel? Isn't she just the best?"

I respond with a tiny nod and, "None better."

Jeri's smile is big, authentic. "How much longer will we have you, Rhonda? We're sure going to miss you when it's time to leave."

§

We get home from the Bakris' about nine thirty. Rhonda is through drinking for the night, but I pour myself two fingers of bourbon. She's already in my recliner. I take a nearby chair.

"Did I mention Charles is a dog?" I ask.

Rhonda turns a confused gaze to me. "Huh?"

"Charles, Jane's husband, remember?"

"Okay, but—"

"He's a dog. Not as in, looks like a mutt. He's an actual canine. She's not married after all."

For a minute or so, all is silent. Rhonda is likely considering the new information and what it implies.

"So, the snipe hunt's back on?" she asks.

I ignore the mythical sarcasm.

"It is," I say. "And I really need your help."

More silence, then, "Here's a logical first step. To someone her age, the music you're obsessed with sounds like cavemen pounding rocks together. You gotta get familiar with some pop stuff recorded after 1990."

"Pop? Don't think that's Jane's vibe." I flash on our recent "Landslide" discussion. "I know she likes the Chicks. Country, right?"

Rhonda's face puckers like she just bit into a lemon. "Ooh. I don't know a thing about that twangy stuff, but everything about anything is on the Internet. We'll hop on tonight and start figuring it out together."

"Tonight, tonight?"

"Yeah, that one. You got a dongle?" Rhonda asks.

In a painful variation of the classic spit-take, I spray bourbon out my nose and onto the marble counter. "Uh, yeah. I'm planning on sticking it into a can of worms, remember?"

"Who said dinosaurs are extinct? Not talking about the gherkin in your manties. A dongle's that little wire tail Apple had to invent when some engineer got high and said, 'Who the hell needs a headphone jack, anyway?' It'll let me connect my phone to your stereo."

"Why?"

"We just said we'd force each other to learn a little bit about Country," she says.

"You remember I have Amazon Music, right?"

"Even better," she says.

"Alexa," I holler, "play 'Cowgirl Landslide.'"

"I am sorry," says the woman in the can, "I can't find anything titled 'Cow GRILL Land SIDE."

"Alexa," Rhonda enunciates, "play 'Landslide' by the Chicks."

"Playing 'Landslide' by Chicks."

A few minutes later, the last note fades and Rhonda asks, "Keep going?"

I nod approval. "They're no Fleetwood Mac, but the cover's not bad. What's next?"

She holds up a handwritten list, a dozen songs Google said are Contemporary Country, including the one we just listened to.

"Alexa, play 'Toes,'" she says. It's an upbeat number that ends in a high-pitched holler. "Zac Brown Band. What'd you think?"

"Okay, you played a couple of songs I didn't hate. But I really don't know if this is going to work," I say. "Getting familiar with ten or twelve redneck songs won't make me into a real country fan."

"Of course not," Rhonda says. "But when she asks if you like some group you've never heard of, you could say something like, 'Sure, but I really love Rascal Flatts. "Bless the Broken Road" gets to me every time.' Speaking of which, let's give it a listen."

It's three minutes later. I turn away and mumble, "Okay." Must not let Rhonda see my eyes overflow.

"Ready for another?" she asks.

"I'm kind of tired. How about we get some sleep and hit it tomorrow?

Chapter 11

Ready to dive in, Danny?"

"Dive in?" I say. "It's eight-thirty in the morning...on a Saturday. What happened to 'good morning, Cousin Danny. May I fix you a cup of coffee?'"

"Good morning, Danny. You remember where the coffee maker is, right?" she says, then hands me a typed list of twelve country titles and "artists."

I brew a cup, then sit down and scan the sheet. "This isn't the same as last night."

"Yeah. I got up early and listened to everything on the first list," she says. "Swapped out a few, but it's still just a dozen. Totally doable, right?"

I offer a noncommittal shoulder hike.

"As you can see, 'Landslide' and 'Toes' are still on the list," she says. "Want to listen to them again?"

"Just 'Toes.'"

The intro is a single picked guitar. Nice. The melody is catchy, and the lyrics crack me up. "Reminds me a little of 'Margaritaville.'"

Cue an evil little chuckle from Rhonda. "He's hooked, now let's reel him in." She poises a finger over the keyboard. "I found another good one. You ever hear of Chris Stapleton?"

A few minutes later, Chris wraps "Tennessee Whiskey."

"Amazing."

"Pretty good, right?" she says.

After a sip of coffee, I say, "Amazing, as in not enough Rs in borrrring." I cover my mouth for a theatrical mega yawn and Rhonda shoots me a look as crusty as artisan bread. Guess I should stop smartassing; she's only doing this because I begged her to.

"You don't have to love every song, Danny, you just have to know them." She turns the page face down on the counter and says, "Name the artist."

"Maureen Stapleton."

Rhonda's not laughing. "Time to get serious, old man."

"Chris Stapleton. 'Tennessee Whiskey.'"

"Very good."

I keep any more clever comments to myself, and we get through the next nine songs in just over thirty minutes.

"So?" Rhonda asks.

"'Jesus Take the Wheel?' Jesus Christ, you gotta be kidding me."

"But you liked some of them, didn't you?"

"Whatever. I'm still more Donny than Marie."

"Let's run through the list one more time," Rhonda says. "There's some prime young hoohaw at stake here."

"But what if she takes it too far?"

"Too far?" Rhonda seems genuinely stumped. "As in, jumps your bones without foreplay?"

"That'd be just right, but it's not what I was referring to. What if Jane and I are speaking country-ese, and she says something like, 'It's so cool we both love "Hello, I'm Gone." What other Trisha Yearwood songs do you like?'"

"We already talked about that, Doctor Horvath," Rhonda says. "I think you're smart enough to talk your way out of that one. Anyway, go get your gym bag. We got more work to do."

I don't have anything like a gym bag, so I change into baggy sweatpants and an old T-shirt.

§

I love exercise, but my style is to get outdoors for a bike or a hike. So this onion-soup-sweat-smelling corner of the country club's fitness area is a light-year or two beyond my comfort zone.

We walk past a seventy-something guy with quads like tree trunks wedged into a byzantine rig. He pauses between grunting leg presses and calls out, "Welcome to the weight room."

"Uh, thanks." But there are no weights, bars, or dumbbells anywhere in sight, just a dozen white and black torture devices, each different, all equally intimidating.

In basketball shorts and a faded Eagles T-shirt—the football team, not the band—Rhonda seems to be in her element. "We'll hit the leg machines later," she says. "Let's start with getting you a bar bod."

"Bar, as in barbell?"

"Bar, as in picking up chicks at the. Start with biceps curls, of course. Young gals love them, I've been told."

"Whatever happened to financial stability?"

"Stability, sure," Rhonda says, "and rock hard bis."

We step to a contraption featuring a two-foot handle attached to black metal plates via a system of cables. Rhonda talks me through three sets of ten curls. I'm awkward at first, but don't really care. The only people in the place are Rhonda and me and Grandpa Thighmaster.

I finish up and glance around. Surprise. One wall is a huge mirror. I raise a fist almost to my shoulder and flex my upper arm. "Oh yeah, baby. Welcome to the gun show."

Rhonda must be undecided about whether to laugh or just roll her eyes, so she does both. "Can you spell cliché?" she says.

"Is it with a Y?"

"Listen up, Ahnold, time to rest that heavy artillery. We're moving on to abs."

"Thanks for all you're doing for me, Rhonda," I say, suddenly serious. "I really need you."

"By the end of the hour, you'll hate me so bad you'll spring for my plane ticket home."

"I just might." I'm joking, of course. The truth is, it's getting harder to imagine life without Rhonda around.

§

It's not Rhonda's fault. I had insisted on wrapping the session by taking over the old guy's leg press machine without adjusting the weight. Now my left quadriceps are throbbing like I just caught a swing from a Nashville Slugger or whatever they call it. Still not into baseball.

§

It's only a little after noon, but I've seen my last patient. A half day on my feet has left me with a left thigh that's aching like a bastard. But there's still one more thing to do.

In a scene reflective of the "Landslide" incident, I stop at the door to Jane's salon, singing along with the music in my Sennheisers. Jane says something I barely hear through the noise cancellation. I pull the phones down around my neck and speak. "What's that? Sorry, Jane, I couldn't hear you over—"

She stands and says, "You okay? Looks like you're limping."

I take my time responding, modulate my voice to low and manly. "It's no big deal. Little incident in the weight room."

"Weight room, eh? Sorry to hear it. Anyways, whatcha listening to?"

"Tennessee Whiskey."

She gives a knowing nod. "Chris Stapleton."

"Yeah, it's one of Chris's best, am I right?"

Her head takes a dismissive little tilt. "Kind of boring to me, but different strokes, I guess."

Can't wait to get back and tease Rhonda with that quote.

"What other ones of Chris's songs do you like?" she asks.

Think fast, Doctor Horvath. "Well, uh, there's, you know…I, I'm kind of…more into female artists right now."

Jane's eyes light up. "Me too! Kacey Musgraves is the best."

"I know. She's amazing, right?" I must sound about as genuine as a Tijuana Rolex.

"I know," she parrots. "What's your favorite Kacey tune? I want to see if we like the same one."

I'd bet a kidney we do. "You go first."

"No, you first, Daniel. You say first."

After an uncomfortably long silence, I stammer, "D…did you know a lot of Eagles songs are…uh…considered contemporary country, or at least crossover?"

She gives me a look I can't quite decipher. Confusion? Disappointment? Pity?

"So, anyway," I lie, "got to get home and let the dog out."
I escape through the front door without another word.

Does this mean I have to buy a dog?

§

Rhonda is cackling so hard she nearly topples off the kitchen
barstool. "So, you choked big time?"

"I guess so, but—"

"Tried to change the subject, then basically just lied and
ran away?"

"What else could I do?"

"Repeat after me. 'It's hard to say, Jane, Kacey has so
many great songs. But I keep coming back to Carrie
Underwood. It's been out a few years now, but every time I
hear "Jesus Take the Wheel," I still get a little teary.' Was that
so hard?"

"Not if you have time to think about it. But in that
moment, I was, I mean... You weren't there."

"You want me to come with you? Feed you lines, like
Cyrano?"

I haven't a clue what she's talking about and I frankly
don't give a—

"Shit!" she shouts. Then again with the laughter.

"What's so funny?"

"Roxane," she manages between chortles. "Roxane!"

"What's Sting got to do with—"

"She and Cyrano are cousins. Like us."

I'm as lost as an Amish grandma in Best Buy.

"Never mind," she says. "Where were we?"

"I have to get a dog, right?"

"Depends."

"On what?"

"You still thinking long-term with this girl or just a drive-by?"

"Drive-by?"

"You know, crash the custard truck then move on down the road."

"Rhonda, sometimes you can really be—"

"Which is it, a one-time thing...or a long-term relationship?"

"I...I think I might be starting to care about Jane."

"We're gonna need a dog," Rhonda says with an overdone eyeroll.

I reach for the car keys.

§

It's like Christmas morning and I'm nine years old.

"Remember all those times Casey tried to follow you to school?" Rhonda is almost yelling to make herself heard over the barks and howls echoing off the little building's concrete interior.

"Yeah. That mutt was as ugly as he was dumb," I say, "but I sure loved him."

"Me too. Did you ever get another dog?"

"Nah. Too busy while I was in school, and once I got married, Lorraine wouldn't even talk about it."

Rhonda nods, then reads the sign on the far wall out loud. "Gimme Shelter. What's the NKS mean?"

"No-kill shelter. These are the good guys. I send them a contribution every year."

A thin woman in her seventies, hippie-ish with long gray hair, frayed jeans, and a tie-dye shirt, approaches. Her name tag reads Margaret: Top Dog.

"Welcome to Gimme Shelter," Margaret says with a genuine smile. "Could I interest you in a low mileage 2014 dachy-poma-schnauzer-poo?"

The next sentence she and I recite in unison. "She's a clean one-owner." Then we laugh and share a friendly hug.

"Good to see you, Daniel. I was so sorry to hear about your wife. You doing okay?"

"I'm good, Margaret, really. This is my cousin Rhonda."

She surprises Rhonda with a hug. "Wonderful to meet you, dear. Daniel loves visiting the dogs. Window shopping, he calls it."

"Margaret," I say, "my window-shopping days are over."

"Are you finally... I mean, actually—"

"I'm getting a dog!" I take both her hands and we jump up and down like kids at recess.

Margaret turns to Rhonda and says, "Isn't it wonderful, dear?"

"It is wonderful, Margaret. It truly is," Rhonda says, without a hint of sarcasm.

§

It has been one of the happiest hours I can remember, looking at, talking about, and talking to each of the NKS's eighteen guests.

"There are three that make the most sense," I announce. "Fergie, Mads, and Huster." All three dogs are females. Fergie's a large retriever mix, tan with dark splotches, Mads a multicolored mutt with a thick, curly coat, and Huster is chihuahua and...something.

"The most sense?" Margaret says. "Sounds like you're not in love with any of them."

I squirm a little. "Not really."

"Come with me," Margaret says.

Rhonda and I follow her into a tiny office where a small dog wakes from a curled-up nap on a ratty throw rug. Then the little guy waddles to my side and snuggles against an ankle.

"Danny, meet Lee-Loo, spelled L-y-l-o-u. Lylou," Margaret says, "meet Danny." She, not he, looks up at me with huge dark eyes.

At first, I'm surprised beyond speech. Little Lylou looks to be mostly, if not completely, French bulldog, a hugely popular—and expensive—breed not to be found in any shelter anywhere. This Frenchie is medium brown with a square black head, a thick inch-long tail, and ears like a fruit bat's. Her rubbery jowls immediately put me in mind of John Goodman.

"What do you think, Margaret?"

"Full disclosure, Frenchies tend to have a lot of health issues."

Rhonda and I share a look. "We'll take Lylou," we declare with a single voice.

It doesn't take long to finish the paperwork.

"That's it," Margaret says. "Get her in for a well-dog check right away. If there are any serious problems, you can bring her back."

"Return our Lylou like a defective toaster?" Rhonda says. "I don't think so."

"Anyway, here's the name and number of a vet I recommend." Margaret hands me a business card for Nicholas Ralman, DVM. "Nick's got the bedside manner of Attila the Hun, but he's the best clinician south of Salt Lake City. You might need that with a Frenchie."

§

"Look at her," Rhonda says. "If that's not a bona fide smile, I've never seen one." Rhonda sits cross-legged on Town Square Park's soft grass. I'm pretty sure I'd dislocate a hip if I attempted her position, so I flop down in an awkward sit-lean, propped up on an elbow, legs stretched gracelessly to one side. Her stubby tail metronoming like a broken windshield wiper, Lylou pants for the sheer joy of blue sky and endless space. Who knows how long it's been since she's seen the outside of that cheerless concrete prison?

"That's a smile for sure," I say. "Don't even try to tell me that the corners of her mouth pull up just because she's breathing hard." Lylou is looking back and forth between her new human friends, grinning like…like I am right now.

Rhonda makes a kissing sound and waves a colorful braided rope. "Lylou know fetch? Know fetch, little Lylou?" she asks in a high-pitched voice. The bulldog barks and jumps at the tempting toy just out of reach.

I chime in, "You like pwetty rope, widow girl?" Of course I'm baby talking, who wouldn't be?

Rhonda tosses the toy to a spot four or five feet out. At first the dog looks confused, but with a little encouragement and lots of pointing on our part, Lylou retrieves the chew rope and drops it on the grass between us. She's snort-panting that huge smile, the pink of her lolling tongue contrasted with jet black lips.

"That's my Lylou," Rhonda coos.

After watching the girls play for a while, I take a few turns throwing the toy. Something—perhaps the filtered sunlight warming my back or the easy repetition of throw-return-repeat—slows the whole world down, calming and comforting me like a favorite sweatshirt. My fuzzy-happy mind wanders into a thought. I had never been able to articulate it before, but this, these few moments of heart-slowing, mind-quieting, drama-free serenity are precisely what I'd longed for, what I'd hoped somehow Lorraine and I might someday have. But I can't recall a single time in the fifteen years we spent together when I'd felt like I do in this moment.

Fifty games of fetch later, Lylou is exhausted, curled up in Rhonda's lap like a baby—a drooling, smashed-nose baby with ears like a fruitbat's.

"You just west awhile wif Mommy," Rhonda says.

"Mommy? Really?"

"Sure," she says. "Think of Lylou as the little girl we never had."

"We?" I'm surprised by how right that sounds.

"Yeah. With Mommy and Daddy as first cousins, this is probably exactly what our baby would look like."

I refuse to laugh. That joke is getting old, and frankly, kind of disturbing.

"Danny," she says, "was there a reason you told me that story about your dad calling your mother a whore?"

The hell, Rhonda? That was out of the blue. "It was just...I don't know...Mom's been on my mind."

"Is it possible she cheated on him?"

"No one could blame her, but I really can't imagine it."

"This is going to sound weird, but hear me out," Rhonda says. "Is there a statistical possibility, however remote, that you and your sister Jocelyn could have different fathers?"

I force myself not to gag. "No way."

"It's unimaginable, I know. But you have to admit the probability is greater than zero, huh?"

"Not by very damn much. And why lose sleep over it now?"

She looks at me without speaking, gold-flecked eyes iridescent in the desert sun.

§

A little after ten that night, I walk into the family room, Lylou close at my heels.

"Couldn't get her to sleep?" Rhonda asks.

"She just shivers every time I try to leave. Anyway, we'll find out tomorrow if there are any physical problems."

Rhonda bends over and picks up our little dog. "You are perfect, Lylou. But who knows what you've been through? Don't be scared, baby, your new mommy and daddy will never leave you."

But that isn't true, is it, Rhonda? Mommy will be flying home to Oregon soon. Much too soon.

I sit down on the carpet nearby. Rhonda takes the recliner, and Lylou curls up snug and happy in her lap. Not sure if we look like a Norman Rockwell painting, but it feels like it.

"Guess I could try one of those DNA tests," I say.

"Margaret from the shelter said she's mostly French bulldog—what else do you need to know?"

"Not for Lylou, for me. To find out if Mom—"

"Earlier today, you said you didn't even want to know."

I shrug a non-answer.

She goes silent, eyes appearing unfocused, likely deep in thought.

"Rhonda?"

She blinks back to the present. "Huh?"

"Where'd you go just then?"

"Nowhere, Danny." Rhonda lowers her head and gazes at the perfect creature snoring in her lap. Her voice is barely above a whisper. "The only reason I'm still here is to find your money. And to help Tarzan get heels to Jesus with Jane. Cousin or old friend, doesn't really matter, does it?"

Cousin or old friend? What is that supposed to mean? I haven't had alcohol in three days, but I'm suddenly dizzy as a drunk. How can I want Jane so badly, and still wish this transcendent moment with Rhonda and our Lylou could last forever?

The dog jolts awake to the pounding chorus of "I Hate Myself For Lovin' You." Rhonda shifts to reach the phone in her pocket, and Lylou hops down and stalks off in a canine version of a huff.

"Mark? Why are you—" I hear about a minute of Mark-talk leak from around Rhonda's ear. But by the time the words reach me, they sound something like "mumbledog-bananaforce-toiletcumulus."

"Mark, just stop for a minute. My future is not going to be late-night office sex and nooners at some Holiday Hotel, so just—"

After a short break, Rhonda blurts, "You what?" Pause "You're an idiot, Mark, a bona fide, one hundred percent, gold-plated idiot."

You appropriated my pet name for the Oregon asshole? Not sure why, but that pinches a little.

Rhonda ends the call and stares at the object in her hand like she's never seen a cell phone before.

"You okay?"

"Not really," she says without looking up. "The dummy just told his wife he wants a divorce."

I hike my right shoulder. "Not your problem."

"He asked me to marry him."

My mind jumps back to the half of the conversation I was privy to. Rhonda called him an idiot. But she never spoke the word 'no.'

Chapter 12

G ot yourselves a French bulldog, huh?" Ralman is tall, twig thin with half-frame readers perched near the end of a nose that's freakishly large for his nearly concave face. "Where'd you get it?"

"Gimme Shelter," I say. "Margaret recommended you."

"Margaret? I thought the woman hated my guts."

Rhonda gives a little palms-up shrug. "She also thinks you're the best vet in southern Utah."

"And you believed her? The woman who stuck you with a Frenchie?"

"We couldn't pass up on Lylou," Rhonda says, hoisting the dog onto the exam table. "Just look at that sweet face, Nick."

"Brachycephalic," he grunts, "And it's Doctor Ralman."

Rhonda gives me a crusty side-glance and blurts, "What?"

"The medical term for short head," I explain.

"Well looky here," Ralman says. "Seems Daniel took medical terminology at some point."

"He did," Rhonda says. "On his way to an M.D. degree. And it's Doctor Horvath, by the way."

"Okay, Doctor Horvath, would you care to tell us what health risks the smash mouth breeds are subject to?"

"I could, but then I'd have to bill you."

"Kill me? Are you threatening—"

"Bill you," Rhonda says. "Jesus, man, Margaret was right, your listening skills are nonexistent."

Instead of registering offense, Ralman breaks into a smile that reveals crooked yellow teeth. "Did she say I had the bedside manner of Attila the Hun?"

Rhonda cocks her head a little left. "May have."

"Then how come," he says, the nasty gash of a grin growing, "in twenty-seven years, I've never had a single patient complaint?" He ejects a snorty laugh through the outsized proboscis.

Atilla the Hun? More like Don Rickles's evil twin.

"You going to examine our dog or not, Doctor Ralman?" Rhonda says.

"Of course," he says, almost cheerily. "Let's start with a look in that mouth, bitch."

Fortunately for all of us, he's addressing Lylou. If he'd so much as glanced in Rhonda's direction when he uttered the B-word, we'd have walked out of the clinic—just after I'd stuffed his stethoscope down that veiny throat. Margaret better be right about his clinical expertise, because as advertised, the man's personality is on the left tail of the bell curve.

Fifteen minutes later, Ralman snaps off his nitrile gloves and rattles, "No problems…yet. Wash its face every day or two. Pay special attention to the deep skin folds of that ugly mug and keep everything clean and dry. This breed does not need a lot of exercise, but a little walk once a day might help keep it from getting fat—fatter. Brachies can't pant for shit, so make sure it doesn't overheat, it could die. Buy a collapsible bowl to help make sure the dog gets lots of water when it's outdoors. Any questions?"

"No," I say. "None I can think of right—"

"Before you leave, make an appointment to get the animal's teeth cleaned—goddamn mouth smells like a ferret cage. The gal up front will give you one of my cards when you pay. Tell her I said to write my personal cell number on it."

He's giving us his personal number?

"Don't hesitate to call if she has an emergency." Ralman's belligerence seems to soften just a little. "Day or night."

Minutes later, we exit the clinic. "Oh, my God," I say. "I don't know if I love or hate that guy."

"While you're deciding," Rhonda says, "bear in mind I've got the hate part covered."

§

"What do you think?"

"It's breathtaking," Rhonda replies.

"Ralman told us to make sure Lylou doesn't overheat, so I thought this might be ideal."

"It's like visiting another world," Rhonda says. "I can see my shadow. At night!"

From behind a sheer sandstone cliff, the full moon has only revealed about half itself, but there's already enough light to hike the dirt road without worrying about Lylou tripping over some unseen stone. I stop for a moment, then start belting the chorus of Cat Stevens's "Moonshadow." Rhonda joins in and we bring it home like a couple of coyotes howling at the sky.

Lylou is looking up at us as if to say, "Not sure what I've gotten myself into."

"Night hiking is my favorite thing about the red rock desert," I say. *Hiking* may be a bit of an overstatement. We parked in the Snow Canyon Sand Dunes lot and the three of us are headed up West Canyon Road, a graded dirt track that parallels the highway from behind a finned rock ridge. Not a stroll in the park, but almost.

We resume walking, and Rhonda asks, "Ever see snakes in this area?"

"Rattlesnakes? Hell, yeah. But they mostly den up at night."

"Mostly?"

I drape an arm around her shoulder and say, "Cousin Danny is here to protect you." For a few more days, anyway.

We hike another twenty minutes, then stop and perch on a low outcropping where Lylou slurps bottled water from her brand-new collapsible bowl. The mottled moon sits directly overhead, a giant pearl with perfect imperfections. I suck-squeeze the last bit of water, swirl it around my mouth, then swallow. Against a rock backrest, Rhonda is partially reclined, face upturned to the night sky. Lylou crawls into her lap and curls into a ball.

"I still need your help," I say.

"Help?"

"You're a younger, attractive woman. Tell me what else I can do to have a chance with Jane. Lose weight? Cool new clothes? What?"

She lowers her head, brow resting against fingertips. "I don't know, Danny. Maybe this whole thing has gotten too...complicated for me."

"Complicated. What does that mean?" I think I know, but for some reason I need Rhonda to say it.

She reaches over and rests a hand on the back of mine.

106

I place my hand on hers. "Yeah. Maybe if things were—" I cut myself off, already said too damn much.

She pulls her hand out and tenderly touches the backs of three fingers to my cheek. We are frozen in a moonlit tableau for almost a minute, then she leans over and kisses the top of my head. "We're cousins, for God's sake. Right?"

Something just below her left eye reflects a dot of moonglow.

§

Next day, I beg off lunch with Ash and make a Sam's Club run. I'm in and out of the store in record time, a bag of Member's Mark Exceed Dog Food over one shoulder and a box marked 23andMe under my arm.

The afternoon seems to drag on forever, but once I finally bid farewell to the day's last patient, I hurry into my office and pull a white box out of a drawer. The 23andMe packaging features a large red and green X and the words "Welcome to you." After opening the package, I retrieve a much-too-small test tube, hide it in my hand, and duck into the nearby staff restroom. After locking the door, I unzip my pants with trembling hands and take a closer look at the collection bottle. No way I pee into that tiny opening without making a hell of— Good God, Danny. You're so nervous your brain's half shut down. I tuck my manhood in and go back to the office to read the instructions.

Generating enough saliva to fill the little tube takes a few minutes, then I go online and register myself and the barcode of my sample. While I'm on the website, I pay an extra hundred to ensure I'll have results in my email within a week.

§

I mail the pouch, then for the rest of the short drive home keep asking myself, Why did I just do that? To remove any doubt that my mom was faithful to her marriage vows, of course. I told Rhonda I didn't want to know, but somewhere deep down, I do. I have to know this about my mother—and myself.

"Hold the fucking phone!" I yell at the dashboard. "This whole thing's got my mind twisted like a pretzel, but that's no excuse for sheer stupidity. My DNA results won't answer the question unless the database includes Dad's info for comparison. And the likelihood that he took the test before his death six years ago? Not greater than zero. Which means I might as well have just flushed that two hundred dollars down the—"

Then something else strikes me, almost more feeling than thought. I suddenly whiplash back to, "Even if there were a way to know for certain if I'm the result of my mom's infidelity, I could not survive a single minute with that knowledge. I choose to believe my mother is an angel on this earth and will not allow anything to change my love for her."

§

My intent had been to keep the whole embarrassing episode to myself, but when I get home, for some reason, I confess my mental lapse—and indecisiveness—to Rhonda over hot dogs and Doritos. We'd recently reminisced on how much we both love a plump frank.

I expect her to hit me with one of her patented zingers, but all she says is, "There's no way to know because your Dad never took the test, right?"

"Yup."

"You sure?"

"Of course. What are you getting at?"

"Nothing," she says. "Grab your shorts and Tevas. We've got just enough daylight for a walk."

§

When we're halfway around the park's perimeter, I hear, "He's sooo cute! Can I pet him?" A five- or six-year-old girl with umber skin and black braids is running toward us from the nearby playground.

"He's a she," Rhonda says. "And she'd love a gentle scratch."

The child kneels in the grass and gives Lylou tickles at the base of her ears. "I'm Ana Sofia," she says to the dog. "What's your name?"

"Ana Sofia," Rhonda says, "meet Lylou."

Our dog issues a happy whimper and rolls onto her back. It's an obvious invitation to a belly tickle, and Ana Sofia obliges.

"Ana," a mother-sounding voice calls. "Time to go home."

"Nice to meet you, Lylou," Ana says. "I hope to see you again sometime."

"Goodbye, Ana Sofia," Rhonda says.

Lylou must have been leash trained at some point in her past; she swaggers along the paved path that circles the park, stopping occasionally at random trees and bushes to check for peemails.

About halfway around, I spy a human form race-walking toward us. The woman is slender, with freakishly large boobs that bounce up and down with each stride. A small pup runs ahead. After a few more steps, we're face-to-face with Jane. She's leashed to a muscular little dog—a Jack Russell terrier, I assume—white on brown, ears flopped forward. Jane's wearing shorts and a jog bra that can't quite contain the twins.

"Jane, it's nice to see you." I go in for a friendly hug but draw back when Charles growls his disapproval.

"Hi." Rhonda extends Jane a hand. "I'm Rhonda. Rhonda Horvath."

"Horvath?" Jane stares at Rhonda like she just stepped out of a flying saucer. "I didn't realize…I mean, no one told me Daniel had already—"

Rhonda laughs. "Danny's not remarried, Jane. I'm his cousin. Flew down from Oregon to, you know, help settle his affairs."

Affairs? Maybe not the best word, Cuz.

"Sorry about that," Jane giggles. "But you do make kind of a cute couple."

"Rhonda, this is…uh, this is Jane Carneely," I say. "She's the clinic's aesthetician."

They shake hands, then Rhonda kneels for a closer look at Jane's dog. No growling, he takes to her immediately.

"This must be Charles."

Oh, shit, Rhonda. You're not supposed to know that.

"Yes. But how did you—"

"Oh, he, uh…he just kind of looks like a Charles."

Was the Charles thing a brain fade? Or is Rhonda having some fun at my expense?

"Lookit. How cute is that?" Jane says.

Charles and Lylou are walking around in little circles, tangling leashes and enthusiastically sniffing each other's butts.

"It is just…too…precious," Rhonda fake-coos.

Maybe I better wrap this up before Rhonda sabotages everything. "Gotta run. It was nice to see you, Jane. And to meet Charles, of course."

"Buh-bye," Jane says. "We have to set a playdate for the kids real soon." She and Charles move on.

Playdate? Kids?

Lylou tugs against her leash, and we resume the walk.

A minute or so later, Rhonda nudges my ribs with an elbow. "Nice boobies. They hers?"

"Silberg specials, bought and paid for."

Rhonda chuckles, then says, "Makeup couldn't quite hide that scar on her cheek. What's the backstory?"

"Told me it was an accident when she was a teenager."

"Car crash?"

"An accident. That's as much as she'll say about it."

"Anyway," Rhonda says, "I can totally see why you'd want a little game of hide the helmet with her. But long-term? She seems a little air-headed to me."

"I don't really need your approval, Rhonda."

"I'm entitled to an opinion—I'm your coach, for God's sake. And p.s., my dog idea is working like a charm."

Not sure how the chance encounter was her idea, but there's no denying Jane and Charles fell for Lylou—and Rhonda.

Chapter 13

I'm picking at a sad salad topped with over-grilled chicken. She swallows a big bite of burger, then attacks a heap of chili cheese fries like they were the last sustenance on planet earth

"Thanks for joining me for lunch, Jane." I'd finally gotten up the nerve to ask Jane on a non-date.

"Nuh, tonk oo." I think it's "No, I thank you," but the words get lost in a mouthful of soggy fries. She washes it all down with a couple swallows of Coke, then continues. "Sorry. Everything is sooo good here. Crown Burger is pretty much my favorite restaurant."

Not sure I'd call this joint a restaurant, but it's clean. Their pastrami burgers are amazing, and... Must not think about real food. Must focus on salad...and maybe baseball.

"It's sorta weird," she says. "I can eat pretty much anything I want and not gain weight."

In this moment, I'm not sure if I love or hate her.

"Just wait a few..." The rest of my statement would have been "years. Every bite of burger will end up on your gut or your butt...probably both." But I catch myself before the words can slip my lips.

"Is Dr. Bakri doing okay?" she asks.

"Pretty much."

"I'm kinda worried about him."

"Me too," I say. "But he's retained an attorney, so—"

"A lawyer?"

"Please don't mention it to Dr. Silberg." Not sure it matters, but still…

"'Kay."

"So, when we going to get Charles and Lylou together for that playdate?" I ask.

"How about Saturday at the dog park?"

"Perfect. Nine a.m. okay?"

"Nine? Sure," she says. "Can't wait to see Rhonda again. She seems so nice."

"Yeah, well, I'm afraid she can't make it. Saturday's her, uh, boxing lesson."

"Boxing? Wow, she's even cooler than I thought."

"Yeah. Don't ever pick a fight with her."

Jane seems unsure whether that was a joke, so she just half smiles and nods her head.

I go on. "She'll be disappointed about missing our date— our dogs' date."

An awkward silence ensues, till I break it with, "What are some of your favorite movies, Jane?"

"I don't like to go to shows alone, so I guess I'm more of a TV person. You into big brother?"

"I, uh, I only have a younger sister."

Her giggles cut me short. "Big Brother? The TV show? Duh."

Really could have done without the duh. But she leans across the table, patting my hand and offering me a great view of hidden valley. All is instantly forgiven.

§

At home that evening, Rhonda gives Alexa the order and Ted Nugent's "Jailbait" plays through the little tower speaker. Not really funny, Rhonda. Then she tilts her head back and laughs at the ceiling. "She said Big Brother? Oh, you're going to hate this so much. Did she mention any more programs?"

I signal no with a quick head waggle.

"So, Big Brother it is."

"What if she wants to talk about other shows?"

"Think we learned it's better to go deep than wide," Rhonda says.

"Huh?"

"Should've taken a deep dive into Kacey Musgraves before."

"Don't think you meant that like it sounded."

She punches my shoulder so hard I wonder if she really is taking boxing lessons. "You know what I mean."

I concede nothing more than an ambiguous shrug.

"Fire up that flatscreen, Danny, and go to On Demand."

§

A little less than an hour later, Rhonda asks, "What'd you think of the first episode? Ready to catch up on the rest of Big Brother season twenty?"

"They made twenty seasons of this junk? Who knew?"

"Millions of fans, that's who. But in fairness, probably not a single one of them is over forty."

"Those millennials are a fucking disaster."

"True enough," she says. "But don't call Jane a millennial. She'll laugh you to scorn. And whether or not she's a fucking disaster? That remains to be seen. If you're lucky."

"Very funny," I say in my best sarcastic voice. "But 'laugh you to scorn?' Who talks like that?"

"Not millennials, that's for sure."

"Yeah. Whoever they are."

"So, we binge-watch the rest of the Big Bro season?" Rhonda asks.

"Let's go out to the yard and play with Lylou."

"I'll bring the fetch rope," Rhonda says. "By the way, you ever set a time for us to hang out with Jane and Charles?"

"N…nope. Not yet."

It's technically true, the planned playdate does not include her. But I feel bad. I mean, I pretty much lied—okay, flat-out lied—to the two most important women in my life. Shiiit, Danny Boy.

§

What's left of my coffee is cold. It's a few minutes till we open the clinic, and I'm still lounging in Reception, wishing Jane would come in early. And missing Ash.

"Screw it," I say, then walk back to my office.

After logging on to the computer and reviewing the medical histories of the day's first patients, I don my doctor costume. Who the hell was it, all those years ago, that decided no one could possibly figure out you're an M.D. unless you're wearing the long white coat with Doctor Fill-in-the-Blank monogrammed over the heart?

"Hey, Danny." Ash is standing in my doorway.

"Hey, bud. What are you—"

He steps aside and gestures a woman through the door. "I'd like you to meet Lisa Monaghan, my attorney." With pulled-back hair like polished mahogany and a navy business suit, Ms. Monaghan looks very professional—and very young.

"Really nice to meet you, Ms. Monaghan." She can't be over five-two, but the handshake is not just firm, it's downright intimidating. Good catch, Ash.

"Please. Call me Lisa, Daniel."

Hell of a catch.

"Lisa and I are headed for my office to review some financial stuff."

"It could take most of the morning," Lisa says. "Join us for lunch, Daniel?"

§

The Cliffside Restaurant is perched on the edge of what St. Georgians call "The Bluff." We're seated next to a wall of windows that offer a spectacular view of the city. Our expensive salads should be here soon.

"Big step up from Crown Burger, Ash," I say. "Literally."

"Yeah, and Lisa's picking up the check."

I don't even try to hide a chuckle, and Lisa surprises me by joining in.

"At least for today," she adds.

"How'd the morning go?" I ask.

"Pretty well, except..." Ash looks to Lisa to elaborate.

"We ran across an LLC with an odd connection to the clinic."

"Odd?" I say. "In what way?"

Lisa continues. "Ash has no knowledge of the shadow company, and no ownership position."

She's definitely going somewhere with this, but I haven't figured it out yet. "And?"

117

"Have you ever heard the name Medical Marketing Services?"

§

After lunch, Ash, Lisa, and I arrive back at the clinic, park the car, then enter via the back door.

Silberg catches sight of us. "What the fuck are you doing back?" He points a finger gun at Ash and growls, "You were suspended."

Lisa steps between Ash and Colin. "I'm Lisa Monaghan, Dr. Bakri's attorney. Who might you be, sir?"

The much taller man glowers down at her. "Dr. Colin Silberg. I own the place."

Lisa extends a hand. "Nice to meet you, Colin."

Something, the vise-like handshake or perhaps hearing the young woman address him by his first name, leaves Colin without a response.

"I'm glad you're here," she says. "Gives us a chance to get clear on a few things."

"Get clear?" Silberg barks.

"First," Lisa says, "my client has not been suspended from his clinic. He's the victim of an error on the part of the Division of Professional Licensing, an error they will soon correct or face a massive lawsuit…along with anyone who may have intentionally made a false report. If there is such a person.

"Second, it's irrefutable that Dr. Bakri owns a fifty-percent share in this establishment. He will come and go as he pleases and will participate fully in all matters of management and administration of the enterprise. That includes access to all records. I repeat, all records, financial, legal, medical, and otherwise. Do you have any questions about that?"

Silberg glares arrows at Lisa.

"And third, exactly what is your role in Medical Marketing Services, Colin?"

Silberg's face pales to the shade of talcum powder, but he does not speak.

Chapter 14

I t's okay, baby. We're almost there." Lylou is in the back seat, whimpering softly and scratching at the inside of her plastic carry crate. She seems to know we're headed for some fun but has no idea where or with whom. I'm betting free run of the Washington County Off-Leash Dog Park with Charles will be a high point of her young life. Of course, I'm just guessing at the young part; there's no way to know for sure how old our rescue dog is.

After parking, I retrieve Lylou from her carrier. The outdoor space is about half an acre of distressed grass surrounded by chain link fencing. Once inside the double gate, I spot Jane setting Charles onto the field. The wiry terrier takes off like a runner from the starting blocks, sprinting out about twenty yards, then whipping around in happy circles. There are other dogs in the park, but so far none of them has noticed the brown and white blur. They seem intent on nosing the ground, reading the Dog Park Times, and occasionally commenting on all the news that's fit to piss.

"Good morning, Jane."

"Oh, there you are, Daniel." Jane steps over and tickles my dog under her chins. "You come a play wif Charles and me, widdow cutie?"

Lylou may look fat at first glance, but she's fifteen pounds of thick muscle. And right now, every fiber is twitching and wriggling to get to the ground and play. When I set her on the grass, she bounds across the park like a gazelle—a low-to-the-ground, short-legged, huffing gazelle. She catches sight of her new boyfriend and they stop long enough for a quick check of respective anal glands.

"How cute!" Jane says. "They remember from the other day."

Identities confirmed, they're off again, taking turns as chaser and chasee. It's unbounded joy, probably beyond anything most humans will ever experience. Wish I had the energy to go out and run with them.

"Shall we make ourselves comfortable?" I motion toward a nearby bench. There's plenty of room, but Jane sits so close we're actually touching. She retrieves her phone and starts shooting video of the happiest two dogs that ever lived.

"This is so fun. Thanks, Daniel."

"Don't thank me, the pups are the entertainment."

"We have to do it again," she says. "But sometime when your Rhonda can join us. I just love her."

"Uh, of course," I manage. First off, she's not my Rhonda. And you love her? You've barely met her, for God's sake.

Forty dog-wonderful minutes later, Jane calls Charles to the bench. Still out on the field of play, Lylou seems briefly confused, but soon lumbers off after a shaggy mutt twice her size.

"Sorry to leave so soon," Jane says. "Charles and I have an appointment with our groomer."

"No problem. I better get Lylou home for some food and a nap."

Jane clicks the leash onto her dog's collar, then stands to leave. "I know you like country, Daniel. Ever go dancing? The Red Dunes Bar has live music every Friday and dollar beers on tap."

Not sure how to respond, I just say, "Sounds great."

I smile and watch Jane and Charles to the car. Her bottom is too small, nearly flat. Never really noticed that before. Guess I was too focused on—

My thoughts are hijacked by urgent, high-pitched squealing near my feet. Lylou's neck and back of her head are nearly covered in blood, her right ear attached by a strip of cartilage no more than two centimeters wide.

§

Minutes later, Rhonda steps to the bench where I'm holding our whimpering pup, injured ear next to my chest.

"Danny, what was so important I had to drop everything and—"Oh, my God!" Rhonda screams. "What happened?" My beige T-shirt is marked with blood.

"I called Ralman but didn't dare put her into the crate. You drive to the clinic, I'll hold her."

Thirty seconds later, we're pulling away, blood dripping onto the tan leather passenger's seat of Lorraine's Lexus.

§

"How the hell could this happen without you noticing?" We're standing outside the door to Ralman's veterinary clinic, waiting for the doctor to arrive. "Too busy looking down boobasaurus's top to see our girl was being attacked?" In the last ten minutes, my shirt has gone from spotted light brown to mostly red. "Let me take a turn holding her,"

Rhonda says, reaching both arms out. We make the delicate transfer.

"I'm not sure, Rhonda. I mean, I guess—"

Squealing tires cut my non-explanation short. Ralman skids his pickup to a stop, throws the truck door open, and hollers, "Which ear?"

"Right," I yell back.

He sprints to the glass door and keys it open, takes the briefest of glances at Lylou, and steps in, yelling back over his shoulder, "Stop standing around!"

I hold the door, and Rhonda carries the dog inside.

"You," the vet growls at Rhonda, "sit down. And for God's sake don't let her scratch at the ear."

Rhonda lowers herself carefully into a faded plastic chair, Lylou in her lap. "It'll be okay, baby," she says. "The doctor will fix you up." Lylou's low moans are pitiful and she's quaking like an aspen in October wind.

"You," Ralman says in my direction, "come with me." I follow him through a door marked Clinic Personnel Only and into a small but well-equipped O.R.

"Sorry to disrupt your weekend, Dr. Ralman, but as you can see—"

"Take one of those gray sterile instrument packs off the third shelf. Place it on the metal cart and roll it over to the operating table."

He's fully gowned by the time I deliver the instruments to his side. He's also gloved.

"You're not going to scrub?" I say.

"Those three minutes might be the difference between saving the goddamn ear or not. Go tell your wife to get the animal in here."

124

"Actually, she's not my—"

"Now!"

Rhonda soon follows me into the surgery.

"Can't do anything until you place her on the exam table," Ralman barks.

"Here we go, sweet doggy." Rhonda lays the pup onto the white sheet. The second Lylou is out of her mommy's arms, she pops to her feet and shakes herself from head to stumpy tail, sprinkling the three of us with blood.

"Shit!" the vet howls. "You." He points his chin at Rhonda. "Keep a firm hand on the back of its neck. One more shake like that and we'll lose the ear for good. Now you, doc. Throw on a gown and gloves. You're assisting."

I'm soon at his side awaiting instructions.

"Take over for your wife. Tell her to go back to the waiting room."

Rhonda leaves. She must be super distressed—she didn't respond to Ralman with something like, "Talk to me directly, you sexist pig. I'm standing right here."

"Lay her on the left side and hold the mouth closed," Ralman orders.

"Mouth closed?"

"Don't want the bitch whipping around and biting me when I administer the injection. What's the dog weigh, six-and-a-half, seven kilos?"

I do a quick calculation in my head. "Yeah. Sounds about right."

Ralman produces a needled syringe, pinches up the left thigh muscle, and gives the shot. "Diazepam and butorphanol," he explains. "In a minute or so, your dog'll be higher than the space station."

§

Two hours later, we're sitting in a small surgical recovery room. Rhonda cradles Lylou who's snuffling into a clear oxygen mask held over her snout by an elastic band.

Ralman steps in and says, "Everything look okay, Dr. Horvath?"

"Not okay," I say.

"The hell?"

"More like perfection. I know a good suturing job from a poor one, Dr. Ralman, and those tiny, even stitches would make a plastic surgeon jealous." Asshole or not, the guy's a virtuoso with a curved needle and silk thread.

He replies with a no-shit shrug, then asks, "What next?" He's testing me again.

"I, uh, antibiotic, I guess."

"You guess? The dog that nearly tore off your animal's ear licks its own ass twice an hour, so yeah, I'll send you home with an oral antibiotic. And pain meds."

"Does Lylou need one of those funnel things around her neck?" Rhonda asks.

"Of course not," I say. "She can't chew on her own ear any more than you or I can."

Ralman opens a door under the sink and produces a clear plastic cone.

"But Lylou could rip the shit out of it with a paw."

Lylou? He actually called the animal by her name.

§

"Pretty sure you can't get bloodstains out of leather."

We're back home, Lylou curled in Rhonda's lap, probably enjoying a codeine-induced dog dream.

"Blood? Leather?" Rhonda says. "What are you—"

"Lorraine's car."

"Oh yeah," she says. "It's a mess."

"And I need the money more than an extra car sitting around reminding me of my dead wife," I mumble, mostly to myself. "I'm going out. Bring you anything?"

"Not that I can—"

"Back in about an hour."

I use an old bath towel to cover the darkening stains of the Lexus's seat, then get in and drive to a local used car dealer that claims, "We buy all kinds of cars, no matter the condition."

After a few minutes of paperwork, an Uber picks me up, and I'm headed home with a much-too-small check in my shirt pocket.

Chapter 15

I've only walked from the car to the bar, but the brand new Tecovas calfskin boots Rhonda bought me are already killing my feet. And I'm supposed to boot-scoot in them? She pushes through the swinging saloon doors and we step into the crowd of suburban cowboys and girls filling the Red Dunes Bar. The place smells like old fryer oil and spilled beer; if it's not a dive, it's pretty damn close. Tonight is Live Band Saturday, but the guy who checked our IDs explained, "The band up and cancelled on us last minute."

Four middle-aged couples in western garb command a pine floor worn slick and wavy. Somebody is sangin' "Achy Breaky Heart" through a buzzy juke box, and the guys and gals execute a heel-toe-clap-turn line dance with military precision.

We claim a tiny table at the edge of the dance area, then look around for a server. There's not a cocktail waitress in sight, so Rhonda offers to make her way to the crowded bar and get us drinks. "Jack and Coke?" she asks.

"Yeah. Thanks."

Next up is a song I was recently introduced to—"Bless the Broken Road" by Rascal Flatts. The slow dancers take their turn.

Rhonda is back sooner than I expect and sets two glasses of beer on the table.

"Where's the real drinks?" I ask.

"It's dollar beer night."

"I know that. Where's my whiskey?"

"This lovely establishment only has a beer license."

I stare at my glass—Something Light, I'm guessing—and take a long swallow. It's weak, almost sweet, and no foam to tickle my upper lip. "Ain't enough of this in the building to get me dancin' tonight."

Rhonda's mind is elsewhere. "You sure Lylou's all right?" she asks. "I feel kind of guilty about—"

"If she isn't still conked out from the doggie drugs, Ash and Jeri are spoiling her like the daughter they never had."

"No kids? I completely forgot to ask when we were over for dinner."

"One son," I say. "Teaches at the UCLA med school."

Rhonda nods, then changes the subject again. "Think maybe Jane the Virgin'll show up tonight?" She's smirking. "I mean, she's the one who told you about this...place."

"Yeah, it was a calculated risk. But even if she does, my street cred doesn't take a hit unless you out me that tonight's a lesson."

The jukebox goes silent, and the dancers slip back into the crowd.

"Don't ever say 'street cred' again," Rhonda says, "especially in a cowboy bar."

"Um, sure."

"And don't say 'out me,' either."

"Okay. I'll just— Oh no, oh my God. Nooo!"

Directly across the dance floor, Jane is taking a seat at a little table like ours. There's a man holding the chair for her. Colin Fucking Silberg.

Wooden chair feet make a scratch-squeal sound against the concrete floor as I slide my seat around, the back of my blue checked roper shirt toward Jane and the asshole.

"What's the matter with you?" Rhonda demands.

Leaning across the table, I croak, "Look across the room. Jane's here, right?"

She bends around me for a look. "Yup. Looks like the love of your life is here with some other cowpoke."

"Silberg, right?"

"Yup. Your Moriarty...or is it Ike Clanton?"

"What are they doing?" I whisper.

"Right now, they're drinking beer. From bottles. And you don't have to whisper, no one could possibly hear you over the crowd noise."

"Bottles? On dollar draft night? Silberg always was a showoff, the bastard. I should probably go over there and punch him in the mouth."

"That's a great idea, Wyatt. Or better yet, challenge him to a gunfight in the middle of Bluff Street." Rhonda allows a moment or three for that to sink in, then continues, "Other than displaying complete jerkitude to your imaginary girlfriend, how do you think the punching story ends?"

"With me in jail for assault?"

She pats the back of my hand. "Boy coulda been a Philadelphia lawyer."

"But what are... Why are they together?"

"He's lookin' an awful lot like a stud pawin' the stall. Could it be your boss man is as interested in gettin' into Calamity Jane's chaps as you are?"

Thanks for that mental picture, Cuz. "Yeah, but...I mean, she would never—"

"Go bushwhackin' with another gent? Why not, Danny? Last I knew, the filly didn't have your brand on her flank."

"Okay, but Colin? Colin Fucking Silberg?"

"I hate him too, Danny. But you have to admit, dude's got a right sexy middle name."

Forcing a sarcastic tone, I say, "Very funny." Rhonda's actually kind of clever, but I'll be damned if I'll let her catch me smiling.

"Anyhoo, pardner—"

"Enough already with the cowboy clichés."

"Okay. Shall we skedaddle outta this saloon before Miss Puss...er, Kitty lays eyes on ya?"

"Yeah. Guess we better." I have more to say but can't trust my voice not to reveal the confusion that fogs my mind like a windshield in the rain.

§

Back home, Rhonda swirls the half-melted ice cubes in what's left of her Jack and Coke and I slam a second shot of Fireball cinnamon whiskey. "Whew! 'Tastes like heaven, burns like hell,' as they say."

Rhonda takes a sip, then says, "So, what happens now?"

"What happens?"

"What are you going to do about Jane?" Rhonda asks.

My mind conjures up a confusing picture of Jane and Silberg at The Red Dunes. I got no plans, not even coherent thoughts right now, just a jumble of feelings, embarrassment at the top of the heap.

"I think you should keep going," Rhonda says.

"Keep going...what?"

"With the reinvention of Daniel Horvath. Even if Jane and Boss Doc are a couple, let's get you ready for the next girl—make that woman—who comes along."

But in this depressing moment, I've got no room for hope. "I dunno, Rhonda, maybe it's just too late for us."

"For us? Leave me out of it, Danny. Jane was just a fantasy, an escape from the boredom of work...and the stress of a gone-to-junk marriage. She was never the love of your life."

The sound of Foreigner's "I Wanna Know What Love Is" drifts across the room like yearning wisps of smoke. Rhonda opens her arms and whispers, "Get over here."

I take the few steps and put an arm around her shoulder. I'm not staggering by any means, but three Fireball shots have left me a bit unsteady. She steers me into the bedroom; the lights are off, but enough moonlight bleeds through the wood-slat blinds to silver the scene like a dusting of snow. Rhonda ducks under my arm and tips me on my left side onto the bedspread.

"Thanks. Don't know what I'd do without—"

"No more talk, Danny." She lies down next to me and surprises me with a little kiss on the cheek. "We'll figure it out. And by the way, your breath could sterilize surgical instruments."

Rhonda curls up with her back toward me. I slip an arm around her waist, and she wriggles her body till she's pressed against mine, back to chest, rump to junk, and knees to knees. "So," I say, "any chance of you and that Mark getting back together?" A fraction of a second ticks by before the blatant stupidity of the sentence slaps me.

"Was there some part of the no-talk rule you failed to grasp?"

There's a thumping sound, another of Lylou's failed attempts to jump onto the bed. I leave Rhonda long enough to hoist Lylou up next to her. By the time I get back into bed, Lylou has taken my place, snoring peacefully.

§

After sleeping later than usual, we load up and drive out of the city for a mind-clearing dose of nature.

"Poor little doggy," I say. "Don't have all your energy back yet, do you?" After about ten minutes meandering between stumpy willows and avoiding yellow-flowered cholla cactus lining the shallow Virgin River, Lylou has simply stopped in her tracks. Our four-legged buddy seems to have decided someone should pick her up and carry her the rest of the way. Happy to oblige, I bend over and hoist the pup, issuing an involuntary groan. "You are heavier than you look, little girl." She turns her wrinkled pancake face up and locks on my eyes, pant-smiling into the protective funnel, tongue dangling from the left corner of her mouth. I'm glad Ralman can't see her just now; the heavily bandaged ear is dark orange with caked-on dirt.

We find a good sitting rock, shaded, near the water. I set Lylou down, and she immediately waddles the few steps to Rhonda's side, an unmistakable message in those big round eyes. Rhonda picks her up and cradles our dog as lovingly as she might a baby.

"You want to talk about last night, Danny?"

"Doesn't seem like there's much to talk about. She's with Silberg."

"I've been thinking about that. Is she really?"

"Really what?"

"With Silberg."

"They were together," I say. "On a date, boyfriend-girlfriend."

"You saw them together—once—and you deduce they're exclusive? Should anyone who noticed you and the girl together at the dog park or snarfing burgers the other day have rightfully concluded that Danny and Jane were a couple?"

My God, Rhonda, can you maybe give the lawyer thing a rest for even a few minutes? "Yeah, I mean, no. So, what's your point?"

"Let me put it in a way you'll understand," Rhonda says. "Let her fly away like Skynyrd's 'Free Bird,' or…*dramatic pause*…'Fight for Your Right.' Of course, if you ask my opinion, which you haven't, I'd cut her loose posthaste."

"Fight? Hell, yeah. I'll kick his ass from here to—"

"Hold on, Mike Tythen. You know we're not talking a literal altercation, right?"

I do now. "Yeah, of course."

"You have to compete for her affection. Win her over, fair and square."

"Thought that's what we've been doing."

"You've been doing. But if you're still in this—which, one more time for the record, I advise against—you're going to have to step…it…the…hell…up. And remember," she says with a wicked little wink, "I'm only around to aid and abet for twelve more days."

Twelve more days? I knew her time here was growing short, but hearing it reduced to days is a bit of a shock. I collect a crumb of courage and ask, "So, um, uh, Rhonda."

She seems to sense my unease and says, "What is it, Danny? Spit it out."

"Remember us lying on the bed?"

"It was a few hours ago. So, yes, I remember."

"Just a friendly cuddle, right?"

"Friendly cuddle? You rode me like a stolen moped."

Oh, my God...did I really...could I possibly... "I know I was a little drunk, but I think I would have remembered that."

Rhonda tilts back her head and laughs to the sky. "Nothing happened."

Not nothing. The closeness, the warmth of Rhonda's supple body was not a booze-soaked dream.

Chapter 16

My house casts a late-day shadow across the yard. The hike from earlier in the day wore Lylou out, so after her three-hour nap, we attempt a much less ambitious outing—backyard fetch. I toss one of her favorites, a stuffed fox with one remaining leg. At first the plastic cone keeps the toy a frustrating five inches from her teeth, but this pup's pretty smart. She soon discovers she can use the headwear like a little shovel, scooping up the chew toy, then tilting her head back to slide it into her waiting mouth. Lylou loves every one of the ten or so minutes, then we settle onto the grass, dog snuggled happily in her mommy's lap for some much-deserved belly rubbing.

"You get those DNA results yet?" Rhonda tosses it out like a discarded tissue, but we both know it's more than idle chitchat.

I pull out my phone and touch the email icon. Sure enough, there's a message from 23andMe: 'Thanks for opting for express service. Results will be in your inbox within a few days.'

"Nope. Can we talk about Jane instead?"

"Sure," she says. "With Lolita, er, Jane, I see you moving down two parallel paths. Track A is making you look good. You're already on that road, kind of, but now it's pedal to the metal. Track B is finding some way to make Colin Silberg look bad. That's less important, and it won't be easy."

"He's a complete asshole. How hard can it be to make Jane see that?"

"We just saw them on a date. He's also her boss, right?"

"And mine."

Lylou issues a little whimper I translate as, "Excuse me? Is there some reason you stopped tickling my belly?"

"Let's start by brainstorming how to make you look good," Rhonda says. "That's a big enough challenge right there."

"That wasn't very nice." I know she's kidding around, but it still kind of stings.

With her free hand she gives my shoulder a little chuck. "This isn't about being nice, buddy. This is war."

"Hell, yeah."

"We want you to come off as smarter...and also physically more attractive. Let's start with the smart part."

"I got it!" I blurt. "Trivia night at Harry A's."

"Harry's is a local bar?"

"Yeah. I've heard they do this quiz game one night a week. I'm pretty good at Jeopardy—I bet I could kill it."

"Ever been to one of these trivia nights?"

"No, but—"

"The questions start off easy," she says, "then get really, really difficult. And they're mostly about pop culture and sports."

"Yeah, well, pop culture maybe not so much. But I do watch sports."

"That right?" she asks. "Who won the Stanley Cup this year?"

"Nice try, but horse racing isn't really a sport, is it?"

Rhonda responds with an exaggerated eyeroll. She knows I'm joking, but she plays along. "Professional hockey is. And baseball. Didn't you tell me you hated baseball?"

"Yeah, well, the only problem with those other so-called sports is that they're not football."

"Okay," she says. "You're not wrong about that."

"Guess I could take her to Salt Lake or Vegas to see the opera or some classical—"

"Has Jane given you any reason to think she gives a dip about anything but goat-roper music?"

"Not really. Hey, here's an idea. I ask her to dinner, and you could act really impressed by everything I say."

"You want me to be a third wheel on your date?"

"Not a third wheel, a double date. You come with Colin, and we'll team up to make him look dumb. Kill two birds, as they say."

"Me and Colin? You're kidding, right?"

I lower my eyes. "Sorry. Can we write off that last idea to dehydration?" Dehydration? Really? We've been outside less than twenty minutes, in the shade, no less. I just handed her the perfect setup, but instead of cracking wise at my expense, she offers a generous nod. In this moment, I want to hug her and tell her she's the most— *Control yourself, Danny Boy. Maybe the heat really has got you confused.*

§

Just after nine that evening, Rhonda steps into the family room and says, "Our little girl went right to sleep."

I'm in the kitchen area standing on a scale that until recently had been collecting dust in the basement. "Already lost a pound and a half," I announce. "And, of course, there's"—I hold a balled-up fist next to my right ear and flex the biceps—"the gun show."

"I'm only going to say this one more time. Unless you're headed to some rented auditorium to buy an AK-47, don't use the words 'gun' and 'show' together. Ever. Got it?"

"Okay, but—"

"I don't have the time to turn you into Magic Mike, so we need to figure out some way to make you seem more macho than you are."

"You left out a word."

"Huh?"

"Even."

"Riiight," she mutters. "You could join a softball league."

"I hate baseball, remember? And don't even try to tell me the bigger ball makes it better."

"Skydiving could be impressive."

"Or…fatal."

"Bungee jumping?"

"Skydiving with a rope? Unh-uh."

"Ever been on a whitewater rafting trip? That sounds fun."

"Hmm. Years back, Lorraine and I did a half day on the Snake River just below Jackson Hole."

"Did you like it?"

"Lorraine was terrified, screamed bloody murder the entire time. So, yes, I loved it."

"You realize I'd have to come along. You know, talk you up to— Oh, hold on! Just thought of the perfect way for you to be the hero. You can swim, right?"

"I'm an excellent swimmer."

"You'd better be, Rain Man."

"So exactly how is it I become the star?" I'm trying hard to sound nonchalant.

"What if," Rhonda says, "one of the rafters were to fall out of the boat, and somebody had to rescue her?"

"Her? Do I have to push Jane into the river?"

"Nobody's pushing anybody. I'll tumble out and you dive in and save me."

"Not sure about whitewater. I'm an okay swimmer, but—"

"Everyone will be wearing life vests, and we'll bribe the guide, make sure he's in on the whole thing."

"Yeah, but—"

"Relax, Danny. This plan is virtually foolproof."

Virtually?

§

It's Saturday, raft day. Thank God we're here. The trip from St. George was a little over two hours, and if I have to listen to one more minute of country radio, I swear I'm going to go "Crazy" -Patsy Cline, 1961.

"So far, not impressed," I say, parking the Forester in front of the world headquarters of Lower Colorado River Adventures, a trailer on a sandy road somewhere near the bottom of Hoover Dam. I'm guessing Lake Mead is about half a mile in the distance, hidden behind the hills southwest of us.

We step into a dusty breeze backed by unfiltered desert sun. "Where's the river?" Jane asks.

"GPS says the launch site is not far from here." I gesture to three vehicles parked nearby, short school buses that look like someone bought them at auction in the seventies and gave them a budget makeover with powder blue house paint. "They'll shuttle us there," I say, trying my best to sound cheerful.

Inside, the LCRA office is nicer than expected. Color photos of their rafts plying the river abound, and an air conditioner in the window keeps the little space at a pleasant temperature.

A fit, heavily tattooed girl in a tank top looks up from the behind the counter. "Welcome to Lower Colorado River Adventures. I'm Sage."

After about twenty minutes for the safety lecture, getting waivers signed, card swiped, etc., Sage says, "Okay let's load up."

Sage is first in. She drops behind the huge, horizontal steering wheel. The bus shows its age, but like the trailer office, it's spotless inside and actually has working air con.

§

After a fifteen-minute bus ride, we exit at a little marina, about fifteen boats slipped at wooden docks near the base of the dam. Craning our necks back, we take in the unimaginable slab of curved concrete looming more than 700 feet above the Colorado River.

Jane gasps at the sight. "It's sooo big. I gotta get a selfie."

"Let me take one of all three of you," Sage offers. We squeeze shoulder to shoulder, and she takes a couple shots with Jane's iPhone. "I guarantee at least one of these will be spectacular."

The "raft" is not what I expected. The one I rode down the raging Snake River way back when was a single piece of inflated rubber with a flat bottom. This thing is basically an aluminum boat between rubber outriggers. Where the Jackson Hole rig had featured an oar for each rider, this one has an outboard motor.

"Sage," I say, "can I talk to you a moment…privately?"

"Sure. What's up?"

"We want to play a little joke on Jane."

"Which one's Jane?"

"The younger. At some point in the rapids, Rhonda, the older woman, will pretend to fall out of the boat, and I'll jump in and rescue her. Where will be the best place to—" Sage starts laughing. "What's so funny?" I ask.

"This isn't a whitewater trip, it's a scenic cruise down what's essentially a narrow twelve-mile lake. Anybody can jump out whenever you want," Sage shrugs. "Just remember, the river's fed by water from the bottom of the dam."

Bottom of the dam? So what?

I wave Rhonda over and explain the no-rapids part. "What do you think, abort the plan?"

"Nah," she says, "I can sell it."

I turn to Sage. "How about a secret signal?" She looks confused.

"When I stand up and stretch, you shut 'er down. Then Rhonda and I will play our little joke."

"Whatever," Sage sighs.

We all climb in. She fires up the boat and points us downriver.

Relax, Danny. This plan is virtually foolproof. The version now playing in my head is tinged with a drop of doubt I'd failed to notice before. Some part of my brain is whispering "Abort," but it's too late now.

§

As if another human voice might break the spell, Rhonda whispers, "Feels like light-years from the Vegas strip." We're thirty minutes into a two-hour tour, and the sheer canyon walls, salmon-colored near the dam, have morphed into rounded mountains, dark cairns of cinders hurled from ancient volcanoes. We're alone on the river, the water smooth as plate glass, not a ripple in sight, and I'm enrobed in a calm that seems otherworldly. Really not sure what's going to cause Rhonda's violent tumble into the water. But she said she could sell it.

"Oo-woo, oo-woo." Jane shatters the tranquility with a holler at the canyon walls. "Echo, echo, echo." But the porous lava just absorbs it. "This is kinda boring," she says. "Where's the rapids?"

I look to Sage whose tiny headshake reminds, Ain't none. Already told you.

I side-glance to Rhonda. She gives a grin and a nod that I read as, Oh, it's on, bitches. Then she steps over the right-side aluminum rail and onto the inflated pontoon. After dropping to a kneel, Rhonda leans way out over the calm water and calls out, "I'm pretty sure I saw an alligator."

An alligator? That's how you're selling it, Rhonda? A fucking alligator in Nevada?

I stand up in an exaggerated stretch then add a loud yawn so our captain can't miss the top-secret gesture. Sage cuts the engine, and the sudden slowing pitches Rhonda headlong into the green water.

"Watch out for the alligator!" I yell. "Cousin Danny's coming to get you." Too melodramatic?

She's selling the hell out of it now, screaming like a middle schooler at some boy band concert. I leap over the rail and execute a perfect surface dive, but the second I hit the water, I realize her screams are real—it's cold as fresh glacier melt. Whimpering and gasping for breath, I finally understand why Sage felt she had to tell me, "Water's right out of the bottom of the dam."

Treading the weenie-shrinking water and hoping for some kind of help, I look up to the boat where Sage and Jane are laughing their respective asses off. I manage to blurt, "It's n, n, n, not funny." But Jane does not seem to hear me over her own hoots. She steps over the rail—omigod, Jane, don't do it—bounces twice on the rubber side, and cannonballs into the freezing stream.

§

Jane's hands flog the water. She's gasping reflexively, huffing "hunh…hunh…hunh." It's not a game anymore, the woman needs help. My leaden legs refuse to move, but in a clumsy version of a front crawl, I manage to windmill my arms and inch in her direction.

Just before I can reach Jane, an orange life ring trailing a rope sails through the air, bounces off the top of her head, and plops on the water. Back on the boat, Sage holds the other end. "Grab on!" she shouts.

Jane stops flailing long enough to wrap both arms around the floating O, then I make a desperate push and grab her by both ankles.

Hand over hand, Sage drags us toward the boat like a fisherman reeling in an old— "Rhonda! Where's Rhonda?" In a painful attempt to look back over my shoulder, I crank

145

my head a quarter turn left. No Rhonda. I let go of Jane's feet and yell to the boat, "Don't worry about me, save Rhonda!" I resume treading water, but it's a bitch without full use of my numb legs. Then I turn my body in a half circle—and I'm staring at my cousin, nose-to-nose. She does not look happy.

"What the hell, man? You couldn't just let her reel us in?"

"Us?"

"Jane, you, me."

"Wait. Were you—"

"Hanging onto your feet for dear life? Yup."

"My legs are completely numb." I tilt my head and mumble into the green water, "Sorry, Rhonda. Now what?"

§

"Really?" Sage says. "You don't want to see the rest of the canyon 'cause you're a little wet?"

It's been fifteen minutes since the alligator incident. We're all now safely back in the boat, stretched out on the bench seats and absorbing the desert sun like lizards on a rock. The passenger vote had been unanimous—make a U-turn and full steam for home.

"It really is spectacular, Sage," I say. "But we're completely exhausted."

"I warned you it was cold."

"Yeah, you did, kind of. In any case, thanks again for dragging us back to the boat."

A few quiet minutes ensue, then Jane issues a little laugh. "Alligator," she says. "That's a good one, Rhonda."

Rhonda responds, "Uh, yeah. Pretty silly, right?"

146

"Everybody knows alligators are in swamps," Jane chuckles. "We're on a river, so it had to be a crocodile."

She's joking, right? I risk a little titter, no more. Rhonda, on the other hand, is laughing so hard I think she may roll off the seat.

§

An occasional snort issues from the passenger side. Jane's seat is fully reclined, and she's sleeping like a beautiful baby. Snuffling softly, Rhonda is curled up on the car's bench seat behind us. We're on our way home.

I preemptively reduce the volume, then turn on the radio and punch the SEARCH button. After three Spanish stations and some guy with an Oklahoma accent *Jee-zussing* all over the place, I recognize Bon Jovi rocking "Livin' On a Prayer," and stop at 97.1. Then I finetune the volume to loud enough to keep me awake and soft enough not to wake anyone else. I hope. Don't dare sing along, so my tired mind wanders off into a question. Was today an abject failure? I certainly didn't come off as any kind of hero, but it was sort of a, a bonding experience, right? And if it was, just who were the bondees? Gotta remember to ask Rhonda.

The song fades to the next tune in the queue, "Crazy Train."

§

Backpack slung over a single shoulder, Jane leans in the passenger side window. "Buh-bye, Rhonda. Buh-bye, Daniel. Thanks for a fun day."

"Bye. See you soon." I wave till Jane's inside her townhouse, then Rhonda buzzes up the window and I drive away.

"So," I say, "was today a success or—"

"Depends on whether you were going for cute, funny guy or macho man of action."

"Let's say macho."

"You made Silberg look like Daniel Craig."

I sort of already knew that, but did she have to phrase it so harshly?

"Okay, what about cute, funny guy?"

"Meh. Maybe an eight or nine."

"That's pretty good, right?"

"On a scale of a hundred."

I reach over and give her shoulder a little slap. "That joke was sort of cruel, don't you think?"

"What joke?" But her poker face cracks, and we share a laugh.

"So, what now?" I ask.

Rhonda blows into her curled hand and says, "Time to stop screwing around."

"What does that even—"

"Did I say stop? I meant start. Anything, Danny. She offered you anything. I get that you're nervous, but stop stalling. You gotta storm that pink fortress before Colin Silberg does, assuming, of course, it's not too late. Bend her over the barrel and show her the fifty states. ASAP."

"Bend her over the barrel" is crass, but I get it. "Show her the fifty states?" Where does she come up with this stuff?

"So, how do I—"

"Call her on it. See if anything includes bumping uglies. And if it does, you'd better rock her world. Anything less and you can kiss that sweet ass goodbye."

"Figuratively, right?"

She responds with a grin and a one-shoulder shrug.

"I have a confession, Rhonda. I've never made love to anyone but Lorraine."

"That's nothing to be embarrassed about, Danny."

"Unless, you know, you include our—"

"We already established digital spelunking doesn't count." She pauses for a moment of thought, then sighs, "Sounds like I'm going to have to convene a class in sex

Chapter 17

Y ou don't have to do this if it makes you uncomfortable, Rhonda." We're at the dining room table and I'm trying to appear calmer than I feel. Bet she is too.

Without acknowledging my "uncomfortable" offer, she hands me a sheet of paper.

"Like the music lesson, this session will be guided by a list."

"A list? This isn't exactly the sixth-grade maturation assembly."

"Don't want to leave out anything important, do we?" Wonder if Rhonda knows how much she sounds like Dana Carvey's Church Lady right now.

"You might only get one shot at this."

I open my mouth, but before I can speak, she says, "Mind out of the ditch, Danny. We have work to do."

Lylou is curled up on my recliner, sleep-snuffles amplified by the plastic megaphone around her head. "Glad you're snoozing, baby girl," I say. "You're much too young to hear any of this."

"It's not Lylou I'm worried about, Danny."

We step to the kitchen and each take a stool, then she lays the list on the counter between us.

"Number one, and it's non-negotiable, is safety."

"But I've only ever been with one woman, so…"

"We know for certain you've been with two people, and I'm guessing a lot more."

My expression must be as blank as my mind. "I told you I've never slept with anyone but Lorraine."

"Lorraine was sleeping around," Rhonda reminds, "and you were intimate with Lorraine. Am I right?"

"Yeah, occasionally, the word occasionally referring to me and Lorraine, not the sleeping around."

"Clinically speaking, Doctor, you've been with everyone she's been with. And frankly, you have no idea about Jane's history."

Jane's history? Never really thought about that before. I mean, she's crazy beautiful, so... "Got it," I say. "I'll get some condoms at the drugstore. Do you still have to ask the pharmacist?"

Rhonda ignores the question. "Always wear protection, no matter where you dip that wick."

"'No matter where?' There's only one—"

"Technically five, but I don't usually count the ears."

"Five? No fucking way." My response strikes her as funny somehow.

"Okay, as a practical matter, let's say three."

I gulp a little. "I'm not really into—"

"This ain't about you, Buckaroo. Your only goal here is to give Janie a night she'll never forget, in a good way, of course. Next on the list is location."

"Thought we just covered that," I chuckle.

"Very funny. We'll get to anatomy soon enough, but right now I'm talking about setting, surroundings. For a woman, this is about romance, not wham bam, thank you, Sam."

"So," I say through a sarcastic smile, "my fantasy of getting it on in the backseat of the Subaru is—"

"No. Make that *hell, no*. The question here is simply your place, her place, or a nice hotel?"

"I'm thinking here at the house, but—"

"Okay, put a pin in it. Now let's talk about romance."

"Of course," I say. "Romance."

"I suggest a very nice dinner. With wine if she likes, but not too much. You want her to remember the night. And you might think about avoiding alcohol altogether."

"No booze?"

"Remember that old saying, 'Alcohol makes you unable to do the very thing it makes you want to do?'"

I've never heard it before, but it does ring true. "And a sexy movie?" I ask.

"Absolutely not. No movie...especially not a sexy one. But let's talk about music."

"Sexy music, no sexy movie. Right?"

"Right. And bear in mind, it has to be something that's romantic to her, not your Billy Idol and his 'Rebel Yell.' I'll create a playlist."

"Thanks. What else?"

"Flowers might be nice."

"Got it. Can we fast forward to, you know, doing it?"

"Sure. You ready for some sexy secrets from Cousin Rhonda's inner sanctum?"

"Sounds naughty already. Please proceed."

"Ahem." Rhonda clears her throat as if she's about to address a jury. "Here's the anatomy stuff."

"Okay, bring it on." Not sure what a lawyer can teach a doctor about anatomy, but I make no attempt to stop her.

"You know what goes where, right?"

"Of course." At least I thought I did until she expanded the possibilities to five. "So, what else is there to know?"

"Let's start with erogenous zones. Those are specific areas of the body that—"

"I know what erogenous zones are, for God's sake."

"Do you know where they are?"

"Anywhere a swimsuit would cover, right?"

"And?"

"And what?"

"The mouth, of course. And some women like being touched on the earlobes, back of the neck...even their feet."

"Feet?"

"Yup. Ever tried shrimping?"

"Like Forrest Gump?"

"Forrest goes shrampin'," she says. "Shrimping is sucking on another person's toes."

"First off," I choke, "that's disgusting. And second, of course it's another person's toes. If I could suck my own toes I could probably— Never mind. Not going shrimp fishing, ever."

"Okay, but if Jane tells you she's into it, what're you going to—"

"Hey, Jane, want me to Hoover the polish off your toenails? Let me tell you something about my mouth, Rhonda. Those words are never coming out of it, and no toes are ever going in. End of crustacean conversation."

"Sheesh, Danny. Open your mind a crack. If you want to give her a hay roll to remember, you have to ask what she wants. And by the way, foot play just might be the least spicy item on the menu."

Before my startled psyche can begin to contemplate what the more piquant dishes could possibly be, Rhonda says, "Next up, the sweet spot."

"Huh?"

"What's the difference between the TV remote and a clitoris?"

"Why would you even—"

"A man can always find the remote." She bursts into laughter so contagious I can't help but get caught up.

"That's an awfully big generalization, Rhonda. I can point out on a medical illustration exactly where—"

"Spend a lot of time with drawings of women's undercarriages, do you, Danny?"

"No. But I got straight A's in anatomy."

"And you have lots of hands-on experience, right?"

"I uh, well, I, I—"

"God. No wonder the woman wanted a divorce."

"In my defense," I say, "I made a few attempts early on, but Lorraine made it clear it was not her thing."

"Okay." Rhonda bobs her head. "Some women do prefer the stick to a flick." She holds up a now-pay-attention finger. Let's take a good look at the pearl in the oyster."

Oh my God, Rhonda! Right here? Right now? I probably should run from the room, but I'm paralyzed—and maybe a little aroused. It's all for science, right?

Much to my disappointment, she opens her MacBook and types something into the search bar. When she presses RETURN, a photo appears.

"See that?" she asks.

"Not really." When I squint a little harder, I can make something out. An actual oyster, maybe? But I thought that was just a metaphor.

"Give me a second." I grab one of a half dozen grease-smeared readers from a nearby basket of glasses and take another look.

The high def image fills the screen, and I instinctively avert my eyes.

"Relax, doc, it's just a picture."

I reluctantly turn my gaze back to a full-color closeup that would make a gynecologist blush. Then a hand moves into the frame. Not "just a picture," it's video.

"Oh my God!" I gulp.

"We're both adults, Danny. Just watch the thing."

From a clinical perspective, the little clit clip is fascinating, but not at all titillating. If this is porn, I just…do…not…understand why they say it's so popular.

"Think you can find the fun button now?" she asks.

Fun button? Really? "Probably," I shrug.

"Probably?"

"Maybe," I say. "But it's still not the same as hands-on experience."

"Hands-on?"

The cheaters have slipped to nearly the tip of my nose, and I push them back in place with an index finger. "I can't see much of anything up close. And since my reading glasses make me look like an old man…"

"You're not an old man," Rhonda says. "Just too old for Jane."

I ignore the remark and ask, "That it for today?"

"Oh, hell no. In this next chapter we'll cover special kinds of kissing."

Shouldn't kissing have been covered way earlier? I mean— "Oh, God no, Rhonda! No…more…videos."

§

"Relax, Danny. You're just asking her out on a date, not requesting written consent to load the clown into the cannon."

"Gotta tell you, Rhonda, your intercourse metaphors are getting weaker. And please, keep your voice down, someone might hear us."

"Look around. They all have those expensive wireless earbuds in, listening to podcasts about ancient aliens and serial killers."

Rhonda and I are sipping cappuccinos at a Starbucks near the clinic. We're surrounded by customers, and yes, every one of them has something in or over their twenty-something ears.

"At just the right point during the evening," she says, "you'll bring up the subject of—"

"Stuffin' the muffin?"

"Now who's stretching for sex slang?" she laughs. "But seriously, you need to phrase it in a romantic but unmistakable way. Something like, 'Jane, I'd love to end this beautiful evening by making slow, sweet love to you.'"

"Thank you, Rhonda," I say, bobbing my head. "That's perfect."

Is that AC/DC's "Highway to Hell" leaking from someone's headphones?

§

"How's that contact lens working out?" Rhonda asks. We're back home, sitting on the carpet in my family room, taking turns tossing the stuffed fox back and forth while Lylou follows it like she can't decide which way to go. "You wearing it now?"

"Yeah." I pull a little blue bottle of Blink eyedrops from my pocket, lean my head back, and drip some in my right eye. "Still not sure why one of those soft lenses wouldn't have worked just as well."

When Rhonda first brought up the notion, I was hesitant. But she ultimately won me over to the idea of getting a single contact specifically for close vision. Despite my earlier doubts, it works fairly well. For the first day, the rigid lens felt like a grain of sand in my eye, but the sensation has now improved from grit to a mere annoyance like a lash under my lid.

"Anyway," I say, "let's get to the plan for that night. No way you going out for a movie gives me enough time alone with Jane. I'll get you a room at the Ramada."

"Why don't you get a room at a nice hotel, something like not-the-Ramada. I'll stay here and watch Breaking Bad reruns."

I give my head a vigorous shake. "No. It's too obvious."

"So, getting in her knickers is some kind of secret? She is over eighteen, right?"

"Come off it. This is not a joke."

"Yet. You hope. Probably."

"Goddammit, Rhonda. I'm nervous enough without you—"

"All right, already. I'll just go bar hopping."

"You're in St. George, Utah. It'll be a short hop."

"I'll be home at one thirty," she says. So, unless you're looking for a threesome—"

"You're disgusting, Rhonda."

"And?"

"And thank you."

Chapter 18

J ane scans the view then takes a sip of her grapefruitcello
martini. "I've never been to the country club before. It's
so pretty here, and the piano player is real good."

We're on the outdoor patio, the balmy night perfumed by
pale pink blooms of hummingbird mint. Just inside the open
French doors, a man plays an elevator version of Slowhand's
"Wonderful Tonight" on a white piano.

"You look wonderful tonight, Jane." I smile, sip my
Perrier. She's way beyond pretty. Golden hair frames her
face, intense blue eyes and full lips blood red against sun-
blessed skin. And the V-neck of her floral print dress leaves
just enough to the imagination. This is perfect, Danny Boy.
Don't blow it.

A vaguely familiar couple passes our table, the wife
making no effort to hide a doubletake I read as, Hasn't his
wife been dead for less than a month? Fuck her...and this
judgmental hag whose name I can't remember.

Our white linen tablecloth is the perfect backdrop for
Jane's delicate hands. I reach over and take one, she gives
mine a gentle squeeze.

"I like touching you." Her whisper is nearly lost in the
music and the breeze.

"Me too," is all I can manage. The night is already the
best of my adult life. Could it possibly get better?

The grilled halibut is served Oscar style, topped with crab, asparagus, and béarnaise sauce. Exquisite. Next we enjoy thick slices of Sachertorte, dark chocolate cake with apricot filling, plated with barely sweetened whipped cream. I lean over and use my napkin to wipe a white dab from the corner of that perfect mouth, and she thanks me with a closed-lip smile. I smile back in a kind of squinty grin—and suddenly my close-up vision is gone.

Shiiit. Did the lens fall out or just slide off my cornea? Based on experience so far, both problems are about equally likely. I blink several times, but nothing changes.

"You okay, Daniel? Is there something in your eye?"

"I, uh, yeah. Think something might've blown in on the breeze. Will you excuse me for a moment?"

"Sure."

The restroom is upscale—cloth towels, a mouthwash dispenser, and that damn low, indirect lighting. I take out my phone and stare at it helplessly. This thing has a flashlight feature, right? A quick press, and wonder of wonders, a bright little beam. I lean in so close my nose smudges the mirror, but I don't see any sign of the lens. Between my presbyopia and the phone blasting light directly in my eye, it's pretty hard to know anything for sure. Odds are it either popped out or migrated around to the brain side of my eyeball.

§

"Everything all right?" Jane asks.

I return to find she's not only finished her dessert, the plate looks like it's been licked clean.

"Did you enjoy dinner?" I ask.

"It was amazing."

It's...*gulp*...time. "Jane, I'm not quite sure how to say this, but—"

She reaches over and takes my hand. "Anything, Daniel. Remember? Anything."

"I...um...I, I'd like to end this beautiful evening by making slow, sweet love to you."

She reaches across the table and gives my hand an affirming squeeze. "Finish your dessert first," she says.

"Maybe just a bite." I use my fork to break off a little chunk. When the smooth, dark icing slides onto my tongue, I can't hold back a happy groan.

"Told ya," Jane says.

The moment I begin to chew, I feel a harsh little crunch between my molars. Inside my own head, it's pretty loud, but Jane doesn't react. So I force a smile, masticate the hard plastic lens to tiny bits, and wash the gritty goo down with three gulps of expensive water.

§

"Your neighborhood is rad, Daniel," Jane says.

"Uh, thanks." I pull in the driveway and stop outside the garage door. Normally I'd park inside and walk directly into the kitchen, but that would mean navigating an obstacle course of boxes, the last vestiges of Lorraine waiting for Goodwill. I open the car door for Jane, and with my hand at the small of her back, guide her to the front entrance.

My key clicks into the lock but the door opens before I can grip the knob. I'm suddenly face-to-face with Rhonda, dog crate in one hand and Lylou on the leash in her other.

"Oh, hi, guys," she says, as if this were a big surprise.

The surprise is actually on me and it leaves me managing nothing more than, "Er, um."

Jane is unfazed. "Hi, Rhonda! It's wonderful to see you. Where are you taking our little Lylou so late at night?"

"Going to a movie...or bar hopping...or maybe for a sleepover at a hotel. We haven't decided yet."

Jane looks bemused. "That, uh, sounds nice...I guess."

"Yep. Just need to borrow Danny's car. Can I have the keys, Cuz?"

I hand them to her and say, "So, Rhonda, what are we supposed to... I mean, if I don't have my car—"

"Give me a call any time. Happy to come back and chauffeur Jane home."

Not sure what kind of game Rhonda's playing, but in this moment, I have no choice but to go along. "You and Lylou have a nice night out," I say through gritted teeth.

My car drives away, and when we step into the house, I hear music. *What the hell, Rhonda?* "Alexa, pause," I command.

"Please, can we hear it?" Jane asks. "I love this song, 'Sweet Jane' by the Cowboy Junkies. I mean, it's all about me."

"Sure. If you—"

"Alexa." Jane calls out. "Resume. Volume seven."

I know Lou Reed's version of the song, but this is something different—haunting, unrelenting, exquisite. "Cowboy Junkies? Is that what you said?"

"Duh. It's on your playlist."

It's difficult, but I ignore the 'duh' and say, "Would you like something to drink?"

"You know you don't have to get me drunk, Daniel." Her voice is like a placid draft that ripples the leaves in some old vineyard.

"I didn't really mean it that—"

Jane answers with a soft laugh. "Just joking around, trying to, you know, put you at ease."

She's trying to put me at ease? No wonder I kind of think I might be sort of falling in love. Well, that and the oversize jubblies I hope to be fondling soon.

"Can I use your bathroom?" she asks. "Take a quick shower?"

"Of course, Jane. I'll show you the way." A shower? Am I supposed to say something like "want me to join you?" But all I can gulp out is, "I'll get you a clean towel."

"And a washcloth, please."

Another gulp, then, "No problem."

"Daniel."

"Yes, Jane?"

"If you're thinking about joining me, forget it."

"It...uh...never crossed my mind."

"You're a little liar," she giggles. "But you can watch, I mean, if you want."

If I want? I'm suddenly dizzy, the result, no doubt, of blood rushing from my brain to other regions now demanding more than their share.

I hope Jane's not offended. I want to perch on the closed toilet seat and ogle her through the rippled shower door. But the word *premature* keeps looming in my mind. So I go to the adjoining bedroom, strip down to silk boxers, and take a seat on the edge of my king bed. I stare at myself in the adjacent mirror and think, Damn. I'd sell my soul to drop thirty pounds in the next ten minutes. Jane is singing something I can't quite make out over the running water, and my thoughts soon turn from Satan's weight loss plan to imagined sights behind the bathroom door.

The water goes quiet, but the singing continues, some country tune about having friends in low places. After three or four minutes, the vocals stop and the door opens. Jane enters the bedroom wearing only a towel. Around her waist. She tiptoes across the distance between us, the unrestrained ivory globes looking back at me from eye level.

Thanks be to God, to the universe, or to whatever, whoever allowed me to live to this day. Thank you, thank you, thank you.

"All clean," she says, "head to…toe."

Did she just punch up the word "toe"?

Jane sits down next to me and cradles my face in still-damp hands. She leans in, the towel pops open, and she gives me a kiss. I instinctively draw back, her thick tongue is nearly gagging me.

Her face contorts. "I'm sorry, Daniel. Did I do something wrong?"

"No, not at all, Jane. Just nerves. You're so wonderful, so beautiful, it's, it's overwhelming."

She stands, takes a step back, and runs the backs of her fingers down her sides like a model. "So, what do you like best?"

"Huh?"

"I mean which part of me? My smile?" She looks down. "My tiny pink feet?"

I lean in, wrap my arms low around her waist and kiss her chest at the exact spot the deep cleavage begins. Her skin is warm as oven-fresh bread; I could linger here forever, but this is just the beginning of our amazing night.

"Of course," she says. "But you know there's more to me than just my little boobies."

Just your little boobies? Natural or not, no one should ever use the words *just* or *little* to describe those world-class breasts.

"Anyways, dinner was wonderful, Daniel. The only thing missing was a nice cocktail."

"But you had two grapefruitcello—"

"Oh, not for me, for you. Maybe a shrimp cocktail."

A cartoonish wheeze escapes my poor mouth.

"And perhaps a muffin for dessert."

Not sure if she expects a response, but I got nothing. In the ensuing silence, a song from Rhonda's custom playlist seeps through the not-quite-closed bedroom door. It's Meatloaf's anthem, "I'd Do Anything for Love (But I Won't Do That)."

God, or the universe, or whatever…help me!

§

"Where the hell did my boxers end up?" After an hour of what some people might call lovemaking, I'm alone in a room that's now a rumpled riot of cast-off clothes and bedding. I fix my gaze on the reflection in the mirrored closet door four feet away, a wretched version of me on the edge of my bed. The post-whatever-just-happened Danny is slumped forward, elbows on knees, chin resting on the back of his hands, naked as the day he was born into this confusing world.

Running water and the sound of Jane singing behind the bathroom door spur me into action. I hop to my feet, snatch a clean pair of undershorts from the drawer, then quickly begin to dress. While I struggle into my pants, the phone slides out of my right front pocket and onto the carpet. I grab it up and text, "Rhonda, get yourself back here. Now." Once I press SEND, I immediately wonder why I said *yourself* instead of *my car*. The explanation just might be that I need a buffer. Got absolutely nothing to say to Jane right now.

I hear the shower shut off and flee the bedroom.

§

Fifteen minutes later—it feels like hours—Rhonda calls from the open front door, "Anybody home?"

"You know I'm home, Rhonda,"—Lylou is slumbering peacefully in her arms, so I keep it to a loudish whisper—"you're looking right at me!"

She's grinning like her face just cracked. "Didn't want to catch anyone off guard, if you know what I mean." She steps over to the crate and gently lays the pup onto her bed.

My mind is racing through options. It's a fifteen-minute drive to Jane's condo. If I take her myself, those minutes will be awkward, to put it mildly. I'm certain Rhonda would be happy to drive her, but the last thing I need right now is to put those two alone in a car.

"Hi, Rhonda." Jane walks out of my bedroom, fully dressed, hair hanging in damp strings.

"Hello, Jane."

The younger woman pulls them into a tight embrace. Over her hugger's shoulder, Rhonda flashes me a taunting smirk, then disentangles, takes a step back, and says, "The car's here. Danny can give you a—"

"Actually," I interrupt, "it might be nice for all three of us to take a little ride."

Hope Jane didn't notice Rhonda's left eyebrow lift. The expression passes quickly, but her message seems clear. I cannot wait to find out what went on here tonight.

The women take their seats behind me like Uber customers. I pull the Subaru out of the neighborhood and turn north onto River Road.

After a few long minutes, Jane breaks the silence. "Hope you and Lylou had a nice evening, Rhonda. What did you end up doing?"

"We caught a movie."

A movie? What the hell, Rhonda?

"I didn't know they allowed animals into theaters," Jane says.

"Well, it was Isle of Dogs, so yeah. But the manager asked us to leave about halfway through. Lylou fell asleep and—"

"She was snoring so loud, nobody could hear," Jane says. "Am I right?"

"It was not so much snoring as the farting."

The back seat erupts into laughter, an improvement over the earlier silence. I guess.

"Can I ask about your night?" Rhonda says. For a split second I consider steering into oncoming traffic.

"Of course," Jane replies.

"My question is…"—Rhonda takes a dramatic pause, for my benefit, no doubt—"…did you leave Charles home alone, or what?"

"Oh, no. He's staying over at Colin's house."

"Colin Fucking Silberg?" Honnnk! I jerk the wheel and swerve back into my lane just in time to avoid getting sideswiped by a pickup towing a horse trailer. *Shiiit, Danny, get it together.* I'm really, really glad my messed up mental state didn't land us in the hospital, or worse. And I really, really wish I hadn't said the CFS thing out loud.

It takes all my willpower to focus on the road, and we make it to Jane's place intact. Parking the car at the curb, I leave the motor running. This parting will be short and sweet. Short at least.

At her townhouse door, I keep it simple. "Good night, Jane."

"Good night, handsome." Before I realize what's happening, she pulls me in for a kiss, long and disturbingly lingual. "See you back at the office."

The office. Of course. I add *coworker* to my mental list of reasons this night had been one big fucking mistake—pun intended.

When I get back to the car, Rhonda is in the driver's seat. Her iPhone is plugged into my AUX input, the heavy bass riff of Nirvana's "Smells Like Teen Spirit" pounding the inside of the vehicle like a triphammer.

"Not funny," I say.

"Oh, it's funny, alright."

I yank the white cord out so violently it snaps just behind the plug. She looks over at the severed cord and says, "I was thinking maybe our chances of getting home alive might be better if I drive. Now I'm certain of it."

She pulls away from the curb before I can get the door shut. "So, Danny, other than blurting out 'Colin Fucking Silberg,' how'd the big date go?"

"Mind your own business."

"You suddenly forget I'm a co-conspirator?"

My head sags and I mumble into my chest, "Koonfnarote."

"You're going to have speak up, young man."

"I couldn't find the remote." God, I hate hearing that out loud.

"As in?"

"As in, I...couldn't...find...the, you know, the remote. And she laughed at me."

"Mean laugh? Fun laugh? Tickle laugh?"

"How the hell should I know? It's not like I could see her face."

"Please, do go on," she says with a snicker.

"Couldn't see much of anything, really."

"You couldn't see anything?"

"Nothing up close, anyway."

"Forget to put in your contact?"

"I ate it."

"Ohh-kay. More detail than I needed, but—"

"I chewed up the contact lens...with a twelve-dollar slice of chocolate cake."

Now Rhonda's really yucking it up.

"Is that a mean laugh or a tickle laugh?" I ask.

"It's an I-just-can't-help-it laugh. I am truly sorry, Danny. I told you this was a bad idea from the start, but the last thing I wanted was for you to be humiliated."

"Yeah, well..."

"So is your little plan deader than Romeo and Juliet?" she asks. "Or do you think there's still a chance?"

Jeff Lowder

"See that 7-11 up there on the right? Pull in—I need a big bottle of Listerine."

Chapter 19

U h, hello." Shiiit. I had hoped to avoid her for a few days after the evening to forget. Now she's standing in the doorway to my office.

"H...h...how are you, Jane?"

She steps in and takes a seat. "Don't you think it's time we had a little talk, Daniel?"

"Not really. I...I..." Probably should have told her to shut the door, but she caught me completely off guard.

"Relax," she says. "It's just sex."

My voice cracks like a seventh grader's. "Okay. Yeah." Just sex? How about just really awkward, humiliating sex?

"I know you're not very experienced, and—"

"Jane, I was married for fifteen years."

She gives her head a sad little nod. "To the same person. Were you faithful to her, Daniel? I mean, we flirted a little, but—"

"I did not cheat on my wife. Ever."

"You okay, Daniel?" she asks. "You're looking kinda red."

Kinda red? My face feels like I've just come in from three hours of sunbathing. I'm guessing, of course; skin docs don't really do that sort of thing.

"All I can say is I'm sorry, Jane. I wanted you to have the most wonderful night of your life, but I...I..."

"Don't be so hard on yourself. You just need more experience."

I have no comeback. A woman in her thirties telling me I need more experience? This is all kinds of fucked up. It's also true.

"I mean, for a doctor, you're kind of clueless." She says it out the left corner of her mouth like some kind of secret.

"I said I'm sorry. Can we just end it at that?"

"We could." She flashes a coy smile. "Or..."

I'm fully flabbergasted. "Or?"

"I've always been a believer in second chances. And you do have potential."

"Potential?"

"You're teachable, right?"

Teachable? "Uh, I guess." This just took one hell of a bizarre turn.

"I could bring a couple of educational videos over— make a big bag of popcorn or whatever. Rhonda might even like to join us."

"Rhonda?" I gulp. "You mean the three of—"

"Jane! Tell me you're not screwing this loser!" Dr. Silberg stands in the doorway, screaming like a scalded monkey. "You work for me!"

§

After work, we take Lylou to the footpath around Tawa Pond. Contrasts of grass green and sandstone orange surround a little lake about forty yards across, a few old men tending fishing poles at the edge of the mossy water.

Lylou tugs at her leash as if to ask Rhonda, "Why you slowing down?"

"Just for the sake of argument," Rhonda says, "let's assume Jane meant something other than a threesome with you and your cousin. I mean, 'make a big bag of popcorn?' That doesn't sound like any orgy I've been to."

"Exactly how many have orgies have you—"

"More than zero, fewer than ten. Now drop it."

You're shining me on, right, Rhonda? "And in fairness to Jane," I say, "before she could explain herself, C. F. Silberg burst in like his back hair was on fire."

"But she was clear about a second chance?"

"We didn't put a sexy time appointment into our calendars," I say, "but she was, uh, pretty clear."

"Pretty clear? Okay, we'll roll with that for now."

We follow our precious pup for a few minutes without speaking, then Rhonda sighs and says, "You two lovebirds can watch all the naughty movies your bigscreen can handle but count Cousin Rhonda out."

"Come on," I say. "Doesn't it sound kind of fun, the three of us lounging on my great room floor, flesh filling the TV, lots of slapping and slurping in surround sound?"

"We tried that."

"No, we didn't. If I'd been in one of your orgies, I'd remember it."

"Ladies and gentlemen, give it up for the comic stylings of Dr. Dan," she teases. "You know I'm not talking about a group grope, just my Intro to Sex seminar. And you flunked the final."

"Maybe if we hadn't skipped the lab…"

A wordless pause ensues, not unlike when the party hostess slips a fart.

"What are you saying, Daniel Horvath?" Rhonda does not sound happy. "That it's my fault? Just because I wouldn't let you, you know?"

"Relax, Rhonda," I say. "Thought we were just kidding around here. You've done everything you could for me. Don't know how I'll ever thank you."

"Glad you noticed. But right now, the most important thing I can give you is loving advice."

"Loving? As in more how to?"

She issues a growl of frustration. "More like tough love. Walk away from this girl, Danny. She throws up more caution flags than a fiery crash at a NASCAR track. I know you're obsessing over her, but this is not the woman you thought you knew."

"But the heart wants what the heart wants."

"Bullshit," she says. "The heart isn't some kind of valentine. It's an internal organ that pumps your blood. You of all people should know that, Doctor Horvath."

"Yeah, but—"

"Screw the heart," she says.

What does that even mean?

"The only connection your heart has to any of this is getting the wrinkles out of Richard. It's time to use that big, beautiful brain of yours."

"Wrinkles out of Richard?"

"Richard Johnson." She slugs my shoulder. "Don't pretend you don't know what I'm talking about."

I'm suddenly desperate to change the subject to something other than my anatomy. "Can we just...I mean, for now, let's enjoy this beautiful day and our Lylou." At the sound of her name, the little Frenchie woofs and walks a little bit taller, a very little bit.

I'm left trying to sort out thoughts that battle inside my big, beautiful brain like marbles in a blender.

§

"Time for a rest," Rhonda announces. We've circled the pond almost three times, and Lylou is panting out the clear megaphone like a middle-aged marathoner. We step to a nearby picnic table and I remove the headpiece so Lylou can lap bottled water from her collapsible bowl.

Rhonda chuckles to herself, then shields her mouth and whispers like a child about to divulge a juicy secret. "We'd have to have some ground rules."

"You totally lost me. And why are you whispering?"

She points at the pup. "I don't want you-know-who to hear this," she explains, as if to an idiot.

"Hear what?"

"We'd have to agree on, you, know, clear boundaries— and a safe word."

Is she saying what I think she's saying?

Chapter 20

Ash surveys the endless desert and says, "This is my church."

"Happy Sunday." I suck tepid water from my CamelBak tube. We finished the thirteen miles just minutes ago, leaned our dusty steeds against a nearby cottonwood, and found a couple of safe sitting spots on a weathered-to-splinters picnic bench. My heart rate is still struggling to recover and my brain is wrestling with last night's Rhonda talk.

"You okay, Danny? It feels like you're off your game a little."

"Yeah. I'm just, you know, just winded. Definitely going to start that diet. Monday. After next."

"Just got some news on that mess with DOPL," Ash says.

"The utah.gov site back up?"

"Not yet. But Lisa finally talked to the investigator. He sat down with the woman who made the complaint—correction—on whose behalf the charge was made."

"What did she say?"

"Nothing coherent. Woman's suffering from early onset Alzheimer's, thought the investigator was her grandson."

"That's sad."

"Yeah," Ash says. "She doesn't even have a grandson. Anyway, since the website's still a clusterfuck, we're going to have to drive up to Salt Lake."

"Tomorrow?"

"I wish. Apparently, there's still a few days of papers to push."

"So what about Silberg?"

Ash perks up a little. "Let's just say Lisa has some pretty damn good ideas about what happens next. Speaking of Silberg, you know yet how much money he squirreled away in that phony company?"

§

That night, I bounce a nervous knee until I can't stand it anymore, then mute Last Week Tonight and ask, "You want to talk about it?"

"It?" Rhonda knows damn well what *it* is, but I'm not going to press her, so to speak.

"We can drop the whole thing," I say. "It was probably a terrible idea from the—"

"Danny." She uses a thumb to point to Lylou. "Not in front of the kids."

I hike my shoulders and unmute the TV in time to catch John Oliver in the middle of a tirade punctuated with profanity. Lylou seems unfazed by that.

After a few minutes, Rhonda says, "Let's step outside."

"Sure." I open the slider and we go out. "Can I get you a sweatshirt?" I offer. The sun's been gone for hours, and it's turned cool.

"I'm fine." Rhonda settles into a nicely padded outdoor chair. "So, where were we?"

I position my seat to face her and say, "Trying to figure out how it is our dog somehow understands human sex talk when simple concepts like 'sit' and 'lie down' go right over her big square head."

That gives Rhonda a little chuckle. "I admit she doesn't fully understand English."

"Doesn't understand English? What does she speak, Mandarin?"

"You want to talk about this or not?" She isn't laughing.

"Sorry."

"Tell me what you're thinking would help the, uh, the situation," she says.

That's a trap if ever I heard one. "You first."

"I might be willing to participate in a brief scientific inquiry."

I gulp a little. "Ohh-kay."

"With specific conditions which I will now enumerate."

"Proceed, counselor."

"Number one: The research shall be limited to a single session not to exceed ten minutes."

"Agreed."

"Number two: The activities shall be restricted to instruction regarding the location of certain female external genital organs, including a brief practicum."

"Okay."

"Number three: The educational session may be halted immediately by either participant speaking a 'safe word' to be agreed upon in advance."

"Is that it?" I ask.

"It is."

"Where do I sign?"

Rhonda says, "Verbal's fine" in a tone that makes me think she missed the intended sarcasm. "Just wanted to make sure we're on the same page."

"Okay."

"We are, and I agree to keep it strictly clinical. This is nothing more than dissecting a pig in med school."

"Not a very flattering comparison, but—"

"Like looking at pond scum through a microscope in junior high."

"Not helping, Danny. And no one's going to need a microscope."

"Animal husbandry at a 4-H Club—"

"Stop with the disgusting metaphors. Let's just call it Grey's Anatomy."

"Why Grey's Anatomy?"

"You'll see."

She allows a moment for me to catch up, then says, "I'm suddenly freezing. Let's go back inside."

I take the couch and leave Rhonda the recliner. She clicks OFF, and the dark screen swallows the scrolling credits from *Last Week Tonight With John Oliver*.

"So, uh, when...I mean...tonight?" I stammer.

"No. First you have to take me out for a nice dinner, buy me flowers, and—"

"This just got kind of weird." Wait...she's laughing.

"How about we give ourselves a twenty-four-hour rescission period," Rhonda says.

"Rescission period?"

"A day for each of us to think about it, change our minds if it's just too over the top. Anyway, you bring an expensive bottle of wine home from work tomorrow, and we'll see."

"When you say, 'we'll see,' do you mean—"

"Get your mind out of my gutter, Danny. I'm going to bed."

§

Not sure why I think our little dog needs me to pitch my voice two octaves higher, but I always do. "Lylou, Daddy's home." No one answers, so I set two one-hundred-dollar bottles of Duckhorn Merlot on the counter and check the backyard. On the grass, just beyond the patio, Rhonda lies on her back in the fading light of day, laughing and half trying to avoid affectionate, and sloppy, Frenchie kisses. In the nearby grill, briquets glow a dull orange.

The girls haven't noticed me yet, so I just stand and watch in awe. It is a moment of unrestrained joy beyond anything I've seen in my forty-six years. I retrieve a white handkerchief from my pants pocket, dab my eyes, then move it lower to muffle a small sniff. If God, the universe, or whatever could freeze time, I'd choose to live in this moment for eternity.

§

"Who da grillmeister, Danny?"

"You are, Rhonda. That may be the best New York strip I've ever sunk my teeth into."

"Don't give her too much. Frenchies can really pack on the pounds."

We're just finishing a wonderful dinner, and Lylou is enthusiastically eating little scraps of leftover steak from the palm of my hand.

"It's okay, she'll walk it off. We'll all walk it off. Tomorrow."

"And thank you for the wine," she says. "It was exquisite."

"I could open the second hunny if you like."

"Honey?"

"As in hundred-dollar bill."

"Let's save it for another night," she says. "Now, about that other matter."

"Uh, yeah." I attempt to sound nonchalant, but the truth is I'm nervous as a third-grade teacher on a field trip to a peanut processing plant. And speaking of field trip, are we about to stumble into a massive blunder? An hour ago, I experienced the sublime in my own backyard. Will this ridiculous plan blow that all to hell?

"You gonna pussy out on me?" she says.

I turn both palms up. "You know a reasonable person could take that sentence at least two different—"

"Allow me to clarify. Button, button, who's got the button. We playing it tonight or not?"

I feel dirty, like I'm about to take advantage of a kind and generous friend, my best friend. God, Rhonda, I've been so lonely for so long—but you'll be gone in a few days, and...

"Think I had too much wine," I mutter. "Let's plan on tomorrow."

I spend the rest of the long night on top of the covers, staring into the darkened ceiling. Everything seemed so clear a few short weeks ago.

§

"On your way to a pick-up basketball game?" Rhonda asks.

"You like it?"

Tonight's the night. Game on.

Dinner was simple, and we agreed to save the wine for one more day. Not sure why I thought it mattered, but I just entered my bedroom wearing the least sexy outfit I could think of—long, baggy shorts, fraying Beatles T-shirt, and brown dress socks.

She sits on the edge of the bed in my white terry bathrobe. No telling what's underneath.

Glancing at my black shorts, she says, "I respect your firm determination, Danny, but try and think of this as nothing more than a science fair project—for adults."

"The autonomic nervous system controls tumescence, I don't." Translation: I'm embarrassed by the polyester pup tent, but it's not under my conscious control. I switch off the overhead light, and the single bedside lamp bathes the room in a soft yellow glow.

"Flip the light back on, Danny. This is a classroom, not a singles' bar."

That guilty buzz is back. "Sure you're okay with this, Rhonda?" Her earlier casual expression has been replaced by a somber look.

"Cousin."

"Believe me, I haven't forgotten."

"It's the safe word, Danny—cousin. If either one of us says that word, any time, for any reason, things stop immediately. Clear?"

"Absolutely." A formal safe word seems silly, but if it's important to her...

Rhonda stands and wriggles out of the robe. She's wearing that familiar Gonzaga Law T-shirt. Just the Gonzaga T-shirt. She lies back on the bed, feet still on the floor.

Oh, my God! The pup tent just became the chief's teepee.

"So," she says, "you up for this?"

"Did you really just...?"

Her matter-of-fact tone turns suddenly sheepish. "Sorry. I didn't mean that the way it probably— Can we just get on with it?"

But I'm paralyzed. A mute statue at the side of the bed, I glance left, then right without moving my head. The details of the room are beginning to melt and run like watercolors in the rain. Without conscious thought, I step between Rhonda's legs, lean over, take that perfectly-lived-in face in both hands. I gaze into her green-gold eyes for what feels like a lifetime, then kiss her long and deep.

I halfway expect poor Rhonda to bolt out of the bedroom like the mattress is on fire, but when I pull back from the epic kiss, she throws her arms behind my neck and draws me in for more.

We finally pause for breath and she says, "Lose the shorts, LeBron."

But from beyond the pulse that thunders in my ears there's an old woman's voice, feeble but undeniable. "She's a blood relative, son. Don't you forget that. Not for a single minute."

I shake my head so hard my cheeks make a wet slapping sound. "Cousin! Cousin! Cousin! You're my cousin."

§

Stretched out on top of the rumpled bedspread, I regard the ceiling with an unfocused stare. For some hours—three, at least—my big beautiful brain has struggled with a mental jigsaw puzzle. There are only two pieces. One is a simple, straight-edged square—the past few weeks with Rhonda have made me feel like awakening from hopeless winter into sun-soaked spring. The second piece is a jagged shard from a dropped china plate which bears a single word: COUSIN.

Lylou's little whimper comes from the other side of the closed door, and I get up and let her into the bedroom. She thanks me with a panting smile then takes a run at the bed. She jumps but falls short and hits the cone on the edge of the mattress.

"You're a really smart dog," I mutter. "How come you always forget you can't make that jump?" A triple epiphany tingles me from toe to crown. First, Jane was a middle-aged man's crazy fantasy, a fever dream that finally broke. Second, I'm never going to find that money I need to retire. Number three comes with a dull chest ache. My best friend will soon be flying back to Oregon for good. Looks like you missed your leap by a mile, Danny Boy. And with that, I feel myself flailing and falling back into the old rut, like the earlier tumble into my dead wife's muddy grave.

Chapter 21

M orning, Danny." Rhonda is hunched at the counter, focused on a plate of scrambled eggs. "How was your night?"

Why are you so infuriatingly flippant? Is this some kind of test? "Think we need to talk, Rhonda. About what happened last night."

She takes a sip of coffee and raises her head. "Nothing," she says.

"Nothing? What's that supposed to—"

"You were there, Danny. Nothing happened." Is she disappointed, relieved? Her blank expression and neutral tone offer no clue. "By the way," she says, "in Oregon, banging your cousin is perfectly legal."

Which, of course, is not the point. As strongly as I feel about Rhonda, as much as I yearn to spend every day for the rest of my life with my best friend and our Lylou, it would break my mother's heart. And after the kiss that Rhonda and I shared, could I ever be happy with mere friendship?

"Rhonda."

"Yes, dear?"

"The thing about last night is—"

A ringing doorbell startles me into silence.

I open up to what could be a page from an Eddie Bauer catalog—a mid-forties man in tech fabric cargos with zip-off pantlegs. The extra-long tail of his untucked polo shirt emphasizes his height and trim, athletic build. It's Caribbean blue to match his eyes.

"Dr. Horvath," he says, extending a manicured hand, "I'm Mark."

Holy shit, this is Mark? I take the proffered hand but forget to let go after shaking, just stand there staring at the movie-star good looks. When I finally release, I can't seem to think what I'm supposed to do or say next, so I bust out with the first thing that enters my conscious mind.

"Piss off, Mark. Get the fuck off my property."

"Wh, uh, what do you—"

"You've been warned, now you're officially trespassing."

The Hollywood smile is gone, replaced by the shock of a ten-year-old whose mother just told him he's getting a new daddy.

"I don't know what they do to trespassers in Oregon, but here in Utah we—"

"Goddammit!" Rhonda pushes me to one side and steps out. "What the hell is wrong with you, Danny?" she says, then gives the door a ferocious slam behind her.

I stand motionless, the closed door less than an inch from my nose.

"What's wrong with me?" I say to the wooden slab. "She kissed me less than... Ah, screw it. Last night was a colossal mistake. Seeing my cousin half-naked one crazy time doesn't give me the right to plant a flag on her ass—her round, firm..." Baseball goal, baseball mallet, baseball arena.

Distressed by the noise and the overall vibe, Lylou retreats to her crate. I kneel next to her bed and say, "It's okay, baby, come on out. Daddy's a big dope and Mommy got a little upset, but she'll come back in just a minute." I think. I hope. The frightened pup steps out, and I reward her with strokes meant to comfort both of us.

Angry pounding on the front door sends the poor dog back inside, curling up and quivering as far from the front opening as she can get.

Not sure if the house door is locked, so I approach it cautiously. The deadbolt is engaged. Must have turned it after the house-rattling slam.

More pounding.

"Give me a second," I yell through the door. "Just getting my gun."

"Goddammit, Danny," Rhonda hollers from outside. "Open up."

I unbolt the door and let her in. She does not look happy.

"Get the fuck off my property? What in the name of all that's holy was that about?"

"You told me it was over, that you hated him."

"For the record, I never said I hated him."

"And we just, I mean, you know... It was kind of a reflex, I guess. Maybe trying to protect you."

"That's, uh, sweet?" At least some of the anger looks to have left her. "But you know I'm perfectly capable of taking care of myself, right?"

"Of course. I'm really sorry if I overreacted, Rhonda. That I overreacted."

She gives my shoulder a friendly punch. "Thanks for caring. I guess."

"So, he's gone?"

"From your property, yes."

"From my property? You didn't tell him to haul his ass right back to Oregon?"

"Danny, the man just drove seventeen hours straight. He needs some rest." She pauses for a moment, then muses as if I weren't in the room. "And if he really does divorce his wife..." She returns her gaze to me and says, "Anyway, I promised I'd hear him out."

"Hear him out? Where? When? Why?"

"Tonight. At the Hampton Inn."

"In his hotel room?" I'm just this side of a scream.

"Jesus, Danny. Take it down a notch."

I suck a deep breath and modulate a couple octaves lower. "Sorry. I just... Is he dangerous? I mean, he's a stalker, right?"

"We're having a drink in the bar...and the man's no more dangerous than you are. Speaking of which, do you really own a gun?"

"Hell, yeah, a twelve-gauge shotgun. I think. Somewhere."

§

Hours later, I'm in the old recliner, Lylou curled up on my lap and snoring like a jowly Darth Vader. "Attagirl," I whisper. "You sleep and let Daddy do the worrying." Worrying about what, I'm not entirely certain. Rhonda left for the Hampton Inn hours ago. She was wearing old clothes and no makeup, but it's Rhonda, so I'm not sure I can read anything into that. Mildly put, I'm concerned that getting back with the philanderer will make her miserable, but she's a bright woman, and who knows better than Rhonda what she does and does not need?

But if I'm unflinchingly honest with myself, my gut is roiling from jealousy—simple, unadulterated dread of losing Rhonda. As is too often the case with my unrestrained emotions, the resentment makes not a scintilla of sense. With or without Magic Mark, she'll soon be headed back to Tillamook. "And when she does," I sigh to Lylou, "how can I ever make you understand, sweet doggy?"

My watch says 2:50 a.m. By law, the hotel bar's been closed for almost two hours. None of my rambling meditations matter. Rhonda has made her decision.

§

5:07 a.m. I awaken to "Help Me Rhonda," the unique ringtone she picked for my number. Lylou jumps down from my lap with a soft woof, and I answer with a tentative "Hello."

"Morning, Danny. Want to unlock the door?" Is this the part where she begins packing?

A few seconds later, she tosses a baseball cap and light jacket on the sofa. Lylou is immediately up on hind legs, gently pawing the front of Rhonda's thighs.

"And you, baby. Gonna miss you something awful."

She's gonna miss Lylou? Guess that seals it.

"Rhonda, are you all right?"

"I'm fine, Danny."

"So, you and Mark are—"

She cuts me off with a look.

"Sorry, Rhonda. I'll just shut the hell up now."

"I know what you're probably thinking, but I haven't been shaking sheets at the Hampton."

"Okay." I'm overjoyed but manage to keep my tone neutral. I take her hand and guide Rhonda to the couch. Lylou hops into her lap, looking up with huge dark eyes that seem to say, "I sense you're hurting, Mommy. How can I help?"

"You might be wondering where I've been."

"Like I said, none of my—"

"I spent the night in West Canyon." She sounds subdued, dispirited.

"West Canyon? Why would you—" The none-of-my-business thing didn't last long.

"Curled myself up on that little rock sofa and—"

I drop my head and mumble, "That was our spot."

"Dammit it, Danny, let me finish. I lay there all night, thinking and wondering. Alone."

"Wondering?"

"What the hell is wrong with me that all my relationships end the same way?"

I open my mouth to speak, but rhetorical flashes through my mind, and I shut my yap without a word.

"It came over me like some kind of revelation." Rhonda's eyes look dull, unfocused. "It hit me I have…a…a…I guess you'd call it a type."

"Tall men? Like Mark?"

"Tall or short, doesn't matter. As long as they're married."

"There were other affairs?"

"One, five years ago." Her chin drops to her chest, and fat tears darken her T-shirt.

Rhonda's a home-wrecker? My body goes rigid, like I've been shot with a taser. "I can't even picture you—"

"Happily married men are my weakness," she mutters, "preferably with children."

194

The imaginary stun gunman dials up the voltage till I'm actually trembling. "You're smart. Beautiful. You could have any man you want, Rhonda. Why go after—"

"Mark showing up here, ready to turn his back on his family?" She shakes her head, flicking flowing tears to the sides. "Last night, I felt like I finally woke up, came out of some weird coma dream. What the hell was I thinking all those years?"

"Maybe you were just—" Shut the hell up, Danny Boy.

"I finally admitted to myself I'd been chasing the perfect marriage," she says. "Doting husband, white picket fence. Like our parents had, or at least I thought they had—the whole idyllic, nonexistent thing." She puffs out a woeful sigh. "But who in their right mind would believe that instead of creating it, she could just steal it? What form of insanity blinded me to what should have been obvious to anyone on the planet? The very act of pursuing that fantasy meant blowing it to shrapnel and leaving a wake of mortally wounded souls. God—and Mark—forgive me."

My heart aches, wishes I could take some portion of the pain from her. I lean over and embrace my best friend. Our Lylou is caught happily in the middle, the only one not weeping like a drippy faucet. In spite of the sadness, or perhaps because of it, this moment of raw honesty feels like the family we've both longed for all these years. But, of course, that can never be.

§

After much-needed naps, Rhonda suggests a hike might help us hit reset, so we drive to a favorite spot just east of the tiny town of Leeds. It's my turn with the leash and I'm gripping the looped handle lightly between two fingers and a thumb. Hooded Lylou leads us along a sandy trail that meanders like an orange river though dark tree-bushes and impossibly gnarled bristlecone pines. The solitude of the desert is endlessly astonishing; we haven't seen another human since I parked the car nearly half an hour ago.

I inhale the juniper-scented air and say, "A place likes this kind of calms the soul."

"It's like nowhere I could have imagined," Rhonda sighs.

That's my cue. "Lylou and I had a little chat after you went to bed last night...make that this morning."

Rhonda cocks her head and regards me with a sort of side glance. "You did, huh? In Mandarin?"

"Le français, bien sûr."

"What exactly were you two—"

"Shiiit!" I holler. "Lylou, come back here!" Leash trailing behind, the dog escapes my grasp and is suddenly sprinting after a jackrabbit that exploded out of the brush nearby and is now darting down the middle of the sandy trail like a— well, like a jackrabbit.

I take off after them, but soon realize that while Lylou may not be back to a hundred percent, I've little or no chance to catch her.

"Lylou," I yell at the top of my lungs, "Lylou, come back!"

Quick as a ricochet, the big rabbit jukes to its right, kicking up a puff of sand and bouncing between tall junipers that line the trail. Seconds later, Lylou makes the same right turn and disappears from view.

Nearly a half minute ticks by before I reach the spot where the animals left the path. I'm bent at the waist, hands on knees, sucking in air as dry as the sand beneath my feet.

Rhonda skids to a stop right next to me and says, "She can't go far, can she?"

"Not really sure, but—"

I'm cut short by the sound of snorty gasps amplified by the plastic head rig. We push branches aside and Rhonda and I bushwhack twenty or so feet to where our sad little girl sits. Lylou is breathing heavily, the attached leash hopelessly entangled in bristlecone branches so contorted they've grown back on themselves.

I bust out a pathetic Elvis while Rhonda frees the breathless hound dog.

Minutes later, Rhonda hoists herself up to a sit a low boulder. I deposit Lylou onto her lap. She's still huffing like a steam locomotive on grade—Lylou, that is. I climb up next to my girls and give her a little side hug—Rhonda, that is.

"You okay, puppy?" Lylou turns her head up to Mommy, and Rhonda gives her gentle scratches just below the head cone. "For a minute there, you were moving pretty fast."

"Not that she could," I say, "but what would our little girl do if she ever caught up to a rabbit?"

Rhonda says, "I imagine her staring at the rabbit's ears and wondering if they were somehow related." We both get a laugh at poor Lylou's expense.

"Yeah," I say. "Then sniffing some bunny butt and thinking, 'Not only is this the ugliest dog I've ever seen, it smells disgusting.'"

We sit in silence for a while, breathing air touched with the scent of expensive gin.

"Rhonda," I blurt. "Don't leave."

"I won't, Danny." She offers a little smile. "Not before we've sorted out all the money stuff."

"No. I mean don't go back to Oregon. Ever." I'm trying to sound serious, but just might be coming off as desperate.

"That's where my job is."

"I know, but—"

"Sooner or later, this place, as beautiful as it is,"—she raises her hand to shoulder height and sweeps in a half circle—"will be hotter than hell's doorknob. And don't even start with 'but it's a dry heat.' My convection oven is a dry heat, and I'm not planning on moving in any time soon."

"You said yourself you don't want to go back and have to face your old—"

"You say fuck buddy again and I'll break your nose."

"You're a good lawyer, Rhonda. You could get a job anywhere."

"You have no idea if I'm good or totally suck. And St. George is a very small city, Danny." Rhonda appears unconvinced, more than a little confused. "Why are we even having this—"

"Lylou needs her Mommy. And I need my best friend."

"Danny, I don't think—"

"You'll have your own room. We'll walk Lylou every evening, eat hot dogs till we're sick of them. And maybe once in a while, dance to Blondie. Bet you never had that with what's-his-name."

Rhonda bobs her head, a smile barely perceptible. "That does sound kinda wonderful." She pulls out a bandanna from her back pocket and wipes away a sniffle. The hanky is red, patterned in blue and white, and for some reason I think of a cowboy pulling it over his lower face, ready to rob an oncoming train.

"You forget about the cousin thing?" she asks.

"I, uh—"

"What are you picturing, Danny? The family you never had—I never had?"

Why does the question feel like a physical door slamming in my face? "M…maybe," I stammer.

"Sharing long, happy walks with Lylou, then ending each evening retiring to separate bedrooms?"

My chin sinks to my chest. "I guess. Yeah."

"How long do you think that marriage lasts, Cuz?" She emphasizes the M-word with a lip-curling sneer. "Just exactly how goddamned long does that work out?"

"I, uh—"

"Sooner than later, we'll toss down one too many shots of that Fireball whiskey of yours and spend the rest of the night riding like a rodeo queen."

A fog lifts, and the stark absurdity of my little plan stands out in crisp relief. What the hell was I thinking? I should probably be humiliated. Instead, I say, "Which one?"

"Which one what?"

"In your sex scenario, are you the rodeo queen—or am I?"

Without warning, our awkwardness dissolves into laughter.

Chapter 22

Rhonda has boxing lessons on Saturday and Sunday?" Jane asks.

"Yes, I mean no, I mean, Sunday is actually…karate."

The dogs are enjoying off-leash freedom, oblivious to their people on the bench.

"Jane, I umm…" Just spit it out, Danny Boy. Tear off the damn bandage already. "I think we should see other people." Of course that timeworn trope is straight out of a Hallmark movie. And anyway, it makes no sense. We are not—nor have we ever been—a couple, let alone an exclusive couple.

"In addition to, or instead of?" Her tone, flat as the top of nearby Smith Mesa, catches me off guard.

"Huh?"

"See each other and other people too? Or just—"

"You're a wonderful person, Jane. You deserve better than this clumsy old guy."

"Charles!" she shouts. "Time to leave." While her dog lopes over to his woman, Jane stands and looks down at me, her facial scar twisted by an ugly smirk. "Get it, Daniel, 'time to leave?'" She turns to walk away, but swivels back and says, "Did I mention you got me pregnant?"

§

"Holy shit, Danny!" Rhonda blurts, "She's non compos mentis."

"Translation?"

"Nuttier than a squirrel turd."

A few seconds prior, I had rocked Rhonda back on her heels with this little gem: "Jane told me she's pregnant."

"Clinically," I explain, "it usually takes a little longer than this for HCG to reach detectable levels."

"Meaning it's too soon to tell, right?"

"Probably."

"But Danny, that's not even the point. You told me when you and the little shaver had your one-on-one time, it was a disaster. I mean, you never actually got it up long enough, that is, for a sufficient length of time to—"

"It was a fiasco, yes...but I never said there was no congress."

"Congress? You telling me you plunged the clunge without a raincoat?"

"If that means what I think it does, then yes. Jane said she'd been tested and was on the pill. She begged me not to use, you know, prophylaxis."

"Guess calling you an idiot isn't helpful at this point."

I waggle my head. Hearing my own words out loud is more than sufficient to remind me how love-dumb I'd been. "So, Rhonda, what do I do now?"

"What do I do now, Rhonda? I'm the one who told you to run away from this girl as fast and as far as you could. Now your pickle's in a wringer, I'm supposed to tell you how to unwind it?"

"Rhonda, please. I need you."

She takes a calming breath and blows it out. "Let's assume for a moment that, knocked up or not, Jane's got a plan."

"A plan?"

"She's either madly in love with you and wants you back—"

"Not likely."

"Not remotely likely." That hurts a bit.

"She might be setting you up for some kind of cash settlement…or maybe angling to marry a rich doctor."

"Whatever rich is," I say, "I'm the exact opposite."

"Jane doesn't know that." Rhonda squints, left thumb stroking her jawline in thought. "Let's start with some things not to do. For example, waiting a few months to see a baby bump is not an option."

"Agreed."

"If you had some of her urine you could test it yourself. You want to unbreak up and have her over for watersports?"

"Watersports?" It takes a couple of seconds for the meaning to register. "Oh my God, Rhonda, that's the single most disgusting thing you've ever— Wait. I got it!"

"Got what?"

"I'm a doctor. Patients provide urine samples all the time."

"Dermatology patients?"

"No. But I work in a multispecialty clinic with other doctors."

"Do I need to remind you that you're talking about shattering multiple laws?"

"I know, but—"

"But what? How you going to provide for Janie and Junior if you're in federal prison?"

The lawyer makes a good point.

"Danny," Rhonda says. "Why not just confront her? Ask for some kind of proof that she's expecting."

"Yeah! And proof that the baby—if there even is such a thing—is mine."

"Slow your roll, Maury. One step at a time." Seemingly deep in thought, Rhonda lets her eyes wander off.

"Was Lorraine spayed?"

"If you're asking if she had a hysterectomy or her tubes tied, the answer is no. But what does that have to do with—Wait, are you saying my spermatozoa may not be viable?"

"That would shut Jane up in a hurry. Were your little aquanauts ever tested?"

"Nah," I say.

"Well, hunt yourself a Dixie cup and an iPad. You got work to do."

§

With the Jane problem pushed to the back of my mind for now, I'm kneeling on the bathroom floor, holding the dog steady for her hygiene session. Rhonda moves around Lylou's jowly mouth, pulling the loose lips back with one hand and brushing her nubby teeth with the other.

"By the way, Danny, was something dinging in your pocket a moment ago...or are you just glad to see me?"

"You've now officially stretched that old joke past its limit."

"Check it if you need to—the phone, that is. But first, can you carry her over to the sink and turn on the water so she can rinse and spit?"

"Sure." Without thinking, I take a single step in the direction of the vanity, then can't help a little laugh at the mental image of our dog sluicing water around in her mouth and expectorating. "Mommy almost had me that time, pretty baby."

Lylou follows me into the kitchen where a Milk-Bone reward awaits. "After you eat your treat, we'll go out for a walk." Like always, she wiggles with happy anticipation at the W-word. While Lylou crunches up the biscuit, I take out the phone and check emails. The most recent notification is from 23andMe, subject line: Here are the results of your DNA test.

The image of my mother flashes through my head. She's the most perfect human being ever to walk the earth. How could I ever have doubted her? And anyway, the test isn't going to answer any questions.

I vacillate for a few seconds, then hit DELETE without opening the message.

"Ready for our walk, ladies?"

§

From a wooden bench, Rhonda and I watch funnel-headed Lylou run around the off-leash park as fast as those stumpy legs will carry her. My mind wanders, pondering if deleting the DNA results was the right thing to do.

"Something on your mind, Danny?" Rhonda asks.

"I, uh, was just—"

A ringing phone rescues me.

"Hey, Ash," I mutter.

"What's going on, Danny? You sound like someone just defecated in your Cheerios."

"Don't really want to talk about it."

"Good," he says. "Let's talk about me. Can you clear your calendar tomorrow? All day?"

"Tomorrow?"

"Yeah. Lisa and I are driving up to Salt Lake to meet with that investigator at DOPL. Thought you might tag along and vouch for me."

"Under oath?"

"Don't think so."

"Good. 'Cause if they swear me in, I'll be hard-pressed to say anything nice."

"Yeah, yeah. You coming or not?"

"I'm in."

"Love to have Rhonda along. We'll pick you two up at seven thirty."

I end the call, and Lylou lopes over to our bench for some water and encouraging pats.

"That's my girl," I say. "You tired, want to go home?" The Frenchie answers with a tiny yip then hustles back into the fray.

"In for what?" Rhonda asks.

"It was Ash. He and Lisa—"

"Lisa?"

"Lisa Monaghan, Ash's attorney. He mentioned her when we were over for dinner."

"Oh, right."

"They have an appointment with the Division of Professional Licensing tomorrow. Asked if we'd like to make the trip to Salt Lake with them."

"Hell, yeah," she says. "And while we're at the office building, let's drop in on the Division of Corporations. The state still hasn't finished that website install, and we need more info on this bogus Medical Marketing Services.

§

After fifteen minutes of paperwork, Ash strokes a check for $11.50 to the State of Utah, and Lisa walks out with a photocopy of the case file, including the name of the person who made the groping complaint: Bessie Weymouth. But a quick glance reveals the complaint was actually "filed on behalf of Ms. Weymouth by a third party." The third party? Lorraine Horvath.

Next we take the elevator up to five and step out directly in front of double glass doors signed Utah Division of Corporations and Commercial Code. The division's nonworking website has wreaked its havoc; the lobby is shoulder-to-shoulder with business and attorney types. Lisa pulls a tag from the Take a Number machine: 357. The lighted overhead sign says, Now serving 328.

"Cafeteria's on two," Ash says. "Meet us there when you lawyers finish up."

"How long do you think it will take, Lisa?" Rhonda asks.

"It'll take as long as it takes."

Ash raises an eyebrow. "Says the woman who's billing me by the hour."

§

It's two thirty and the cafeteria, not much more than an employee lunchroom, is deserted but for Ash and me.

"How's the soda?" I ask. I'm nursing my second iced tea, and he's drinking caffeine-free Coke Zero from a can.

He shrugs and turns his palms up. "It's cold."

"Did I ever tell you why that stuff is like making love in a canoe?"

"Yeah, you mentioned it a time or— Looks like the lawyers are back."

Grinning like they hold winning lottery tickets, the two women approach us in purposeful strides, then take the remaining chairs at our little table.

"Ready to have your minds blown?" Rhonda asks.

"Always," I reply.

"The president, CEO, and fifty-percent shareholder of Medical Marketing Services, Inc.," Lisa begins, "is Colin Franklin Silberg." She pronounces Fucking wrong, but I let it go.

"That shouldn't shock anyone here," Ash says.

"No, but this might. The vice-president and owner of the other half is none other than…"—Lisa nods and Rhonda commences a table-top drum roll—"…Lorraine Horvath."

"Wow!" I say. "Guess I shouldn't be surprised, but still."

"Do you realize what this means, Danny?" Rhonda seems to take my blank expression as a no. "Lorraine is dead."

"I kind of already knew that."

"Danny, you are her sole heir, including to her share of whatever this company is."

"She had fifty percent ownership, right?" I ask.

"Exactly," Rhonda says.

"So, if Silberg hasn't already swept every nickel from this MMS, I might get half my goddamn money back?"

§

"Buckle up." Lisa pulls away from the 7-11 pump island, her candy-apple-red Infiniti Q50 fueled and ready for the four-hour run back to St. George.

Rhonda and I share the back seat, and I ask, "So how long will it take to find out if there's any money left in the Medical Marketing account?"

"I'll FedEx a death cert tomorrow along with a formal demand to recognize you as the heir."

"Remember," Lisa says over her shoulder, "I'm here if you need me at some point."

"Thanks, Lisa," Rhonda says. "Back to your question, Danny. I hope to have access to all financial records within a week."

Lisa punches the accelerator, and we rocket up the on-ramp and onto I-15 South. "Remember," she calls, out, "Ash gets hit with a four-hundred-dollar surcharge if anyone spills their Gulpy-Gulp in my new car."

Chapter 23

Who's she?" Silberg barks. A massive walnut desk separates Dr. Colin F. Silberg from Rhonda and me.

"I'm his attorney, Rhonda Horvath."

"Horvath?"

"She's also my cousin."

"So, what do you Horvaths want?" he growls.

"To introduce you to your new business partner," Rhonda says, "and demand you immediately provide him with all financial records for Medical Marketing Services."

"I don't know anything about any Medical Marketing Services."

"Silberg," Rhonda says, "cut the crap." Like a matador challenging a bull, she stands and waves a sheet of paper. "This is a printout from the state Division of Corporations. It says you're the CEO and fifty-percent shareholder of Medical Marketing Services LLC. The vice-president and owner of the other half of the company is recorded as the late Mrs. Lorraine Horvath...*dramatic pause*...but you knew all that, didn't you?"

Silberg attempts a so-what shrug, but the sweat sheen on his forehead and a little tremor of his pinky ring give him away.

"All of which means you now have a new partner. Daniel Horvath."

"That zit doc is not my partner."

"The law says he became your partner the moment his wife died. You remember that moment, I assume."

"You bitch!" Silberg screams.

In a voice as flat and solid as the table, Rhonda says, "I'm giving you until four to produce the records. Happy to pay a reasonable copying fee."

The tall man leaps from his chair and heads for Rhonda with violence in his eyes.

I move in front of her and signal Colin to stop with an upraised hand like a traffic cop's. He surprises me by actually stopping.

"You so much as touch her," I snarl, "and this will be your last day on earth."

"Get the fuck out of my office!" he shrieks. "Now!"

"Of course, Dr. Silberg." Rhonda's voice is still emotionless. "See you at four o'clock. If you fail to hand over the records, Dr. Horvath will have no choice but to file a criminal complaint of fraud. Have a nice day, sir."

C. F. Silberg follows us to the door and slams it so hard a glass-framed copy of the clinic's business license rattles off the hallway wall and shatters on the tile floor.

§

"What's under that?" Lisa asks. Rhonda and I are in the lawyer's red Infiniti, just pulling into the physician parking lot of the clinic. She parks next to a car-sized canvas cover.

"Silberg collects Chevys from the fifties," I say. "He'll occasionally drive one of his babies to work. When he does, one of the receptionists goes out and puts the cover on it."

"The receptionist?" I can't see her eyes, but I'll bet they're rolling. "Really?"

"Anyway, thanks for coming, Lisa."

"My pleasure," she responds. "Quite literally. May as well give Colin one more reason to abhor me. Rhonda, you were clear about him handing over the materials at four, right?"

"She was clear, all right," I say. "Clear as vodka."

Rhonda glances at her watch. "And it's almost five."

"Think he'll turn them over without a fight?" Lisa asks.

"If I thought that," I say, "I wouldn't have invited you."

That gives Lisa a chuckle. "All right, then. Time to engage the enemy."

We storm Silberg's office to find him anchoring the far side of a completely empty desk. "You're with them?" he barks at Lisa.

"Good afternoon, Colin." Her tone is surprisingly affable for someone who just one minute ago referred to this meeting as "engaging the enemy." "Will you be providing the records in electronic or paper format?"

Silberg's reddening face squints up into a malevolent smile, but he does not speak. Instead he flicks a business card with his middle finger. It glides across the desk and onto the floor at Lisa's feet.

"Can I assume it's your accountant's?" she asks.

I squat and retrieve the card. Warburton Warburton and Stignell, Attorneys at Law. G. Frederick Warburton II, Esq. I look up and growl, "Silberg. If you think—"

"Time to go, Danny." Lisa takes an elbow and ushers me through the door.

Once outside, she takes the card from me and says, "Freddy Warburton is the sleaziest lawyer south of Salt Lake

City. Before this is over, I'll have his license on my wall like a scalp."

"Amen," I intone, and we share a high-fifteen, or whatever you call a three-way hand slap.

Rhonda and I drop arms to our sides. Lisa keeps hers in the air, balling it to a white-knuckled fist.

§

A few minutes later, Rhonda and I sit side-by-side in Lisa's back seat. "She's been mumbling to herself since we left the clinic," I whisper. "You getting any of it?"

"Maybe a word here and there."

Lisa steers into our driveway and shuts off the ruby Infiniti. Without the soundtrack of wind, engine noise, and tire whine, the muttering comes to us as actual words. "Oh, you'll see. You're damn right I'm meeting with your attorney, Colin. And if the fat ass tries jerking me around, I'll—"

"Thanks for the ride, Lisa." My words seem to break a kind of trance.

"Oh, uh, no problem."

"You okay?" Rhonda asks.

"Fine. Just psyching myself up for a confrontation with a banana slug in a bolo tie."

"Got it," I chuckle. "See you in the morning."

§

"We're home, sweet baby." I close the front door behind us and listen. Silence.

Rhonda calls, "Where's my little—" She runs to the crate to find the dog cowering against the back. Rhonda coaches Lylou out and scoops her up.

"What's wrong, girl? Are you sick?" The dog gradually calms, settling into her mama's arms. I step over and give a gentle scratch under the pup's sagging chins while I glance around the room.

"Oh, shit!" I exclaim. "We got a problem." A little breeze whooshes through a jagged hole in the glass sliding door between the kitchen and the back patio.

The great room area looks undisturbed, so I run to my bedroom, skid to a stop at the door, then survey the room as carefully as I can without entering. The mess reminds me of TV footage of a tornado's aftermath; emptied drawers are scattered around, the floor knee-deep in stuff. My first instinct is to run around and check the rest of the place. But the fucker who did this could still be in the house, right? I back away and do a quick one-eighty.

"Rhonda," I yell, "take Lylou and get out. Call 9-1-1 and report a break-in."

"What about—"

"Just go!"

I step into the kitchen and grab one of the handles protruding from the pine block next to the sink. Its serrated blade reflects a shaft of sunlight. I'm disappointed with the rounded end—guess it's technically a bread knife.

Once I'm back at my bedroom door, I holler out in the manliest voice I can muster. "Cops are on the way, asshole. Now's your chance to get the fuck outta here." Nothing.

Knife hand extended, I enter the room at the approximate speed of the Mendenhall Glacier. The space is redolent of something unpleasant, but there's no one here.

I move room to room. Once I've convinced myself I'm alone in the chaos, I slide the bagel cutter back into its place in the block. A deep breath and the sound of distant sirens help slow my jackhammering heart—no one is getting shot or sliced today. I turn my attention away from the possibility of a gruesome death and focus on that overwhelming odor. The smell is familiar, like, like—

My house reeks of Axe cologne.

"Estelle, you wicked bitch," I say to the empty house. "What the hell are you and Tony Soprano still looking for?"

Less than a minute later a car screeches to a stop in my driveway. I take a step in the direction of the front entry, then freeze. The door to the coat closet opens a crack, and a meaty, tattooed hand sticks out—Estelle's bodyguard. Holy shit! He was here the whole time? Where's my bread slicer when I need it?

He comes out of the closet, takes a split second to give me a menacing look, then whips open the front door and steps outside... into the arms of two very young cops, guns drawn.

"Down on the ground. Now!"

Once Mongo has been handcuffed and locked into the back seat's metal cage, Officer Gerwitz walks me to the black-and-white for a closer look. "You said you've seen him before, right, Mr. Horvath?"

"Yeah. He was here a few days ago...with my mother-in-law."

"I'm going to need you to sign a statement, sir. Can you follow us to the station?"

§

"That her, Mr. Horvath?"

Rhonda and I and Officer Gerwitz stand at a one-way window. I have no idea how they managed to round her up so quickly, but in the tiny room on the other side, Estelle sits rod-straight in a Costco folding chair.

"Yes. That's Estelle Anders, my late mother-in-law."

"Late?"

Rhonda jumps in. "His wife, her daughter, passed away recently."

Gerwitz nods. "Sorry to hear that. Anyway, the guy we arrested at the house is Tommy Breckner, a small-time skell out of Vegas. He's got half a dozen outstanding warrants, plus we just caught him red-handed in a B&E in possession of a firearm, so the dude's going away for a while."

"He was carrying a gun?" My legs are getting rubbery.

"Yeah. This thing could have turned out a lot worse. Anyway, you'll probably be called to testify at his trial."

"I...um..." My thoughts are still on the gun.

"Mr. Horvath?"

"Yeah, sure. No problem. What about Estelle?"

"Breckner already flipped on her, says she hired him to bust in."

"Did he say what he was after?"

"A suitcase."

"Suitcase?" Rhonda blurts.

"She told him to look for any box or luggage that felt heavy, then bring it to her without opening it. Theoretically, the DA could charge her with some kind of conspiracy, but—"

"Let me guess," Rhonda says, "prosecutors have bigger fish to fry?"

Gerwitz confirms with a little palms-up gesture.

217

"I'm not looking to punish her," I say. "Just want the woman out of my life."

"I'll pass that along," Gerwitz says. "In any case, she'll be stuck in jail for a few days while they sort things out."

I can't help but smile. I'm betting a few days in lockup will scare the old biddy off for good.

§

We arrive home from the police station and Rhonda hurries in to check on our little girl. "Lylou's still trembling," she says. "Let's get her out for some fresh air."

"You hold our pup while I sweep up the glass. The rest of the mess can wait till we get back."

Once the floor's safe, I prop an old card table on its edge, covering the broken pane. Then Rhonda and I maneuver my heavy recliner to hold it in place. "Good enough," I declare. "I'll call a door guy tomorrow. You up for a drive to Snow Canyon?"

§

"Still beautiful," Rhonda says.

"Not as dramatic as it was under the full moon, but the West Canyon Road makes a pretty good dog path."

We've been walking about twenty minutes, and Lylou is huffing—and drooling a lot more than usual. I drop to one knee and look into her panting face. "Little girl need Daddy to carry her?"

"There's our favorite sitting rock," Rhonda says. "Let's all take a water break." She settles onto the sandstone ledge worn nearly smooth by a thousand weary hikers, and I heft Lylou into her lap.

"Sorry about the doggy spit," I say, then scoot myself next to the girls. "Think she's still a little—"

"The whole thing's still got us all a bit shook up," she says. "Maybe talk about it later?"

"Sure."

"On a completely different topic, Danny," Rhonda says, "you ever hear back on that DNA stuff?"

Not sure why she brought it up right now, or at all.

"Everything takes longer than they say, right? And it doesn't really matter, so…"

"Stop being evasive. Have they emailed you the information or not?"

"Technically, yes."

"Technically? Hand me your phone."

"No. This is my private business."

"Do you really think this is just about you?" Her anger surprises me. "Hand me the damn phone."

Why not? The email's worthless, and it's long gone. I unzip a pocket on my hiking shorts and fish out the aging iPhone.

"It's too late," I tell her. But she makes a grab for it and misses.

We both gasp as the delicate instrument clatters across the rock shelf and into the dirt.

"Oh, Danny. I'm so sorry." Rhonda passes Lylou to me then hops down and picks up the mobile. After wiping most of the dust off with her shirttail, she holds up my phone. "Just a couple of scratches, nothing too— Dammit!" Upon closer inspection, the screen is tightly webbed with cracks.

"Rhonda, what I was trying to tell you is the phone won't help. I already deleted the email."

"But you read it first, right?"

I tuck the damaged phone back in my pocket. "Never even opened it."

§

We'd stopped at JDawgs on the way home. Lylou is now hydrated and curled up in her bed. But the second Rhonda opens the oil-stained paper bag, the pup lifts her head and snort-sniffs the unmistakable molecules.

"Maybe just a bite or two?" I venture.

"No way! Last time you fed her Polish sausage she walked around in a fart cloud for two days straight."

"Sorry, Lylou. Mommy's feeling mean, so no hot dog."

"Feed her if you want," she says. "But she'll be sleeping with you tonight."

"Mommy and Daddy say no hot dog tonight, Baby."

I set paper plates and napkins on the table. Rhonda takes out the food and we tuck in. The franks are done to perfection, latticed with dark grill marks and extra-napkins juicy. They're also huge, but we eventually finish them and sit staring at empty plates in a grease-induced torpor.

"Sorry about your phone, Danny."

The sudden shift catches me off guard. "Oh, uh, no worries. The thing's at least six years old. What's that in techno years?"

"Somewhere in the low- to mid-one hundreds, I think. Can I take a look? Maybe it's time for Cousin Rhonda to buy you a new one."

"Nah. It's okay. Probably"

"Let me see. I promise not to drop it again."

"Knock yourself out," I say, and hand it to her.

She gives it a once-over. "Hmm. Seems the screen's still cracked."

I feign surprise. "Still? Dammit!"

"Let's see if I can test it without cutting myself on the broken glass." She carefully pokes and prods. "Well, look at that."

"What?"

"You deleted a recent email from 23andMe."

"Like I told you."

"You do know how to empty your email TRASH, right?"

"My what?"

"It's still here, Danny. Buckle up, 'cause I'm about to read it to you."

"Rhonda, I don't really want to—"

"Pay attention." She holds the phone up and reads, "It says here you're twenty-five percent Mongolian."

"No damn way."

"And twenty-five percent Mayan."

"Mayan? What the hell is that?"

"You know, Mayans, Central America, child sacrifice?"

"You're thinking of the Inca. Let me see that." I reach for my phone, but she yanks it away too fast.

Rhonda smiles and looks back to the crack-laced glass. "Yup, you're Mayan, also fifteen percent Greenlander and twenty percent Antarctican."

"Nobody even lives there in Antarctica."

"Not anymore, maybe. Anyway, here's the biggie." She pauses to flash a cheesy grin and perhaps do a calculation in her head. "Fully thirty percent of your DNA can be traced back to the Neanderthals."

"Neanderthals, eh?" I shake my head but can't hide a chuckle. "FYI, that's a hundred fifteen percent. You realize no one can be more than one hundred percent, right?"

"Yeah, well...perhaps not average people. Are you average, Daniel? I think not."

That gives me a good laugh. "The email was gone, wasn't it?"

"Nope." She holds up the phone. "It's right here. I'll pull up the actual graph and—"

"Still don't care. My dad never took the test, so there's no way to know about Mom."

"Did Jocelyn take it?"

"My sister? I have no idea."

"If she did, she'll show up on your report as either a sister or half-sister." Rhonda is still holding my phone. "This'll be easier if I forward the email to my address. With your permission, of course."

"Told you, I don't really care."

About a minute later, Rhonda slides her fingers across her MacBook's trackpad, issuing hmm, ahh, and hunh sounds under her breath. I make a conscious decision not to look over her shoulder, but in spite of all I said about not giving a shit, something in my chest flutters each time she vocalizes.

"Dammit, Rhonda. What am I...really?"

"Come around where you can see the computer." The screen is filled with a world map surrounded by several concentric rings. Some are full circles, some are fragments, all are shades of blue. The right half of the page lists the percentages the rings represent.

"It's pretty much what I thought: English, Scandinavian, and a little southern European. Not a stick of Neanderthal or Antarctican in the woodpile, by the way."

"There's a possibility," she says, "I misread it on that busted screen. Okay if I take a look at the list of relatives?"

"No."

Rhonda turns her palms up in surrender, then says, "You all right, Danny? You look like you're about to pass out."

I'm not about to faint, but I do feel like I'm being physically torn apart. What if my sister is in the database? I may be about to learn the final truth about my mom.

She ignores the earlier "no" and navigates, I guess is the word, to somewhere else on the site.

"The heading on this screen is Relatives in Common. Listen up."

"Rhonda, I don't know if I can—"

"Three people are listed. One is designated a fourth cousin, the other two are fifths, and all the names are completely foreign to me. Your sister Jocelyn does not show up."

"Which means she hasn't taken the test, right?"

Rhonda's eye contact makes a subtle change to unfocused stare. She gives a thoughtful little scratch to the side of her neck. "She, uh, probably didn't."

Chapter 24

The offices of Warburton Warburton and Stignell, Attorneys at Law are in a medium rise building, 421 West St. George Boulevard.

After passing through glass double doors, we step into an overdone lobby—indirect lighting, designer furniture, two saltwater aquariums surrounded by paintings and metal sculptures with a southwest theme. The psychology of lavish spending to impress clients or patients never made sense to me. Do they think we're too damn dumb to know who's really paying for it?

Lisa announces herself to the receptionist, a young man named Geoffrey in a pinstripe shirt and bowtie. He walks with us to the elevator, then we exit on floor two where he ushers us into a conference room, then disappears. The space features an entire wall of windows that frame a view of the spectacular rust-colored bluff to the north. The light oak table, thirty feet if it's an inch, is surrounded by swivel chairs done in soft leather the color of ground cinnamon on a Starbucks macchiato. Oh, now I get it. The obvious excess is not just to impress clients, it's also meant to intimidate the hell out of the poor souls on the wrong side of the table.

The three of us seat ourselves on the west side of the boat-shaped conference slab—and wait and wait.

"We've been here twenty minutes," Rhonda says. Where's this G. Freddy Junior?"

"Probably thinks making us wait is some kind of power play," I offer.

"I'll nip that in the bud," Lisa says.

The door opens, and Jabba the Hutt in a tan western suit with blue leather shoulder and elbow patches waddles in. G. Frederick is not the regal barrister I was expecting. He's midthirties, no doubt the younger of the Warburtons. The tight suit and bolo tie look ridiculous on his five-foot-six, 250-pound frame. The room may be imposing, but the dude looks like he barely finished the online law program from ASU—Altoona Southern, not Arizona State.

The man and his chair share a groan as he takes his place across from us at the oak table. I instantly detest G. Frederick Warburton II.

Without so much as a hello or a handshake, he begins thumbing through a manila folder, muttering, "Sorry I'm late. You know how it is."

"Screw you, Freddy," Lisa says.

He looks surprised, maybe even hurt. "What? How about a little respect, Lisa?"

"Respect? Is that what you call making us wait on your fat ass for half an hour? Expect a bill for my time which, as you know, is not cheap."

"Lisa, come on. Let's just hit reset and—"

She cuts him off with, "And for Dr. Horvath's time, which, by the way, is triple my hourly rate. Now stop stalling and hand over the Medical Marketing financials."

G mumbles something under his breath then pushes the folder across the table. Lisa opens it and goes straight to the last of a dozen pages. There's a long silence, which she breaks with, "This is unalloyed fraud, Freddy. When I'm finished, you and Silberg will be sharing a cell in the Utah State Prison."

She slides the single piece of paper to Rhonda who takes a quick glance, then passes it to me. According to the notarized document, Medical Marketing Services LLC has cash reserves in the amount of $142.68.

§

Later in the day, what I've come to think of as our little family watches the sunset from my back grass. I give a drool-dampened stick a heave, and Lylou—sans cone, finally—takes off after it.

"What happens now, Rhonda?"

"It's an embarrassingly obvious crime. I'd like to say it won't take long for Lisa and the AG's office to get to the bottom of it, but you really never know with these things. We'll just have to let them— Yuck." Lylou drops the slimy stick in Rhonda's lap and the Frenchie barks a request to throw it again. Rhonda gives it a good toss then turns back to me. "We'll just stay out of the way and let Lisa work her legal magic."

"Got it. Thanks again for everything you've done." I want to lean over and smother her perfect face in kisses, to beg her never to leave my side. But the fates have decreed a different ending for our story, as if there ever was an *our story*.

The dog drops the saliva-soaked stick onto Rhonda's lap again, then looks up with that signature panting smile, big round eyes radiating pure love. Rhonda responds with tears and Lylou licks away the fat drops before they can roll off her cheeks.

"Mommy has to go away, sweet girl," Rhonda says. "But Daddy will always be here to…to play fetch, take you for lots of walks, and"—her voice lowers to just above a whisper—"let you sleep next to him in bed every night for the rest of your life."

I tell myself, command myself, not to shed tears of my own. But my heart—or is it my big beautiful brain?—refuses to obey. In spite of, or perhaps because of, those miserable, fucking fates, everything just feels so…God…damned…wrong.

Chapter 25

I am placing you on leave, Dr. Horvath, for the duration of the investigation." I haven't seen my first patient yet, but here I am in Silberg's fancy office, that big-ass desk between us. If anything, he's smugger than last time I was here. "Of course, I could fire you on the spot if I wanted."

"You're accusing me of sexual harassment?" This is unbelievable, even for Colin Fucking Silberg. "Someone's been blowing smoke up your ass. Jane, perhaps?"

"I can't divulge who reported you."

"Bullshit."

"My attorney told me we're obliged to keep the victim's name confidential. Best for everyone concerned."

"How the hell is that best for me? Anyway, we both know this is all you, using Jane Carneely to try and intimidate me. Well, fuck you! And fuck her."

A haughty grin cracks Colin's miserable face. "Unfortunate choice of words, Dr. Horvath."

"What's that supposed to mean?"

"My lawyer told me to warn you not to make contact with anyone you think may have made the report."

"Oh, and fuck your lawyer too."

"You could be charged with retaliation," he says.

Charged? I take a deep breath, try and force at least some of the anger out of my voice. "So, what am I supposed to do?"

"I'm not here to give you legal advice," he says with finality. "Maybe you should talk to the bitch you call an attorney."

"She's kind of busy right now," I hiss, "preparing to toss your lying ass in prison." I spin around, poised for a dramatic stalk-out, then stop and turn back. "Just got my results."

"Results? What results?"

"Lab says I'm one hundred percent sterile."

"What does that even mean?" Colin asks.

"You know exactly what it means, Big Daddy."

I march straight over to Ash's office and close the door behind me. "Tell me you're not in on this, Ash!" I yell.

"What the hell are you talking about?"

"The suspension. Jane. Sexual—"

"Calm down, Danny," Ash says. "You're not making sense."

"Silberg just placed me on something he called 'investigative suspension' for sexual harassment."

"Sexual harassment? First I've heard of it. Who made the accusation?"

"Supposed to be a big fucking secret, but it has to be Jane."

"Jane?" After a thoughtful pause, Ash continues, "Did something happen between you two? You finally get into her bloomers?"

"Bloomers? Really, Ash?"

"Did you and Jane have sex, Danny? Or anything like it?"

"Both." I feel my face flush.

"Both what?"

"We had sex...and a couple of things like it. But it was completely consensual."

"Says you."

"I swear it was."

"Any witnesses?"

"Rhonda was there just before and right after."

"But not during, correct?"

"You are disgusting, you know that?"

"Did you make one of those tapes? You know, like the celebrities."

"No!"

"Was Lylou in the room?" He finally gives himself away with a little laugh.

"Goddammit, Ash, there's nothing funny about this. When I broke it off with her, she—"

"You broke up with her? I thought winning Jane was your life's goal."

"It was, until..." I don't seem to be able to finish the sentence.

"Until? Until what?"

I tilt my head and study the floor.

"Rhonda?" Ash breaks into a massive grin. I avoid his eyes. "Jeri was right, you guys have a thing for each other."

"There's no thing, Ash. We're cousins."

"So what?" His grin has somehow widened. "I mean—"

"It's...it's unnatural."

"Unnatural? My nephew married his boyfriend last year and no one north of the Mason-Dixon could possibly give two shits." Ash's face now is serious. "Look at me, buddy. Do I look unnatural, like some kind of freak?"

"Of course not, but—"

"My mother and father are first cousins. In Pakistan at the time, that was more the rule than the exception."

"But that was in a Muslim country."

"I don't know if you even consider yourself a Christian, but did you know some people say Joseph and Mary were cousins?"

"Okay, but Joseph wasn't Jesus's real—"

"Father? If you say so." We both have a good laugh.

"Anyway, Jane suddenly came up with this ridiculous claim that I impregnated her."

It seems to take a second or two for Ash's train of thought to return to the Jane problem.

"Oh my God," he says, "you really are in deep stool, brother. Talked to Lisa yet?"

"She's my next stop."

§

Actually, next stop is home. Rhonda and Lylou are just returning from a morning stroll around the neighborhood. I hop out of the car and join them in the driveway. "Rhonda, I have to talk to you."

"I'm standing right in front of you."

"Not out here."

The three of us go inside where Rhonda slips off the doggy harness and pink leash. Lylou shakes herself like she's just gotten out of the bath, then makes a beeline for her water bowl.

"You look like you just saw the ghost of your late wife," Rhonda says over the dog's loud slurps. "What's going on?"

"It's Jane."

"Jane Eyre-head?"

"The same. She ratted me out to Silberg—now I'm on something called 'investigative suspension' for sexual harassment."

"How much of the horrifying details did she share with him?"

I shrug a don't know. "He won't even admit Jane's the so-called complainant. But it has to be her."

"You sure, Danny? Is someone else at the clinic you might have diddled...and forgot to mention?"

"Not really funny, Rhonda. This is serious as a quintuple bypass."

"Didn't know a fiver was even possible. But should I take that as a no?"

"No. I mean, yes. What do I do now?"

"You have Lisa Monaghan in your phone contacts?"

"I do."

"Then why the hell are you wasting time talking to me?"

§

Three hours later, Rhonda and Lisa and I are at the very expensive Cliffside Restaurant, looking over the menus and the view.

"Order whatever you want," Lisa says. "I'm picking up the check."

"Keep it under twenty bucks," I counter. "We all know who's paying for it in the end."

We order, and the moment our waiter walks away with the menus, Lisa retrieves a pen and legal pad from her briefcase on the floor.

"Speaking of in the end," she says, "you must have some idea who made the SH complaint."

"Got to be Jane," I blurt.

Lisa glances left, then right, then puts a finger to her lips. "Careful, Daniel. You don't want to add a defamation suit to your troubles."

"It wouldn't be a problem," I say, "if we were in your office instead of in the middle of a crowded restaurant."

"But here we are," she shrugs. "Shall we continue?"

I whisper, "Jane Carneely."

"She works at Danny's clinic," Rhonda says. "Pretty woman, fifteen or so years Danny's junior, with a rack seldom seen outside a porno."

Lisa leans in and mutters, "Did anything happen that she might have misconstrued as a pass or sexual advance?"

I whisper back, "I sucked her toes."

"Her toes?"

"Oh," I say, perhaps a little too loud, "and I fucked her."

"Waiter," Lisa yells, "cancel the order!"

§

Three minutes later we're in Lisa's idling Infiniti, AC on high. "So," she says, her eyes on mine, "what's this about engaging in sexual congress with the hired help?"

"Jane and I had sex...and stuff. But it was completely consensual, I swear. And she's not technically a clinic employee."

"Not an employee? What is she?"

"Aesthetician. Independent contractor."

"Okay," Lisa says. "Pretend I'm a judge—convince me the sex was consensual."

"At the end of a dinner date, she agreed to go back to my house. She asked to take a shower and—"

"Were you in the shower with her?"

"No, but—"

"But what, Danny?"

"She invited me to watch. And after that, she initiated some, uh, sex-type activities."

"'Sex-type activities' is pretty vague. Sorry, Danny, but I'm going to need you to reconstruct the entire evening, from picking her up to dropping her off at home, in detail."

In horrific, embarrassing, disgusting detail.

"Rhonda, you may want to step out for a few," Lisa says.

"I'm not going anywhere."

"Daniel?" Lisa looks to me for a decision on ejecting Cousin Rhonda from the game.

"She can stay."

"I've heard it all already," Rhonda says.

The bunch in my gut tugs itself a little tighter. Actually, Rhonda, you haven't heard it all. But at this point, what the hell?

Ten excruciating minutes later, Lisa asks, "That everything?"

"Every decadent detail."

To say the last few minutes were humiliating would be an understatement on par with the Beatles have sold some records. I just want to get the hell out of here, go home and curl up in bed after a cocktail or four.

But Lisa is not finished. "Tell me more about this Jane Carneely. Any reason to think she has an ulterior motive?"

Rhonda explodes into boisterous chortling. Once she catches enough breath to speak, she says, "Hell, yeah. She's trying to shake Danny down by lying about being pregnant with his—"

"Pregnant?" Lisa says.

"Not by me," I say. "I have motility issues."

"Huh?" The word doesn't seem to register with Lisa.

"Every swimmer in this lazy river lost his flipper," I say, pointing to my general lap area.

"He's got the test results to prove it," Rhonda adds. "And don't forget Silberg."

"He and she tight?"

"If Jane really is knocked up," I say, "the kid is definitely Colin Fucking Silberg Junior."

"We'll circle back to that," Lisa says. "For now, our focus needs to be on the money. I'll pick you two up at nine tomorrow. Bring three official copies of the death cert."

Chapter 26

Althea Gouden, vice-president of Southwestern States Bank, is a small black woman in a crisp charcoal business suit. Ms. Gouden slips on her gold-framed glasses while Lisa pushes Lorraine's death certificate and my driver's license across the glass desktop.

Althea takes her time inspecting the larger page. She holds the license up to compare my face to the photo, then slides the documents back. "Lorraine was quite a woman, Daniel." She smiles and shakes her head. "That thing last month was the most excitement we'd had here in a long time."

Rhonda is staring like she just saw a flying saucer. Lisa leans over and whispers behind a sheltering hand, "What is she talking about?"

"Ms. Gouden," I say. "What thing was that?"

"The withdrawal, of course. Sorry you had to make the trip to Salt Lake."

"I have no idea what you're talking about."

"Oh my God," she blurts. "That wasn't you in the car?"

I shake my head, but Lisa speaks first. "Please tell us what happened. From the beginning."

"Lorraine—Mrs. Horvath—, made a large withdrawal from the company account."

"How large," the three of us ask, almost in unison.

"Seven hundred fifty."

"Seven hundred dollars is a lot of money here?" I ask.

"Seven hundred fifty…thousand."

I'm certain everyone in the room can hear me gulp.

"Of course, we had nowhere near that much cash on hand, so—"

"Cash?" Rhonda exclaims.

"So we arranged for her to pick it up at our main office in Salt Lake City. I was worried sick about the bank handing over such a large amount of currency, but she said something like, 'My husband will drive me. He has a concealed carry permit and a loaded .45.'"

§

Back in Lisa's car, Rhonda says, "So Lorraine took the cash and what, stuffed it in a pee-stained mattress somewhere?"

A thought slams me with a force that physically snaps my head back. "Estelle!" I shout. "She and Bluto weren't looking for a keepsake, they were after the money."

"Estelle?" Lisa asks. "Who's Estelle?"

I bring Lisa up to speed on the recent break-in, and she asks, "You think they found the cash at the house?"

"The guy was empty-handed when the police cuffed him."

"If that's the case," Lisa says, "it could be in a safe deposit box, certificates of deposit, some phantom account in her or Silberg's name…the possibilities are nearly endless."

"Let's dig her up and see if she jammed it in her ass," I offer. Not entirely sure I meant the crack to be facetious.

"Nah," Rhonda says. "If it had been there, Colin would have found it."

"And speaking of Colin Silberg," Lisa says, "he walks away from this whole ugly thing unless…"

§

Lisa, Rhonda, and I step into the big Warburton conference room. Apparently, G. Frederick wanted to spare himself another tardiness tongue-lashing—he's here waiting for us. We take seats, and Lisa says, "Hello, Freddy. Can I assume you invited us here to give my client's stolen money back?"

"Not exactly," he says. I force myself not to reach across the table and slap the smirk off his puffy face. "You've seen the balance sheet. Medical Marketing Services has no money."

"So where is it?" I yell.

Rhonda digs fingernails into my thigh, a pretty clear message to shut up.

"You'll have to ask Mrs. Horvath," he says.

"You fat fuck!" I jump up and lunge, but the table's too wide—plus Lisa and Rhonda are pulling me back by my belt loops.

Freddy pushes his chair well back from the table. His index finger is poised over his phone. "C…can you control your client, counselor? Or do I call 9-1-1 and report an assault?"

I flop back against the high seatback, feeling Lisa's white-hot glare.

"Not one more word, Daniel," she loud-whispers. "Promise me right now you'll sit there with your hands in your lap or get the hell out."

I stare at my lap hands without looking up. "Promise," I mutter.

"And Freddy," Lisa says, "you will conduct yourself with a modicum of civility or I'll call the cops myself and charge you with first-degree assholery."

Warburton clears his throat loudly, then says, "MMS has virtually no funds because Lorraine Horvath bled it dry."

Lisa stares arrows at him. "Tell me something I don't already know."

"At its peak, the balance was in excess of $750,000," he says. "But last month she wrote a large check to herself and—"

"And Silberg drove her to Salt Lake to collect the cash. The Southwestern States Bank. Am I right?"

G. Frederick offers a noncommittal shrug.

"So, Freddy, where's the money now?" Lisa glances at her watch. "At exactly this moment in time."

"Like I said, you'd have to ask—"

"Finish that sentence and I'll strangle you myself," Rhonda says.

Tear him a new one, Cuz!

"You must have done the research," Freddy says. "Where were the checks deposited?"

"Freddy,"— Lisa gives an exaggerated headshake—"you know damn well she cashed them and walked out of the bank with the currency."

"If you say so. Look, the record shows that my client was not involved in even a single transaction. If anyone's a victim, Colin Silberg is."

"What is that supposed to mean?" Lisa demands.

"My client is a full partner, entitled to half of the missing money. As Lorraine's surviving spouse, Dr. Horvath inherited that liability."

NOW LORRAINE HAS GONE

§

We return home from the Warburton meeting to find an anxious pup. Lylou hears the word "walk" and begins a little spin dance accompanied by happy whimpers. "We're just making a lap or two around the block," I tell her. It doesn't dampen her dogthusiasm one bit, but we already established she doesn't speak English, so...

Once she realizes there's no car ride associated with today's stroll, Lylou heads down the driveway to the sidewalk, square head held high.

"What now, Rhonda?" I ask.

"Find the account or accounts where she stashed the cash."

"What about the aforementioned pee-stained mattress?" I ask.

"Then we better find the mattress before someone else does."

"When we do, I'll see Silberg in hell before he gets half my—"

A text ping interrupts. It's from Jane.

§

"Lucky girl gets two walks today," Rhonda laughs. From a nearby bench, we watch Lylou sniff around the Washington County Dog Park like a four-legged Sherlock Holmes. "It's ten after. You think she'll really show?"

"She initiated the meeting, so— Oh, there she is."

Wearing plain polyester shorts and an oversize tee that can't hide those freakish, pendulous breasts, Jane is following Charles through the double chain-link gates.

"Hi, guys," she calls out. Considering how our last meeting went, the woman seems oddly upbeat. She clicks off the leash, and her dog shoots out like a brown bottle rocket in Lylou's direction.

"May I?" She nods at a spot on our bench.

"Of course, Jane," Rhonda says. "Please join us."

She sits next to Rhonda and says, rather sheepishly, "Bet Daniel was surprised to get my text."

Surprised? Try dumbfounded. Or maybe gobsmacked, if that's really a word.

"Is everything okay?" Rhonda asks.

"Of course." But her welling eyes belie the words. "I just...just..."

She's full-on weeping now. I should probably feel at least a hint of empathy, but she was nearly giddy thirty seconds ago. Is this some sort of game, Jane?

"What's wrong?" Rhonda drapes an arm around her shoulders.

The younger woman snuggles in, resting her head against the consoler's neck. Rhonda glances over at me and we share a *what-the-hell* look.

"I'm so sorry, Rhonda. I had to talk to you, to confess..." She turns her head just enough that Rhonda's shirt is now absorbing the tears and, I assume, snot.

Confess? Confess what, you pathetic child? And why the hell are you apologizing to Rhonda? I'm the one you screwed over, so to speak.

"I lied to the lady about that sexual harassment stuff."

"What lady?" I blurt.

"The one from the state discrimination thing. I didn't want to, but Colin said I still owed him." Her head drops, and Jane goes quiet.

We wait silently. When it seems Jane may have rallied, Rhonda ventures, "Owed him? For what, Jane? Did Dr. Silberg threaten you?"

"You probably didn't know that my boobies are fake."

Those super-sized Whoppers aren't real? Everyone who's ever met you better prepare for a shock. And you still haven't answered the question about owing Silberg for something.

"And," she adds, "that I'm kinda gay." Rhonda removes her arm from Jane's shoulder and slides closer to me.

Hallelujah! I'm not a bad lover, Jane's just not into men!

"Kinda?" Rhonda says.

"I'm not a lesbian."

How do you un-hallelujah?

"I like both kinds."

"Bisexual?" Rhonda ventures.

"I guess."

I say, "Sorry for what Colin's put you through, Jane."

"And he's a lousy lay. Makes Daniel seem like Brad Pitt."

Please go on, Jane dear.

"Or Angelina Jolie, if she still…you know."

That's enough.

"Anyway, wanted to get this off my chest."

My thirteen-year-old self giggles without sound. She said "off my chest."

Jane continues. "I care about you two. Sometimes I even think about the three of us—"

Rhonda cuts her off with, "You mentioned owing Silberg for something?"

"There's more to the boobies story."

"More?" Rhonda asks.

"Dr. Silberg performed the surgery."

We offer encouraging nods.

"No way I could afford it, so he offered to do it for free if I'd—"

Rhonda cuts her off. "In exchange for favors?"

"Yeah." Tears are gathering. "Sex-type favors—and lots of 'em."

"Jane," Rhonda says, "I am so sorry."

Jane seems to take that as a cue to re-close the gap between her and Rhonda.

After a beat of silent empathy, Rhonda asks, "Does he ever brag about money or maybe his business deals?"

"What he brags about are his old cars."

"He loves his classic Chevys," I say. "Won't shut up about them."

"Yeah, right? A few days ago, he took me out to the big garage where he keeps the fancy cars. Said he always wanted to do it in the backseat of his '55 convertible. It was a beauty, shiny black and chrome. We did it, but I kind of broke a window with one of my stiletto heels."

I'm repulsed by Jane and despise Silberg, but damn if that isn't a sexy mental picture.

"He was real angry, yelled at me and said I must be retarded. But it wasn't my fault. I mean, there just wasn't enough room for, you know. And I didn't want to do it anyway."

I cut her off with some aggressive throat clearing. "I guess that's all we need to know."

"Jane, you said you didn't really want to have sex with Dr. Silberg," Rhonda clarifies. "So, why did you do it?"

"This time or all the other times?"

All the other times? Not really a surprise, but still.

"You said you had sex with Dr. Silberg against your will. Did he physically force you?"

"No," Jane whispers. "I told you I was paying him back, but somehow it's never enough."

"Paying him back?" Rhonda says. "For the breast augmentation?"

"Yeah. I kinda told you that already."

I say, "But Jane—"

"Anyways, after, you know, he said a strange thing. Don't know what it means, but I felt like I should tell someone."

Rhonda says, "Weird sex talk?"

"Nah. It was after that stuff was over. He pointed to one of the cars and said, 'See that car over in the corner? I sort of inherited it from an old friend. Can you believe it's worth three-quarters of a million dollars?' I don't know if it was supposed to be a joke or what. I mean, it was a rusty old wreck, the only car in there that didn't look like brand new. I'm sorry, I, we really gotta go."

"You've done a brave thing, Jane," Rhonda says. "Would you be willing to tell your story in court?"

"In front of other people?"

"Of course."

Jane looks suddenly to be in the grip of some temporary catatonia.

As if he'd read his person's mind, Charles lopes over to our bench. She unfreezes, hoists him onto her lap, and mutters, "Time to head home, buddy." While she's walking away, Jane calls back over her shoulder, "And I'm not really pregnant, that's just what Dr. Silberg told me to say."

No shit, Jane.

Out on the field, Lylou is playing with a brindle-coated mutt. The game looks to be keep-away, the object some half-shredded, cast-off dog collar.

Rhonda adjusts her position to make eye contact with me. "You thinking what I'm thinking, Danny?"

"That it's still not too late for that threesome?"

"That was not at all what I was thinking," she says. "But if you really want to—"

"God, I'd rather binge watch 'Downton Abbey.'"

"Colin has a car worth exactly three-quarters of a mil?"

"And a crap car, at that," I add.

"Bequeathed to him by an 'old friend?'"

"Let's pick a time when he's in surgery," I say. "Sneak over for a closer look at the miracle jalopy."

"Not without a court order."

"We won't steal anything, just see what we can see."

"Criminal trespass is a class A misdemeanor, Daniel. And if you break a lock or a window to access the garage, it's B&E."

"B&E?"

"Breaking and Entering. A felony."

"You're a total buzzkill, Cuz."

"Yup. But I've kept you out of jail. So far."

My iPhone dings, and I read the text out loud. "Dr. Silberg & Dr. Bakri would like to meet with you tomorrow at 7:30 a.m."

"Hope Lisa's an early riser," I say.

Chapter 27

H ave a seat," Silberg says.

Lisa and I remain standing across the desk from CFS and his overweight attack dog, G. Freddy Warburton. And why the hell is Ash sitting between them?

"What's this about?" Lisa demands.

Freddy clears his throat. "We've concluded the sexual harassment investigation," he says. "Dr. Horvath's employment with Southern Utah Medical Partners, dba Red Rocks Multispecialty Clinic is terminated effective immediately."

"Last I knew you were not an officer of the company, Freddy," Lisa says. *You* can't terminate anybody."

"You're fired, Horvath," Silberg spits. "Pack your shit and get out."

I haven't taken my eyes off Ash, and he hasn't taken his eyes off the desk.

"What the fuck, Ash? Does Silberg have photos of you with underage farm animals?"

He finally looks at me with an old man's eyes. "Goddammit, Danny. Why couldn't you just keep your pecker in your pants?"

"Ash, don't you see that Silberg—"

"So, Colin,"—Lisa is literally rubbing her hands together like some cartoon villain—"care to tell us who made the complaint?"

G interrupts. "Lisa, don't—"

She stops him with a stare. "And who put her up to it?"

§

I'd begged off a day hike in Zion by telling Rhonda I had a doctor's appointment. I feel a little bad; it's true, but I'll be making a house call. And with a little luck, the doctor won't be in.

I've never been invited to Silberg's for anything, never even seen the area where he lives. So the first pass is a reconnaissance cruise down Manzanita Lane, an area of older, upscale homes. Each property looks to be at least an acre, and a couple of horses seem more the rule than the exception. Going too slow might look suspicious, so I drive by my target with barely a glance. Right now, I'm mostly interested in the neighborhood. How close together are the houses? Anyone out working in their yard? Someone walking a dog? Subtle hints of people at home in the middle of a weekday. No signs of human life—so far.

The next time by, I pause at the curb in front of a two-story Tudor that looks like it belongs in the rainy English countryside, not the Utah desert. I grin at the dark brick and steeply pitched gables, comically out of place among the graceful curves and light earth tones of the adobe-style homes surrounding it.

"You gotta be kidding me." Next to the front door is a massive bronze plaque, a coat of arms depicting twin rearing stallions, front hooves resting against a shield bearing a huge

S. As far as I know, Colin is the only S in the manor—his last wife fled four years ago. But a guy can't be too careful. I pull away slowly, turn right at the end of the block, and soon park near a shade tree in the parking area of a nearby church.

Decision time, Danny Boy. The entrance to I-15 is less than a mile from here. You can be home in fifteen minutes with no risk of spending the night—maybe a whole bunch of nights—in the Washington County jail.

§

SLOWER TRAFFIC MUST STAY RIGHT the sign says. That's me, riding the outside lane and keeping the Subie a couple of miles under the limit. I know it's irrational, but I'm experiencing some kind of weird apprehension that if a Highway Patrol trooper were to pull me over for speeding, he or she might somehow divine my previous evil intent. Maybe it's the word that has me a degree off-kilter. Apprehension, that is. My offramp looms, I flick the signal, slow even more, and turn onto Exit 26 northbound.

At the bottom of the ramp, I experience a sudden surge of courage. "Fuck it!" I yell at the windshield, then make a tire-squealing left under the freeway and another left onto I-15 southbound. I stomp the accelerator and push the little SUV to eighty-five.

§

Not sure why I close the door so slowly. I'm two blocks away from Manzanita Lane, there's no one around to hear, and what's the big deal with a slamming car door, anyway? I don sunglasses, walk through the church property, and turn right onto the sidewalk that soon brings me to Silberg's street. The dark glasses are unlikely to fool anyone, and my bearing might not project the nonchalance I'm going for. This whole don't-notice-me-I'm-just-out-for-a-stroll act would look more authentic if I'd brought Lylou along, but of course I couldn't take the risk that our little Frenchie might end up in doggy jail. *Doggy Jail? Focus, Danny Boy, you're not thinking clearly.*

As if I needed reminding, a sign warns, PRIVATE DRIVE NO TRESPASSING. Silberg's driveway is fashionably stained the color of butterscotch, a long stretch of stamped concrete terminating at a three-car garage that matches the house. Behind the dark glasses, I turn my eyes left then right without giving myself away with any head moves. The neighbor's horse watches intently, but no humans are within my view, so I swivel on one heel and racewalk down the access. Thank Zeus I'm not being chased by trained attack dogs. Yet.

A row of small windows runs along the top edge of the garage door. I stretch tip-toed and peer in. Lots of lawn and garden equipment. Where the hell are the cars?

Stepping back, I take a quick glance around. It had been hidden by the house at first—a red metal building double the size of the nearby garage. Most of the front is sliding barn doors secured with a welded hasp and padlock the size of a Crown Burger Double. A walk around quickly confirms my suspicion. There are no windows. Abort mission.

A fourth of the way back to the sidewalk I pause and turn back. That's the end of that stupid idea...assuming, of course, I make it back to the car without incident. But something catches my attention. From this perspective, I can see skylights—framed windows that stick up about four inches above the plane of the storage building's gleaming roof. This changes everything.

§

Whether it's good luck or bad remains to be seen, but there's a ladder at the back of the outbuilding. I tip it up and climb to the edge, but before stepping onto the roof, perform a quick assessment. The pitched roof is unpainted, corrugated steel or perhaps heavy gauge aluminum. My dark glasses help a little, but the metallic silver reflects the desert sun like a dusty mirror. I test the surface. It's warm—make that hot—to the touch, but not unbearable.

Your mission, should you accept it, is to make it to that roof window and look down to see if there's a rusty, car-shaped treasure chest inside. I take a deep breath and whisper, "I choose to accept it."

Transitioning from the ladder is more precarious than I expect, but I'm soon on all fours, bare palms and bare knees on the roof. The surface is waaay hotter than I'd expected. *Holy shit!* I'd kill for a pair of gloves right now...and what made me think this was a good day for shorts? Better unass this roof before second-degree burns set in.

Without looking back, I raise my right foot and probe for the ladder. It's a little left of where I thought. My shoe grazes the vertical rail, and a hellacious sound instantly brands my consciousness, the metal-on-metal screechrattle of an aluminum ladder sliding across the roof's scalloped edge, then slamming the ground. *No time to think, Danny Boy. Your hands and knees are on fire. Make a damn decision now or you are fucked.*

"My shirt!" I take one hand, then the other off the scorching metal. The back-and-forth provides some relief, but removing the sweat-stuck tee is precarious—make that terrifying. It's finally off, and I maneuver the shed shirt until it's a kind of hot pad under my roasting hands, then do a little push-up to get off my knees and onto the tips of my shoes. Thankfully, I'm wearing my Salomon trail runners, the ones with the cleated rubber sole that wraps up and over the toe box.

With both hands on the protective fabric, I begin a precarious four-point scrabble in the direction of the skylight. *Shiiit!* For about five seconds, the cotton had spared the palms of my hands from a grilling, but the garment is drenched in sweat, and the stovetop-level heat is now penetrating my Tom Petty T-shirt like steam through a wet oven mitt. Think, dammit!

I flip the shirt out of the way and go for the one and only remaining option—my shorts. I somehow manage to wriggle out of the khaki cargos, but in the process, my iPhone slips out of the front pants pocket. I have no choice but to let it slide away.

Fuck it. It's already cracked…and, Danny Boy, the phone, the money, and everything else are totally worthless if you tumble off this roof and wind up some kind of -plegic.

The skylight is thirty or so inches on each side, about fifteen feet above me. In this moment, I couldn't give two shits about whether I'll see the crap car. I need an oasis, some way to get myself up off the roof, which is beginning to remind me of the flattop at a Denny's. I start scrambling, but a thin layer of dirt renders the surface as slick as wet tile. Goddammit! Rubber toes don't fail me now.

I somehow make it. Almost. The dust-dulled glass is just below the peak on my side, now no more than two feet above me. For a fraction of a second, I consider a hail-Mary pounce, but that thought is erased by a mental image of me missing the mark and sliding backwards over the roof's edge, naked but for an electric blue pair of loose-legged satin briefs.

Much sooner than I expect, searing heat makes it through the cargo shorts. My fingertips suddenly feel like I'm unscrewing a hundred-watt bulb I'd forgotten to turn off. If I can just fold the fabric double, I think I can make the last—

"Noooh!" I fumble the khakis, and they launch themselves down the slick ribs and over the edge to rejoin the phone.

Hail Mary, full of grace.

Inside the Salomons, my toes are cramping. I slide my left foot forward into an awkward stance, probably more wounded ballerina than the sprinter-in-the-starting-blocks I was going for. I lean back just a little to get more weight on the shoe tips and push off with as much power as my trembling calves can muster.

§

The shower of broken glass seems to have ended, but I wait an extra few seconds before opening my eyes. I'm flat on my back, staring up at bright specks of dust dancing in a column of sunlight emanating from a square opening fifteen or so feet directly above. I sit up and shake my head. Instead of mental cobwebs, tiny cubes of glass jingle from my hair.

I'm not currently bleeding to death because the skylight is—was—safety glass, like a car window. The little cubes are still tinkling down, losing themselves in the inch-deep layer already surrounding me on this…what? What am I sitting on?

Gingerly, I brush some glass nuggets out of the way, then place my palms down. It's a cloth convertible roof, the framework of metal ribs underneath the fabric the obvious explanation for a pretty damn hard landing. I press down in an attempt to raise my butt and scoot to the edge. What the hell? It feels like someone clubbed a spot near my neck with a bowling pin. I drop back to my butt, then use two fingers to very carefully trace the length of the left clavicle. Halfway across I discover a lump—just touching it sends another agonizing jolt. It's a diagnosis even a skin doc can make—that fucker's fractured.

Holding my left arm tight against my ribs, I manage to climb down from the top of a gleaming black convertible—1955 Chevrolet, I'm guessing.

I miss my pants and shirt but thank God I still have the Salomons between my feet and the glass. Soles now firmly on the floor, I take in the scene. There are two other Chevys, both familiar, a 1956 Nomad wagon in red and white and a baby-blue '57 Bel Air. It seems odd that neither has a car cover, but as far as I can see in the dim light, their gleaming paint is nearly dust-free. I turn back to survey any damage to the ragtop that broke my fall and my collarbone. A few glass bits remain on the roof. Hundreds litter the nearby floor, but I don't detect any harm to the car. A small judder passes through me at the thought of Silberg coercing Jane into sex in the car's cramped back seat just to indulge some pathetic teenage fantasy.

In spite of the pain, I feel a sudden rush like I'd found a shipwreck loaded with Spanish gold. Just as Jane had reported, beyond the black Chev, a car-shaped pile of rust and dust hugs the back wall. Time to see if that old hulk hides the treasure. I take one step, then freeze.

A booming bass guitar invades the space and Axl Rose's sing-scream is unmistakable. But where the hell is "Welcome To The Jungle" coming from? Before I can investigate, the music fades and is replaced by spoken words.

"Where, pray tell, are your clothes, Dr. Horvath?"

What the ever-loving fuck?

"I sincerely hope you haven't damaged my baby," the disembodied voice continues. "This particular car has a certain, shall we say, sentimental value."

I swivel my head but can't see another human being in the garage. "Where the hell you hiding, Silberg?"

"Southwest corner, just below the roof."

I squint in the direction my still-reeling mind guesses is southwest. Where the roof meets the wall, a lens protrudes from a white box half the size of my fist. With a soft whir, the camera and its blinking red light move a few degrees left and a little downward, pointing itself directly at me.

"I'm watching you from my smartphone. Isn't technology great?"

I don't see the speaker he's talking through, but one thing's for sure, the asshole can see—and hear—me. So I show the lens my middle finger and shout, "Fuck you, Silberg," then take a step in the direction of the mystery car.

"Stop right there, Horvath."

"Or what? You'll shoot me with a laser beam from your fucking phone? I think I'll just take a closer look at the rusty heap by the back wall. What is it, make that *was* it? An old Nash Rambler?"

"You're being recorded, Horvath. Don't be stupid."

I ignore the threat and walk to the rear of the car to find the trunk lid suspiciously free of dust. An old-style T-handle sticks out the back; it turns easily, but the hinges respond to my tug with a banshee's screech. Inside is a single white Bankers Box. Pulling the lid reveal bundles of cash, each one-inch stack wrapped with a single paper band, white with double purple stripes. In the same purple ink, *$2,000*. The container is filled with, I'm guessing, three-hundred-seventy-five-ish more bundles. I instinctively reach for my pocket and the camera phone. Damn! Nothing but flimsy boxers.

"Touch the money and you're headed straight for prison, asshole."

"Someone's going to jail, but it sure as shit ain't me." I arrange myself between spy cam and cash, grab a stack and tuck it under the waistband of my boxers. The elastic doesn't hold, and it slides through the loose fabric and plops onto the concrete floor. Duh.

"Put my money back, Horvath."

"Okay, okay." I squat and retrieve the cash, then turn and make a show of setting it back in the box and replacing the lid. Hope he didn't see me pull a single bill and stuff it in my mouth. I use my tongue to wad up the evidence, tucking it as far back and to the left as possible, then slam the trunk and turn back and show empty hands to the all-seeing eye.

"You slatisfied," I say, trying to sound like there's not a clump of wet paper in my mouth.

"Not yet. Open wide and say ahh."

I manage to swallow the wad in a single gulp. The moment I jack my mouth open, there's a soft sound I take for the camera zooming in.

Silberg says, "Did you know US currency is mostly cotton?"

"What?"

"In twenty-four hours or so, the hundred you just swallowed is coming out as nothing but shit. Nice try."

Left of the camera, I spy an EXIT door equipped with one of those crash bars for emergency egress. I step over and try it. Locked, of course.

"How you going to get out, Horvath?" he asks with a humorless laugh. "It's a long way back up to that broken window."

"Eh, I'll figure it out." I lean in for a closer inspection of the exit mechanism.

"Got a proposition for you."

"Fuck your proposition."

"This one could keep you out of prison." His tone is maddeningly casual.

I stop midstep and prick up my ears. Prick? Ears? That's about right.

"I can unlock the exit from here," he says. "You walk through it, forget the whole unfortunate incident, and all is forgiven."

"And if I don't agree?"

"How long do you suppose an adult human can survive without water, Dr. Horvath?"

No more than three or four days in this heat, as any well-prepared mountain biker could tell you. "You're pure evil, Silberg, but I can't believe you'd stoop to murder."

"Murder? How could I have known you'd break into my building? And it's not like I go out there to check on things more than every week...or two. So, you know..."

"Burn in hell."

"Keep your pants on." He spends the next few seconds giggling like a kindergarten girl. "Pants on, I love it! Lighten up, Horvath, we're just having a little fun here. I'd never do you like that."

"Riiight."

A metallic clunk issues from the metal door. "Walk out now," invisible Silberg says, "or the next sound you hear will be approaching sirens."

§

"How's the pain?" Rhonda asks.

"Not bad."

The sun is now low in the sky, and we're following Lylou for the second lap around the park, leash in my right hand, left arm suspended in a navy-blue sling. A few hours ago, an orthopedist friend had x-rayed the shoulder and pronounced, "Good news. It's a crack, not a through-and-through break." After delivering that fucking wonderful information, he hooked me up with some Percocet and this strap. "The equation is simple," he had said. "The less you move that left arm and shoulder, the less pain." I'd already kinda figured that out.

"There's no probable cause for police to search his garage," Rhonda says.

"Of course there is. I saw the money with my own eyes."

"You claim to have seen it, but only after breaking into a private residence."

"Not a private residence, just an outbuilding near the—"

"No difference."

"And I really did see it."

"May I remind you, Dr. Silberg almost certainly has video evidence of the crime against his property."

"Yeah. Including me finding the money."

"Think that'll be on the thumb drive he gives the cops? The only good news is that the physical evidence of your theft is crap. Literally."

I'm outta yeah-buts.

"So, what now?" Rhonda asks.

"Hi, Lylou! Remember me? I'm Ana Sophia." Deep into the conversation, neither of us had noticed our little friend approach. The Frenchie stops and nuzzles the girl's outstretched hand. Ana kneels and gives her canine friend a big neck hug.

"Can I walk her a little? If I'm real careful?"

"Of course, Ana Sophia," Rhonda says.

"I can do it all by myself. I mean, if you trust me."

"We do, Ana Sophia. Is your mother here?"

The girl points to the busy playground. "She's over there, watching my little brother."

I hand off the leash. "Let's walk over and make sure she says it's okay."

After a chat with her mom, Ana Sophia and Lylou are soon strutting down the path, as proud a pair as I've seen.

Rhonda joins me on the bench. "It wouldn't be the end of life as you know it," she says.

"You lost me. What are we talking about now?"

"Silberg. The money."

"And exactly what is it that wouldn't be the end of life as I know it? Prison?"

"Actually, that would be the end. But just walking away from the stolen money? Do the math, Danny. The house—your paid-off house—is still on the market, right?"

"I still need a place to live."

"Yeah, but three thousand square feet in a gated community? There's a lot more than $750,000 in your 401(k). You pull down a paycheck most of us could only dream about and—"

"I'm currently unemployed, remember?"

"With all your loyal patients, you could open a practice tomorrow. And don't forget, if Lorraine were still alive, you'd already have flushed a lot more than this, not to mention a ludicrously large check going out month after month after month."

"But it would kill me to know that fuckwad won, Rhonda." I just realized my jaw is sore from grinding my molars.

"Danny, you have every right to be upset. I mean, we both wish Silberg a slow, agonizing death. But you can survive this."

"How?"

"Tell me exactly what it is you're faced with. Keep it simple."

"What?"

"A brief summary of the problem. Humor me."

"My dead wife stole my money—"

"Some of your money."

"A shit-ton of my money, and now the man she cheated on me with is threatening to send me to prison if I make a move to get it back."

"So what?"

"Huh?"

"So what if it feels like the asshole's winning? You gonna waste the rest of your life crying about it?"

The fingernails of both clenched fists dig into my palms.

"You get to choose—have to choose—rot in prison or let the money go. Do you really need to ponder that for more than ninety seconds?"

"But the thought of Silberg—"

"Screw Silberg. This is a corner you painted yourself into, Danny."

"I want a second opinion."

"Okay," she says. "When Ana gets back, we'll drop Lylou at home and go see Lisa."

§

I park the Forester in the circular drive behind Lisa's Infiniti. The house, in a gated community along St. George's eastern foothills, looks to be less than a year old. Lisa answers the door and we follow her into a tiled foyer with clerestory windows twenty feet above us.

"Welcome to my home office," she says. "The office part is on the right."

We enter the inner sanctum and take chairs around a dark oval table. The ground floor office has French doors that open onto a seclusion garden complete with koi pond. There's also a small wet bar anchored by a De'Longhi Eletta espresso maker exactly like the machine I had refused to spend two grand on for Lorraine. No reception area, no cavernous conference room, but it's definitely a law office— luxurious carpet, solid walnut furniture, legal tomes filling built-in bookcases like a mini law library. It's small, but if impressing clients is the point of this place, it's working for me.

We take seats at the table and Lisa says, "What's going on?"

I stumble through the story of Danny breaking bad.

"I'm sorry, Daniel. It's a hot mess," Lisa says, "but you created it all by yourself. Not sure there's any more I can do for you."

"But what about—"

Lisa cuts me off with, "Any move we make, Silberg will just counter with a threat to hand over video evidence of the break-in to the authorities."

"There may be one strategy left," Rhonda says.

"We're listening," Lisa says.

Rhonda continues. "Jane Carneely claims Colin Silberg forced her to have sex."

For a few seconds, Lisa seems unable to speak, then, "Let me make sure I got this. The woman told you Silberg raped her?"

"Not raped," Rhonda clarifies. "She said the sex was payment for a favor."

"What favor?"

"A free boob job."

"This could be bigger than your garden-variety sexual harassment," Lisa says. She is suddenly smiling. "If someone can confirm it, we may just have him by the walnuts."

"So, we can blackmail him!" I effuse.

Lisa shows her palms. "Let's agree here and now that no one utters the B-word ever again."

"Agreed," Rhonda and I say in almost-unison.

Lisa continues in more cautious tones, "Even if there is some kind of substance behind it, what makes you think she'll let us use the information?"

"Jane's really angry at Silberg right now," Rhonda says, "and—"

"And what?"

"And," I interject, "I think she might have a little crush on Rhonda."

Lisa looks a bit confused. "Jane has a crush on Rhonda?"

"In any case," Rhonda says, "I think I'm the one who should talk to her."

"Give it a try if you want," Lisa says, "but don't use that forbidden word, and for God's sake don't— Sorry, Rhonda, you're an attorney, you know the hazards."

Chapter 28

Twenty-four hours later, we're back at Lisa's table, sipping steamed milk off frothy caramel lattes. "So, you talked to her?" Lisa asks.

"Yeah," Rhonda says. "But she's afraid of losing her job."

"Silberg could lose his license to practice medicine," I say. "Right?"

"He could and should," Lisa says. "But back to the key question, can we get Jane to cooperate?"

"She hates Silberg," Rhonda says. "But the woman's frightened as a fawn about going public."

"At least for now," Lisa says. "But if we can't convince her, Ash is facing the loss of his license and the clinic."

"The clinic?" Rhonda says.

"Yes," Lisa says. "The partnership agreement is very specific—if one of the partners has his license revoked, he forfeits his fifty percent share to the other. That was part of the urgency to clear Ash's name with DOPL."

"That's insane," Rhonda says. "Why would Silberg agree to something like that?"

"Because," Lisa says, "he planned to use it to get rid of Ash. In the words of John Lennon, 'Ain't karma a bitch?'"

"Don't think that was Lennon," I say. "In any case, Ms. K is coming back around to bite Silberg's lying ass, and the bitch's teeth ain't rubber."

"But remember, guys," Lisa says, "this is nothing but smoke in the wind unless Jane's on board."

Chapter 29

I'd gotten up to pee a couple of minutes ago. Not sure how I'd missed it the first two bathroom trips, but this time I notice a light on in the family room and come out to flick it off. Instead I discover Rhonda tickling the Mac's keyboard like a reporter about to miss a critical deadline.

"It's four in the morning, Rhonda."

"Uh-huh." She won't stop typing, doesn't even look up.

Not wanting to interrupt whatever zone she's in, I quietly brew myself a cup and settle into the recliner without further question or comment.

About the time I finish the coffee, she says, "Got it."

"Got what, exactly?"

"Just memorialized my discussion with Jane. Wrote down everything I remembered in as much detail as I could. Can I use your printer?"

"Of course," I say. "But I'm not sure I get it. Why did you go to all that trouble?"

"For the legal record. I'll get it notarized when the bank opens."

"Yeah, but it's secondhand. If Jane won't—"

"It's all we have for now, Danny. And I have an idea how we can leverage it."

§

"Thanks for coming, Freddy," Lisa says. "I think this is the first time you've deigned to visit my office. Do you approve?"

G. Frederick Warburton II sits across from Lisa and me at a table an eighth the size of the one back at his place.

"It's fine," he mutters.

"I thought Dr. Silberg would be joining us. He's not ill, I hope."

"He's in surgery. What's so important I had to drop everything and drive over here?"

"Thought you should be aware of this." Lisa taps the thin manila folder in front of her.

"Am I supposed to ask you what it is?" Can't tell if his churlish response is born of confidence or an attempt at covering concern.

"No need," Lisa replies. "It's a sworn statement that your client, Colin F. Silberg, provided cosmetic surgery in exchange for sexual favors and that—"

"Says who?"

"I don't have the patient's permission to disclose her or his name at this time."

"That's a hell of a serious allegation, Lisa. You expect me to respond without knowing who made it?"

Not sure about the ethics here. Every word Lisa has spoken is true—and designed to lead her adversary to the wrong conclusion. Indeed there is a statement in the folder, sworn and signed, not by the patient, but by Rhonda Horvath. Hearsay, if I remember my TV law. Don't know if the paper would be worth anything to a judge, but it's sure got Big G's attention.

"Believe me, Freddy, if we wind up in court, you'll get every disgusting detail. That's if we wind up in court."

"On behalf of my client, I most strenuously deny the allegation."

"That's mighty bold coming from someone who hasn't yet discussed the matter with Dr. Silberg," Lisa says. "Or just maybe...you already have. Did you see this coming, Freddy? Has Silberg confessed a crime to you?"

GFW 2.0 pushes his chair back and escapes the room without another word.

Once he's out the front door, I say, "God damn, Lisa. You could play poker for a living."

"Poker's no fun, the stakes are only money."

§

"Try and relax, Danny. I got this." Rhonda stands behind my recliner, gently massaging the knots out of my neck and shoulders, the gentle harmonies of Extreme's "More Than Words" playing in the background. I take a deep breath and blow it out—try to surrender to the moment, whatever the hell that means.

"These past few weeks have been a rowdy ride, haven't they?" she says.

I roll my head in a circle and something in my neck makes a sound like boots on gravel. "Rowdy is one word for it." What about terrifying, insane, or plain old shitty? My wife is dead, I have no job, and Silberg's getting away with three-quarter mil of my money.

"I'm not sure there's any more for me to do here," she says.

And of course, there's that. The only woman I've ever truly loved, my cousin, for God's sake, will soon be out of my life forever.

"How soon are you thinking about leaving, Rhonda?"

Her calming touch moves out to my deltoids and down my arms. After a minute or so, she steps around and sprawls across my lap. I'm surprised, but don't protest.

"Soon," she says.

"I love you, Rhonda," I breathe into her ear. Shiiit! Saying it out loud was stupid…and agonizing.

"I know, Danny." She wriggles further down in my lap.

"But—"

"Let's not rehash the buts. You're a good guy who would never do anything to hurt or disgrace his mother. I respect that…I guess."

"You guess?"

"And shacking up with your first cousin,"—she kisses me—"no matter how beautiful and sexy she is? That would be impossible for Aunt Martha to get her Christian mind around." She kisses me again. "Even though she lives three hundred miles away and might never know unless someone felt compelled to tell her."

"Rhonda, I…I wish things were different, that I could marry you tomorrow without shame or lies."

"I get it already." She pulls my head down and kisses me long and hard. "How about a roll in the hay? Our little secret."

"Not really interested." I beg to differ, says the turgid manhood pressing against her backside.

She stands, pulls me out of the chair and in the direction of my bedroom, cooing, "I want you to remember—for the rest of your uptight little life—what could have been."

I respond with the most difficult words my mouth has ever formed, "I can't, Rhonda. I…just…can't."

She retreats to the guest bedroom and through the open door I hear the unmistakable sound of a suitcase zipper. Minutes later, she's headed for the door.

"One more day, Rhonda, please. I need to be alone today, do some serious head clearing. Can we talk tonight?"

I get no verbal response, but she rolls her carry-on back into the bedroom. It's no guarantee she'll be there when I get back, but I choose to take it as a good sign.

I grab my car keys off the kitchen counter.

§

Four hours later, I'm making my way through the yard jungle. The front door is locked. *Good for you, Mom.* I press the bell and hear the eight-note chime that may be the most memorable connection to my childhood. Through the door, I can hear my mother wheezing and I feel bad about making her stand up.

We're soon settled, elbows on the old Formica table, hands steepled over steaming cups of rosehip tea.

"What a wonderful surprise," she says. "If I'd known you were coming, Daniel, I'd have made funeral potatoes."

I cringe. Funeral is pretty much the last word I want to hear from my ailing mother.

"Mom," I venture, "I need to tell you something."

"Okay."

"Sorry. This may be a little awkward."

271

Her smile flees and Mom's forehead wrinkles with concern. "Not sure what to say to that, Daniel. But if there's something you need to say, I guess you'd better go ahead."

I command my nervous knee to stop bouncing. It does not obey. "You know what a wonderful person Rhonda is."

"We already had this conversation, Daniel." Her voice is beginning to crack.

"We did, Mom, but—"

Mom's head sags onto her forearms and she commences crying. Physically, she's fragile as cracked crystal, but up until this moment, I thought she still possessed the emotional strength of the younger Martha Horvath. I step next to the chair, place my hand on her back now heaving with sobs, and wait.

After a minute or so, she rallies. "Daniel," she says, "y…you and—" Once again, Mom slips into sobs. But this time is different, her crying is backed by something like…laughter? Not a happy cackle, but a wheezy bark just this side of hysteria.

I lay my hands on hers and say, "Mom, are you okay?"

"Daniel." She struggles to continue. "You and Rhonda can never, ever, be together. Never."

"I'm sorry you can't accept it, but I'm not here to ask for permission."

"Daniel," she blubbers into her arms, "God forgive me, I, I…" Once more, the shuddering sobs overtake her.

I pat her hands, lean in and whisper in her ear, "It's all right, Mom. I'm right here."

"It's not all right. I, I…cheated on your father."

My sweet mother was unfaithful to Dad? My crazy dream-memory was real? I forget to breathe and my vision narrows to a dark tunnel. "Why?" I mutter.

"Your father could be so cruel, and somedays I just—"

"Of course, I understand completely, Mom. But why tell me now, after all these years?"

"Because...because...you and Rhonda."

Somewhere deep in my big, beautiful brain, the pieces are coming together. "Are you saying Dad might not be my actual father?"

"No, I mean, yes, I mean—"

"So there's a chance Rhonda and I are not related—at all."

"No, Daniel, I—" The hacking returns, stealing her speech.

"I can't imagine how painful it must be to rip open this ancient wound. I love you, Mom. Nothing could ever change that."

"But I...*cough*...I...*cough*...I cheated with...Deloy Horvath."

"Uncle Deloy?" The words hit like a cinder block ricocheting off my head. "Dad's brother?" The hit of elation, the hope I'd felt just moments ago, is gone in a puff of despair.

"Yes," she whispers into the tabletop. "Rhonda's father." My mother gives her head the saddest shake. "It lasted for almost two years, just before you were... There's no way to tell if you are..."

I get it, Mom. You can stop now. "Does Jocelyn know?"

"Your sister has no idea. Bernie was certain there'd been some kind of infidelity, but he went to his grave without a clue it was with his brother."

My immediate reaction is straight from the gut. "I wish to God I hadn't asked." But that was never really an option.

§

Mom's bizarre confession has recalibrated my entire mindset. Suddenly, the idea of Rhonda and me as a cousin-couple is almost comically trivial, but thank whatever gods may be we never took it further than a kiss.

I'm driving home to tell the woman I love I could be her brother. If that ain't a deal breaker, I don't know what is. Technically, half-brother, but I'm pretty sure the distinction won't give Rhonda a single shred of comfort. And the possibility that we might not be siblings? Doesn't mean a goddamned thing. The odds are straight-up fifty-fifty—that's a bet no one would take.

The cruise is set for just under the speed limit. I'm not in any hurry to get back, in no rush to have the conversation. The Forester crests a little hill, and the small town of Beaver comes into view. It's close to six p.m., and a few "city" lights, mostly fast food joints and gas stations, twinkle in the distance. Must have left the radio on—when the lost FM signal returns, the sudden sound of "Let It Be" gives me a start.

"Let it be? Fuck you, Paul McCartney!" I scream. "Fuck you and this whole fucking—"

The bouncy intro of "Help Me Rhonda" layers itself over my cursing and Beatles' music. I switch off the radio and grit

274

my teeth. I'll wait it out, let the call go to voicemail. But I can't stand it one second longer. "Hello."

"Hi. Danny. Thought you'd be back before this, so I, um, I'm just checking on you."

"Everything's fine, Rhonda," I lie. "Headed back from Salt Lake."

"Salt Lake? Why in the—? Tell me you didn't drive up there to ask your mother's permission to—"

"Rhonda," I interrupt, "we can't ever be together, you know, in that way."

The line holds silence for what feels like forever. "Of course, Daniel, of course." Her voice is dark and flat as a midnight two-lane. "We knew that all along, right?"

"I'll be home soon. Can you just—" But the line is dead.

§

The dashboard clock reads 8:30 when I press the button to close the garage door behind me. Once I'm inside the house, I call out, "Rhonda. You here?" But the only reply is Lylou's welcome home bark-whimper…from inside her crate. I walk over and kneel down. The second I open the wire door, she leaps out and smothers me with licks.

"Where's Mommy, Lylou? Did she run to the store?"

I imagine Lylou replying, "Run to the store? Are you a complete idiot?" Our dog stops with the kisses and heads for her water dish. Before I can stand, I notice something I'd missed before. Near the back of the enclosure sits a white envelope with one hand-scrawled word: Danny.

Not sure how much time has gone by, but I'm still on my knees, staring at the unopened missive on Lylou's blankie. I'm not stupid—I know it's not a shopping list.

"Thank you, Rhonda. I guess. You spared us both a talk I feared worse than long, agonizing death." I reach in for the envelope.

At a nearby wastebasket, I tear it once and watch the halves flutter to the bottom of the empty can.

Chapter 30

One more crank, next breath...one more crank, next breath... Gasping for my very life, cracked collarbone throbbing, I reach the top of the sandstone slab that looms over Church Rocks. The monolith feels like an old friend, a buddy who's determined to whip me into shape—or kill me. I unclip both feet and stand astride the bike's top tube, heart still racing like a hummingbird sipping Mountain Dew. It takes a couple of minutes to return my breathing to something near normal.

The next part should be simple—just swing my right leg back over the bar—but I'm still babying the sore shoulder. My shoe catches the saddle and I tumble sideways in a tangle of man and machine. Too exhausted to do anything else, I lie there for maybe three minutes. When my pulse feels like it's slowed to the mid-100s, I skootch out from under the wounded bike. Then I settle in to a four-point stance, two chamois-padded butt cheeks and the heels of my bike shoes. Once settled, I carefully rest scraped elbows on dinged-up knees.

To the east, far below, traffic flows mostly southbound along I-15. Here the high desert begins its slope to the northeastern end of the Mojave. The long downhill means vehicles are smooth and quiet, except the big rigs. The truckers engage their Jake brakes, the compressed exhaust exploding like rolling thunder through the heat-rippled air.

At least three miles beyond the interstate, Smith Mesa rises up from the desert floor. Even from a couple of miles away, the flat-topped massif dominates the scene like a Kilimanjaro with its jagged peak neatly sliced away. Dramatic rock formations and red-orange sand complete the panorama. But for the gray-green frost of endless sage, there's not much evidence of thriving life.

I look back to my bike resting on the lichen-laced rock and I do a quick damage survey—without getting up, of course. There are a half-dozen places where unforgiving stone has scraped the red to bare metal, but I don't see anything that would prevent me from pedaling back to the car—if and when the damn collarbone stops throbbing like a gigantic toothache.

The plan had worked for a while. When a guy is just this side of an infarct, it's impossible to think of anything except the next breath. But my respirations are slowly recovering, and the disturbing thoughts forcing their way out of my mouth.

"It's your own damn fault, Danny Boy. The thing with Rhonda was doomed from the start, but you were too stupid to let it go." I issue a snorty laugh. "Thank the gods we didn't do what I desperately wanted to do the night of the anatomy lesson!"

The memory of the night is suddenly back, and it's in full color, high-def. "Stop right there!" I command the growing bulge in my Spandex bike shorts.

§

"Toys on top, toys on top." I force down thoughts of Rhonda and repeat the incantation out loud, remembering to stop the car before I can total the expensive mountain bike on the low garage entry.

I unload, and the second I'm inside the house, an excited dog is all over me. I get down to Lylou's level, scraped-up knees creaking in protest. The only living thing on earth that loves me without judgment circle-dances, happy-barks, and lays a dozen wet kisses on my salty face. For the moment, at least, it feels like life might be worth living. We roll around in a mild version of roughhousing, then I stop and hold Lylou's big square head in both hands. "Too late for a walk, girl. It's dark outside."

She responds by running to her crate and wiggling inside with a joyous whimper. I'm guessing the only word that registered in that canine brain was walk. And dark sounds a lot like park. "Sorry, baby. Daddy's going to soak in the tub…and perhaps get good and drunk."

§

Morning clouds are rolling in and the temp drops enough that I put on the emergency sweatshirt I keep in the car. I didn't think to bring Lylou's sweater, but she seems fine, barking at a fat robin and sniffing the air for the latest news. Always before, I'd found the little Frenchie's enthusiasm irresistibly infectious. Not today. Today, all my slightly hungover brain can process is how much Rhonda loved the walks and how she must miss our baby girl.

About halfway through the second lap, I hear a familiar voice.

"Lylou! Lylou! I missed you so much." Ana Sophia runs over, and our dog—my dog—puts the walk on pause, rolling over for an enthusiastic tummy rub.

"Hello, Ana Sophia. It's nice to see you."

"It's good to see you, too, Mr....uh, uh."

"Danny. You can call me Danny."

"Mr. Danny, can I take Lylou for a walk all by myself?"

"May I come along?"

"I can do it all alone, remember?"

"I do remember, and I'm sure Lylou does too. You take the leash, and I'll just tag along with you two girlfriends."

"Speaking of girlfriends and stuff, where's Lylou's mommy today? I hope she's not sick or nothin'."

§

How many hours ago did I plop my ass into this old recliner? Enough, obviously, for the sun to set and the room around me to fade to near darkness. Probably ought to get up and turn on a light or two, but I'm sunk deep in the chair, Lylou asleep in my lap. And who even gives a shit? Speaking of which, there are a few reasons I can't just sit here forever— biological urges, of course, and the need to pour another shot of Fireball. But right now, pulling the side handle to unrecline would take more energy than I care to expend. And the thought of actually standing up? Fuck it. I'm way too busy feeling sorry for myself.

Ding-Dong.

"Go away," I mutter. "Didn't your mother teach you no lights means nobody's home?" Mother.

But Lylou jumps down and begins sniffing the threshold, barking delight at the prospect of new friends. The ringing repeats. And repeats. And repeats.

"Give the damn doorbell a rest." I struggle out of the chair, ready to give the Girl Scouts or the Mormons or whoever a piece of my foggy mind. But it's not a pair of white-shirted teenagers, it's Ash. The goddamn, worthless traitor, Ashan Bakri.

"We're here to check on you, Danny," he says.

Before I can tell him to piss off, Jeri steps around and shoulders her way into my house. Uninvited. He follows right behind. Uninvited. She flips on a light, and my eyes snap into a squint.

"You look like shit," Ash says.

Jeri tags in. "And the house is a disaster. When's the last time you ran a load of dishes?"

With the lights on, I realize there's nothing to be said in my defense, so I just stand here in the grip of aphasia, watching Jeri attack a pile of filthy plates.

Ash retrieves the old Kenmore canister vac from the coat closet and calls out "Alexa, play 'Waterloo,' max volume." The audio equivalent of cotton candy spins from the cylinder speaker. I hate ABBA, and he damn well knows it.

They just entered my domicile without express permission, right? That was Rhonda's definition of criminal trespass. I think. Should probably call 9-1-1. But instead I scorch my esophagus with two Fireball shots then sag back into the big chair...and restless sleep.

§

"Daniel? Daniel?" Jeri is nudging my good shoulder. "Think we're done here." I open my eyes to a home that looks and smells like it belongs to someone who actually gives a damn.

"Uh, thanks, I guess." Did I sleep a lot longer than I thought, or did Jeri and Ash summon help from small forest animals? Either way, I gotta pee like a Clydesdale.

I come out of the bathroom to a mild surprise. The Bakris are perched on kitchen chairs relocated next to my recliner.

"I thanked you already. Now get the hell out."

"Sit down, Danny. Please," Ash entreats. "We need to talk."

Can't muster the energy to tell Ash to fuck off, so I take my spot. The recliner's leather is still warm.

"Danny," Ash says, "I know how angry you must be about the termination."

"Ya think taking away a guy's livelihood might just piss him off?"

"I had no choice but to go along. You took advantage of your position to screw the help."

"Already told you," I say, "she practically begged me for it."

Jeri stammers, "I, I think I'll go out to the patio and straighten up a bit. Oh, and Daniel, I found a letter when I emptied the kitchen trash. It's torn, but I thought it may have wound up in the garbage by accident."

Somehow "mind your own damn business" comes out as "Okay. Just leave it on the counter."

"Outside, Lylou?" Jeri and the dog step through the recently-repaired patio slider.

As soon as Jeri shuts the door behind them, Ash says, "Jane said she only went along because you were her boss. Sexual harassment, cut and dried."

"Yeah, well, fuck her and the Jack Russell she rode in on. And you, too, Ash-hole."

He stands and rests a hand on my shoulder, the busted one. "Oww! Take your goddamn hands off me!"

"Sorry, buddy. Thought it was the other side."

"Fetch me a Percocet; bottle's next to the sink. At least it was before you two broke in and rearranged everything."

"Not with all that alcohol on board, Danny."

I respond with a barely audible growl.

From somewhere, Ash produces a yellow legal pad and pen. "Let's summarize where everything stands right now."

"Everything?"

"I only have one pad of paper. Maybe if we keep the list to just your employment, financial, and legal problems. Think those will be enough?"

"Very funny, Ash."

"Nothing funny about it," he says. "But I'm here to help, if you'll let me. Where shall we start?"

"With me explaining why it's much worse than you're imagining right now."

"Worse?"

"As in, looks like I'm going to prison worse."

"What the hell, Danny?"

It takes about ten minutes to convince Ash Jane had lied about the "coercion," ten more to bring him up to speed on just how deep my dung is, and another five to commit it to paper.

He holds out the pad, but I hesitate taking it from him, as if seeing it in black and white—or black and yellow in this case—might make it more real, force me to stop pretending that if I just keep on drinking and sulking, all the shit will somehow fix itself. Hmm, maybe putting me face to face with the realities was probably Ash's plan all along.

I take the pad and read:

Unemployed

Options-

Find new job
Open independent practice
Figure a way to come back to clinic employment
Screw it all and go full homeless
Find dirt on Silberg

<u>Silberg threatening criminal charge</u>
Options-
Do the time and start life over in three to seven years
Walk away from the clinic and the money
Hire a hitman
Find a way to extort the extortionist

<u>Silberg hiding my money</u>
Options-
Walk away (see above)
Hire a hitman/burglar (see above)
Blackmail Silberg (see above)

"Notice something interesting about the options we brainstormed?" Ash asks.

"No sure what you're—"

"The problems go away, all three of them, if we can find dirt on Silberg. But it's gotta be something big, not shoplifting a can of Shasta when he was in fifth grade."

"I told you, he made Jane set me up."

Ash seems lost in an unfocused stare. "We might be able to get your job back. But we really need something bigger."

"Is trading a boob job for fucking a patient-slash-employee big enough?"

"Holy shit!" Ash says. "That happened?"

"Jane Carneely said it did."

"If you can prove that, he loses his license." After a thoughtful pause, he continues, "And just like that, I own the clinic outright."

I'm rallying a bit. "Love for that to happen, Ash, but—"

"But what?"

"The license may be my only bargaining chip."

"Meaning?"

"The threat of losing it might bring him to the table. The whole thing's kind of like global nuclear war."

"Nuclear war?"

"If either of us actually pulls the trigger, it's mutually assured destruction."

Ash looks mildly confused. "Okay," he says. "I need to sleep on it. Lunch tomorrow?"

Chapter 31

The least I could do is thank Ash with a pastrami burger, so I'd set today's meeting at our old haunt. He surprised me by showing up with Lisa, and in spite of our determination to introduce her to the pleasures of the flesh—cow flesh, that is—she is eating grilled chicken from a large, undressed salad.

"She already said no," Lisa reminds. "What makes you think Jane might change her mind and stand up to Silberg?"

Ash swallows a bite of burger and says, "He fired her."

I say, "Old news, Ash."

"Ash," Lisa says, "did he consult you before the termination?"

"I first heard it from her, on her way to her car with a box of tchotchkes. She was pissed at me till I explained I knew nothing about it."

Lisa scratches an eyebrow with a thoughtful thumb. "Angry enough to testify against Silberg?"

Ash hikes his shoulders. "What's she got to lose?"

"Perhaps," I say, "her dignity."

Ash and I keep quiet while Lisa scribbles a few notes. "Think it's worth taking another run at her?" she asks.

"Hell, yeah," I blurt. "We just established she's joined me on the list of people who have nothing left to lose."

Lisa makes another note, then says, "It's unethical for me to approach her. God, I wish Rhonda were still here." She looks to me for an amen, but I bite my lip.

"I'll do it," Ash says.

"No way," Lisa says. "You owe a fiscal duty to the clinic."

A tiny tilt of his head says Ash agrees.

"Sounds like it's all up to me." Those are words I hoped never to hear myself say.

Lisa nods. "Yeah, I guess so. Think you can pull it off, Daniel?"

"Absolutely. Probably. Maybe."

"Tread lightly. You have plenty of problems without adding a retaliation charge. If the conversation starts going south, wish her a good day and get the hell out. Immediately."

"Okay. I'll make the call."

Chapter 32

W e must look a little silly, Dr. Horvath."

"Yeah. Not a dog in sight, and here we sit."

Not sure why she insisted on meeting at this location—without the dogs. Despite the bright sun, a fall breeze nips. It's early afternoon in the middle of the week, but hey, it's not like either of us had a job to go to.

"How is Charles doing, Jane?"

"He's fine. Where's Rhonda?" Her tone is brusque.

"She's in Oregon, had to get back to work."

Jane's voice softens. "Aww. I bet Lylou misses her."

"She really does."

"Why did you let them fire me, Dr. Horvath? You always said I was the clinic's best employee."

"It was all Colin, Jane. You know he fired me, too, right?"

Her mouth hangs open. "Dr. Silberg told me you quit."

"Nope. Terminated me for sexually harassing you. Said you told him our, uh, encounter was not completely consensual."

"You know it was consensual, but he made me say it wasn't. Looks like we both got screwed, eh?" The unintended joke hits her with a little tittering.

Silberg made her say it? Now we're on to something.

"Jane, if there were a way to get your job back, would you even want it?"

"I worked there almost ten years. That job and my work friends are all I have—had—and Charles, of course."

"Is that a yes?"

"Only if someone could promise Dr. Silberg would leave me alone and never talk to me again."

Oh yeah, Jane! You agree to testify against CFS, and we'll have him by the scrotal pouch so tight he won't be able to squeak.

"I think my attorney can make that happen. If—" I close my mouth and wait for her reaction.

"If what, Dr. Horvath?"

"If you affirm what you told Rhonda is true."

"What I told Rhonda?"

"About Dr. Silberg trading an augmentation mammoplasty for unwelcome sex."

Jane stares into her lap for a few uncomfortable seconds, then, "I didn't even want the surgery. But Colin kept telling me no one could ever love me with my flat chest."

Goddammit, Silberg. I hope there's a hell just so you can burn in it.

"I used to love running with Charles, but now it just hurts." Jane's crying. "Everyone stares at me, and I…I can't get through a day at work without feeling like my bra strap is cutting me in half. I never should have let him do it. I hate that man."

"Are you willing to swear in court that Dr. Colin Silberg performed the surgery in exchange for sexual favors?"

"In court? In front of people?"

"That's right. I have a very good attorney who can help you. A woman." I hand her Lisa Monaghan's business card.

She gazes at the card for several seconds, then takes a deep breath and huffs it out. "Not without Rhonda."

§

"So, what does she mean, she needs Rhonda?" Lisa asks.

Back in Lisa's office, I've just reported on the Jane thing.

"Jane needs to consult with Rhonda before she agrees," Lisa asks, "or she'd need Rhonda by her side to testify?"

"That wasn't clear, but I'll bet my cowboy boots it's the latter."

Lisa grins and says, "You have cowboy boots?"

"Long story. Anyway, saying those intimate things out loud and admitting what a fool she's been in front of a room full of strangers? Think she'd need some female support."

"Did you mention your attorney is a woman?"

"I did. Gave her your card. And she seemed fine with at least sitting down with you, 'woman-to-woman,' she called it."

"Good," Lisa says. "I'll use Rhonda's affidavit, put it in Jane's first-person. If she agrees everything is accurate, I'll ask her to read the statement a few times out loud. That might get her comfortable with the idea of testifying under oath."

"In court?"

"No," Lisa says. "A deposition in my office."

"With Colin's troglodyte attorney present?"

"Of course."

"I don't think she'll do it."

Lisa stares off, lost in thought, I assume. "Perhaps we can avoid that altogether. A videotaped affidavit may scare the boys enough to bring them to the—" She stops midsentence to answer her ringing phone.

"Lisa Monaghan," she says into the phone. "Take a couple of deep breaths, then tell me from the beginning."

The side of the conversation I can hear ends, "I completely understand why you're upset, Jane. Can you bring it to my office tomorrow at nine a.m.? Okay, okay. Now is fine. I'll text you the address and you come right over."

Less than twenty minutes later, Jane Carneely arrives, hair in tangles and the cheek scar throbbing red. Lisa invites her in.

"Jane," she says, "I think you know Dr. Horvath."

She offers a weak nod.

"He was here in a meeting when you called. Are you comfortable with him staying in the room?"

"I don't care," Jane mumbles. "Here it is." She hands over a wrinkled sheet which Lisa smooths out against the edge of the maple table.

"That son of a bitch!" Lisa says, then pushes the paper to me.

Western States Adjustment Bureau
444 W. Paseo Verde
Henderson, NV 89183

Dear Ms. Jane Carneely,
The following bill from the Red Rocks
Multispecialty Clinic has been consigned to us
because of nonpayment:

Augmentation mammoplasty $4,036.16
Interest and fees accrued to date $3,184.34
Total Payable to Western States Adjustment
Bureau, Inc. $7,220.80

340 days past due
To avoid legal action, including garnishment of
earnings, please remit
no later than 14 days from date of this letter.

Thank you,
S. D. Trager, Assistant Manager, Collection

"That slimy son of a bitch!" I blurt.

"Do I really have to pay?" Jane blubbers.

Lisa says, "Leave the letter with me and don't give it another thought. This is nothing more than a ploy, and frankly, the sleaziest one I've seen in my legal career."

"Can't you just subpoena the clinic's records?" I ask. "They should show Jane was never billed."

"That's what they should show. But at this point, Daniel, you really think that's what we'd find?"

I feel my jaw clench. "Of course not. That slimy son of a—"

"We already established that."

"Yeah, okay. Now what?"

"Jane," Lisa says, "are you ready to sign a sworn statement and start preparing your testimony?"

"I, I…I need Rhonda." She's beginning to sound like a toddler. "Rhonda's the only one that understands."

Lisa produces a phone and says, "You can talk to her right now, if she's—"

"Not on the phone. I need Rhonda here."

§

After having spent fifteen futile minutes attempting to calm Jane and talk her out of the must-have-Rhonda-here mindset, Lisa finally says, "I'm so glad you came over, Jane. I know how upsetting this must be."

"It sure is."

Lisa opens her arms, and Jane falls into them, staining the lawyer's silk blouse with her tears. They stand like that for several seconds, then Lisa pats Jane's back and pulls out of the hug. "You try not to fret. I'm going to fix everything. I promise."

Jane produces a tissue and blows her nose with a decidedly unsexy honk.

That's one hell of a promise, Lisa. Hope you can deliver, for all of our sakes.

"Thanks, Lisa," Jane says. "You'll let me know when Rhonda gets here?"

Lisa escorts the disheveled young woman to the front door, then returns to the conference room.

"Want to call her right now, Daniel? Or maybe wait to…"

"I, uh, sort of can't make the call."

"What? Why not?"

"It's kind of—"

She stares at me like she's divining something hidden behind my eyes.

"Omigod, you…and Rhonda? That's why she left so abruptly!"

Goddammit, Lisa, just let it go. "Whatever. I'll text you the number."

"I have it, remember?"

"Lemme know what she says," I say, on my way out the door.

§

"Give me just a second," I yell in the direction of my ringing phone. Lylou and I had fallen asleep on the floor, the pup lying on my outstretched right arm. I reach for the cell with my left hand and the movement sends shocks of pain radiating from the wounded shoulder.

"Wake up, baby. Time to move." I free the good arm and grab the phone. "Hello."

"You okay, Danny?" Lisa's voice says. "You sound kind of—"

"Sorry, Lisa. Took me a minute to get her off me."

"I don't even want to know."

"Lylou. Fell asleep across my arm." The one that's still sting-tingling like a finger in a light socket.

"Like I said, don't even—"

"Remember Lylou, our French bulldog?"

"Ours?"

"Mine, I guess. What's up?"

"Rhonda agreed to babysit Jane, so I'm flying her down late Friday. Right now her plans are to go back sometime Sunday."

I don't have an immediate response.

"You still there, Daniel?"

"Yeah, uh, got it."

"I assumed she'd stay at your place, if that's—"

"I'll book her two nights at the Hampton."

Chapter 33

Come in, Daniel." We step into the meeting room where a video camera on a tripod is pointed across the table. Lisa clips a wireless lavalier mic to the collar of Jane's baggy sweatshirt.

"Hello, Jane," I say.

"Hi, Lylou!"

Jane pushes her chair back, kneels on the carpet and clucks, "I missed you, sweet girl." She hugs the Frenchie around the neck and says, "Your mommy is going to be so happy to see you."

Lisa leans in and whispers, "Brilliant move, Daniel."

It wasn't a move. Lylou would never forgive me if she found out Rhonda was in town and I didn't hook them up.

"Lylou! Sweetest!" Rhonda comes through the door and joins Jane in loving up the pup. She takes our dog's face in her hands and purrs, "I missed little Lylou so much."

Contending emotions are playing tug-of-war, and I'm the frazzled rope. I ache to take Rhonda's face in my hands and tell her I've missed her like an amputated limb, but saying it out loud is unthinkable.

Lisa allows a few minutes for the mother-child reunion. It's a glorious moment, to be sure. Just wish someone would at least acknowledge that I'm in the same room.

"Okay then," Lisa says, "let's get started, if you're ready, Jane."

"Can Lylou stay?" Jane asks.

Rhonda looks my way without speaking.

"Of course," I reply. "I'll keep her right here by my—"

"Not him," Jane says with finality. "Just Rhonda and the dog."

It's hard not to take it personally. But, come on, why would Jane want an ex-lover in the room with the things she's about to say? Without a word, I turn for the door.

"Danny," Rhonda says, "how about later we take Lylou to the park?"

"Um, sure" comes out of my mouth. I try to make it sound like no more than lunch plans with Ash, but in my mind, I've already begun to count the minutes until the three of us will take one last walk together.

§

"Her ear is healing well," Rhonda says.

Dressed in her black sweater with orange pumpkins, Lylou guides us along the Tawa Pond pathway. The setting sun gilds the eastern mountains, but we are already in cool shadow. I zip my jacket higher around my neck.

"Wimp," Rhonda says. "You call this cold?"

"It is for around here." I force a smile. So far, we're doing a good job of keeping everything smartass casual. "Thanks for flying down on short notice."

"Happy to help."

"So, how've you been?" Do I really want to know? I wish for her to be happy, I truly do, but...

She gives her head a couple of shallow nods, then says, "I'm okay. You know, back to real life, work and all that. How about you?"

"Well,"—I leak a nervous laugh—"guess it depends on how the meeting with Jane went."

"She held my hand under the table for the entire taping," Rhonda says. "But she was credible, did a really good job of explaining the sex-for-surgery arrangement and the other abuse." She snickers. "I'd love to be a horse fly on the wall when Silberg and his crooked attorney watch the video. I predict some big-time brick shitting."

Lylou is pawing at something on the grass. "What you got there, baby?" Rhonda asks.

"Looks like what's left of a little fish," I say.

"Yuck! Lylou. Drop it, leave it be." The Frenchie turns away from the carcass and trots on. "Good girl. Mommy loves her sweet puppy."

I say, "Been doing some thinking, Rhonda."

"And?"

"Would you like to take her home to live with you?"

"Lylou? With me in Oregon?"

"She misses her mommy," I say. "Every night she searches the entire house hoping to find you."

I know in this moment Rhonda aches to scoop up the little bulldog and dash for the airport before I can change my mind, but she does not respond.

"I need to tell you something," I say. A battle rages inside me. Almost more than anything, I want to blurt out, 'Maybe the cousin thing shouldn't have kept us apart. I haven't stopped loving you, but there's something else, something so much bigger, and it means we can never, ever, worlds without end, be together." But a single step down that revelatory path would lead her to a mind-shattering realization—she shared a passionate kiss with a man who may well be her brother. And that's a poisonous pit I cannot, will not plant in her mind.

"Tell me what?"

"It's just, I wish things were different."

"You wish?" Her tone is suddenly tight, angry. "You had your chance and blew it all to hell."

"No. I can't. We can't."

Rhonda's head sags. Without looking up from the pavement just ahead, she mumbles, "Drop it. Leave it be." The command is not meant for Lylou.

For several minutes we walk in silence, interrupted only by our doggy barking at a quail. Then Rhonda stops walking and turns to me. "Danny, I, I suppose it's all for the best. Still friends?" We seal it with an A-frame hug and pats to the back.

Perhaps someday I could learn to love her like a devoted brother cares for his sister. *Who the hell are you kidding, Danny Boy?*

§

"See that hole?" Ash is pointing at a tiny flat plug just below my TV screen. "Just stick it in there...and make sure it's right-side-up."

Apparently, my TV is smart. Once the thumb drive is securely inserted, Ash works some magic with the remote, and a picture fills the screen—Jane seated at Lisa's conference table.

"Okay," I say. "Roll it."

Twenty minutes later, Ash turns the TV's power off, and we both sit staring at the dark screen. Jane had surprised me, answering Lisa's questions thoroughly without notes, stopping just once for a sip of water and a couple of times to gather her thoughts. Of course, I'd already known most of the story, but hearing it in Jane's voice was chilling. Colin Silberg is no ordinary asshole, he's a fucking sociopath.

"Have Silberg and his attorney seen this?" Ash asks.

"Lisa gave Fat Freddy a copy yesterday."

"Holy shit," Ash says. "Part of me wants to watch again. I mean, there's so much disgusting stuff in there that I feel like I may have missed something important."

"If you really want to."

"Better not. One more viewing and you'd have to stop me from going over and putting a sharp object in Silberg's demented head."

"One more viewing, and I'll drive. Stop at Walmart for an ice pick."

"I'm sorry, Danny," he says. "I owe you an apology for not believing in my friend. And the clinic owes Jane—and you—your jobs back. At a minimum."

"Thank you, brother. That means a lot."

"And of course," he says, "Colin Fucking Silberg should never be allowed to touch another patient as long as he lives."

I wish, Ash. I wish it could go that way. But that's not the plan.

Chapter 34

L isa suggested a suit, but today it's jeans, a pale blue river shirt, and my trusty Salomons—I'm well beyond caring about good impressions. I ignore a fleeting temptation to calm my jagged nerves with a Fireball shot, but it's nine thirty a.m., and that's a line I've not crossed. Yet.

"Lylou," I call. "I need my sweet little—" But she's at Lisa's place with Rhonda, of course.

The glass I fetch from the cupboard is spotless. Thank you, Jeri. I'm on my way to the water cooler, looking around the room for nothing in particular, when it grabs my attention. Both halves of Rhonda's envelope, each bearing yellow Rorschachs of dried garbage mustard. Since the day Jeri rescued it from the trash, I'd intended to tear it into smaller pieces and consign it one last time to the shit-can. But with my feelings raw as road rash, I've avoided even looking in its direction. Today I tie up loose ends and finally move on, so what the hell?

I pick up one piece of envelope, shake it till the half-sheet drops out, then repeat. After unfolding the halves and sliding them together, I see it's a copy of a webpage headed *23andMe—Rhonda Horvath*. Rhonda took the DNA test?

The subhead reads: *Relatives in Common.* My legs wobble and I grab the counter to steady myself. Siblings or cousins? The crumpled papers in front of me will settle it once and for all. But it doesn't really matter, does it? Either way, there is no Rhonda and Danny. "Fuck it," I say to the empty room. "I don't even want to know."

But my eyes mutiny and I read on— *Mary Ann Chritchlow, half-sibling.* I take a few breaths, then read every word…carefully… deliberately. Then I read it again. And again. I've never heard of a Mary Ann Critchlow. She took the test a few weeks after I did, but Daniel Bernard Horvath, my name, does not appear anywhere in Rhonda's report. Not half-sibling. Not cousin. Nothing. "But how is that even…" There must be a simple explanation, but right now adrenaline fogs my brain. And I can't be late for the most important meeting in my life.

§

"I hate this place."

"Me too, Daniel," Lisa says. The elevator dings, and the door slides open. We step into the hallway and pause in front of a tall wooden door signed:

Warburton Warburton and Stignell.

Conference Room Two

"As if there's a number one," I sneer.

"It'll take just a few minutes to wrap this up, then you'll never have to see the inside of WWS for the rest of your life."

"Lisa, tell me again I'm doing the right thing here."

"You're doing the right thing, Daniel, I promise. You were lucky to get the offer; it's frankly more than we could have hoped for."

"Of course," I sigh. "But it still feels like indentured servitude."

"Stop with the whining. You're keeping your job and getting a pile of money…minus my fee, of course."

"Getting my own money back."

"Oh, and that little matter of not going to prison? You should be worshipping at my feet."

"Sorry, Lisa. You're absolutely right."

I push the door open with my good arm. Silberg and Warburton stand waiting.

"Dr. Horvath," Freddy says, extending his right hand. Out of habit I shake it, then immediately wish I'd thought to bring a little bottle of sanitizer.

After he and Lisa shake, Freddy says. "Please sit down." My lawyer and I take places quickly, before anyone can suggest shaking hands with Colin Fucking Silberg.

The attorneys spread a few papers on the table and Warburton says, "This shouldn't take long. Both parties—"

"Where's Ash?" I demand.

"Dr. Bakri had a medical emergency."

"Bullshit."

Warburton ignores the vulgarity and continues. "He's read the agreement and concurs in principle. I'll obtain his signature and messenger an original to Ms. Monaghan by end of business."

"Before going any further," Lisa says, "I'm going to take a couple of minutes to summarize."

I don't need a summary, Lisa. I just want the goddamn thing done. But before I can speak, she touches an index finger to the document and says, "Dr. Silberg agrees to pay Dr. Horvath $750,000."

"Which the parties agree is not owed," Warburton says, "but rather a signing bonus as part of a five-year employment contract with the clinic."

I clear my throat to catch Lisa's eye, then give her the circular "move it along" hand signal.

"Dr. Horvath agrees to withdraw his complaint to the Utah Division of Occupational and Professional Licensing. And Dr. Silberg affirms he has no cause for any criminal complaint against Daniel, er, Dr. Horvath."

Warburton holds up a thumb drive, brushed bronze on a silver keyring. "This is the only remaining copy of certain, ahem, video footage. It's not mentioned in the contract, of course, but I'll hand it over to Ms. Monaghan the moment the parties have signed."

"What about Jane?" I blurt.

"Huh?" Freddy looks like he just found a spider in his SpaghettiOs.

"Jane Carneely. She getting her job back?"

"Not your problem," Colin mutters.

"No. It's yours. And unless you—"

"She's been offered a, you know, her own employment contract," Freddy says.

"Okay, but what about—"

"Drop it, Daniel." Lisa says it with finality. "Let's get this done."

Freddy pulls paper clips off both copies of the contract, moves the signature pages from the back to the front, slides the stacks to Silberg, and taps near the bottom. "Just sign here." His sausage finger moves to the second stack. "And here."

But Colin is staring out the window to the rocky bluff. Right elbow on the table, he holds a Cross ballpoint, flat-black with a gold pocket clip, near the side of his head, clicking repeatedly.

What the fuck, man? You gonna sign it or not?

"Three-quarters of a million," he mutters to himself. "That is a hell of a lot to just walk away from." A few more clicks. "And, God, would I love to see Horvath in an orange jumpsuit."

If you back out now, Silberg, they'll be adding aggravated homicide to my breaking and entering charge.

Two more clicks. "Fuck it." He scribbles his signature on both pages and slides the piles to me.

Lisa reaches for the contracts and gives the signatures a close inspection, probably confirming the pervert wrote Colin F. Silberg, not Lick My Balls.

Now it's my turn. I hover the pen tip just over the first signature line and try without success to clear a phlegm nugget from the back of my throat.

Shiiit. Thought this would be easier. I get my money, keep my job, avoid going to jail, for God's sake. Signing as fast as I can is the very definition of a no-brainer. It means I get my old life back—my safe, predictable, meaningless old life back.

I swallow the lump and sign both copies. Freddy hands over the thumb drive, and Lisa zips it into a pocket of her briefcase. Whew! No prison time for Danny Boy.

The second I set the pen back on the table, the Beach Boys ringtone breaks the silence.

"Rhonda? Is Lylou okay?"

"She's fine, Danny." The sound of her voice shoots through me like a hit of methamphetamine. I'm guessing on the meth thing. "Sorry to interrupt. I have to leave by two o'clock at the latest or I'll miss my flight. I didn't want Lylou to be alone for very long."

"We're about to wrap up. If I'm not there, just leave her in the crate. Okay?" I end the call without waiting for an answer.

The others in the room are staring at me. Is it possible they can sense the electrical current now buzzing through my brain and body? And why would I give a shit if they did?

The room is suddenly stifling as a sauna, and I can't draw a full breath. Without permission, my mind leaps back to the confusing papers on my kitchen counter, and it hits me like a stray golf ball. Whatever permutations of adultery, adoption, or abandonment might explain it, Rhonda and I are not siblings, not cousins, not anything but two people in love—if I haven't already lost her.

I leap to the window end of the table and pick up a thousand-dollar chair, not an easy task with one arm in a sling.

"Free at last, free at last, free at last!" I scream at the top of my lungs. Then I throw the heavy seat at the plate glass. I'm half expecting it to just bounce off, but with a boom just this side of thunder, steel and leather explode the massive window and sail into the desert afternoon. The room's crushing atmosphere rushes out, replaced by authentic air...wholesome and warm, tanged by nearby sage.

The three onlookers stand like lawn gnomes while I grab both contract copies. It takes six seconds to tear up the papers and send the shreds out the ragged gap in the glass.

A breeze catches the oversized confetti and swirls it in strange circles.

"Danny," Lisa says, "are you clear that you just tossed $750,000 out that window?"

My face is stretched into a grin so wide it hurts. "Clear as vodka."

"Then I hope you're happy." There is not a hint of sarcasm in her voice.

Mouth agape, Colin Fucking Silberg stays frozen—for three seconds. "Give back the video," he screams, diving across Lisa and grabbing for her briefcase. "This fucker's going to jail."

She yanks it away. "No," Lisa says. "But you very well might, after you lose your license to practice medicine."

Thank God she has a two-fisted death grip on the handles. My freedom—and Silberg's downfall—depend on the tiny memory drive zipped into a side pocket.

In the second before I can reach him, he snarls, "You bitch," and slugs the side of Lisa's face with a balled-up fist. The impact snaps her head nearly a quarter turn, but she hangs on.

I step away from the window and take a wild swing in Silberg's direction, by sheer luck connecting with his jaw. Can't tell if the resulting crunch is his mandible or my metacarpals. Either way, he flops back and slides down the chair, puddling onto the floor.

Lisa's reeling a bit, but still has the case. I take her elbow and help her to her feet.

Warburton makes a half-assed attempt to approach, but I shoot him a violent glare, and he thinks better of it. "Who's going to pay for my window?" he whimpers.

I fill my lungs with fresh air, spin on one heel, and Lisa and I stalk out.

Just before the heavy door closes behind us, Lisa calls back, "The man just gave you three-quarters of a million dollars. That should more than pay for a window, you sleazeball."

§

One ring and my call goes straight to voicemail. Shiiit! "Rhonda," I say into the phone, "I'm in the car, headed to Lisa's. Wait for me. Please. I'll be there as fast as I can." A glance at the dashboard clock: 1:43.

1:49. A single ring, then direct to voicemail again. "I love you, Rhonda. Please don't get on the plane." Is she on a long call? Has she blocked my number?

1:53. If Rhonda's gone by the time I get to Lisa's, it'll be too late. So I change plans, steer up the nearest on-ramp and power onto I-15 southbound. The St. George airport is on the Arizona border, about twelve miles ahead.

An attempt at another call is answered by, "The voicemail box is full."

2:11. My little SUV leans hard as I exit the freeway too fast. The overhead sign on Highway Seven says, "St. George Regional Airport 3.8 miles." Damn! In my panic, I'd forgotten the airport was another four miles after the interstate exit.

2:14. The Subie's tires screech me to a stop along a curb marked:

PASSENGER PICKUP ONLY
DRIVER MUST REMAIN WITH VEHICLE

I jump out, leaving the engine running and my car door wide open.

"So sorry. This is an emergency." I push my way to the front of a seven-person line and blurt, "The two thirty flight to Portland. Am I—"

A sturdy black woman manning the counter snarls, "Sir. You need to go back to the end of the line. Now!"

I hesitate for a split second.

"Sir! Do I need to call security?" I turn to walk away and hear her voice behind me. "That plane has already left the gate."

In a head-down shamble, I make my way back to the pickup curb. The black Subaru is nowhere in sight.

§

"Daniel? Mr. Horvath?"

"Uh huh."

"I'm James, your Uber driver." James is a seventy-plus David Crosby wannabe, right down to the bushy white mustache and knit watch cap. I settle in to the back seat of his immaculate 1990-something Buick LeSabre, he confirms the address, and we pull into airport traffic. One of my late dad's favorites, Crosby, Stills & Nash's "Wasted on the Way," is playing through a pretty good aftermarket sound system, but this particular song is just adding to my anxiety.

"Would you like a mint or a bottle of cold water, Daniel?"

"No!" I bark. "And turn the goddamn music off."

In the rearview, the driver's crinkled eyes reflect surprise and disappointment. "What the hell, man?"

"James," I say. "It's James, right?"

"Yeah," he mutters.

"I'm sorry for snapping at you, James. It's not you. I'm going through the most insane day of my life and I just need to sit here quietly and think. Okay?"

"Whatever," he says, turning the music off. "I'll have you home"—James glances at the GPS screen on his oversized phone—"in twenty-four minutes." But the address in his system is not my home. Lylou is waiting for me at Lisa's.

You told the man you needed to think, so take a deep breath and start thinking, dammit. A few deliberate breaths later, my heart rate slows a beat or ten. *That's right, settle down, Danny Boy. Rhonda didn't leave to colonize Mars, she's just flying home to Oregon. At some point, you'll be able to get a call through.*

But a call won't do, will it? I need to look straight into those gold-speckled eyes when I tell her, read in her perfect face if we're to be or if I've smashed everything into so many pieces it can never fit back together.

For a moment I consider telling the old guy to turn around so I can catch the next flight to Oregon. But I can't just abandon our Lylou.

§

I'm finally on Lisa's doorstep. Behind me, squealing tires and the roar of the Buick's big V8 signal Grandpa Crosby's need to put some pavement between him and what was no doubt his worst fare of the week.

"Daniel?" Lisa seems surprised to see me. "Are you all right?"

"I'm, uh..." My brain is awash in a bizarre admixture of hormones, and in this moment, I can't quite remember why I'm standing at my lawyer's open door.

"Come in, Daniel." She turns her head to reveal a cheek overtaken by an angry purple lump.

"My God, Lisa! Your face."

"Looks worse than it is. Thanks to you." She guides me by the elbow to the nearest chair.

"Lylou," I manage. "Here to pick up our dog—my dog."

The puzzled look returns to Lisa's damaged face. "Rhonda took her."

A board to the forehead could not have hit harder than this news. "What the hell? I mean, I guess I did tell Rhonda Lylou could go live with her in Oregon. But she never answered one way or another, so I assumed—" Shiiit! Is it too late to change my mind and get back my old life—and the seven hundred fifty-fucking-thousand dollars? But the bedrock truth is the old Daniel Horvath is dead and gone. The sale of my home is closing in a week, and the new Danny is moving on, with or without Rhonda.

"I'm so sorry, Daniel." Lisa's voice yanks me from a sort of trance. "I thought you knew. Can I get you anything? A cappuccino?"

"Got time to give me a ride home?"

"Where's your car?"

My chin drops to my chest and I shake my head. "Some impound lot. I hope."

"I'll get my keys."

§

"I'm worried about you," Lisa says. "Sure you're going to be okay, Daniel?"

"Of course," I lie. "Thanks for the ride."

I give Lisa a feigned smile and tiny nod as she backs out and drives away. Then, reaching for house keys in my right front pants pocket, my fingers find nothing but cotton. Shiiit! The airport. The keys. In the ignition. Engine running. Not sure why I assumed earlier it had been towed—stolen is more likely. Anyway, maybe, just maybe, I left the new patio slider unlocked and can get in through the back.

My feet do a slow shuffle across the driveway and into the side yard while I study the ground below me, hoping, longing, to spot some reminder of our blissful family hours with Lylou—an abandoned chew toy perhaps, or even a little mess deposited on the blue-gray buffalo grass.

I'm almost to the rear corner of the house when something stops me midstride—a muffled, happy woof.

On the lawn just beyond the patio, Rhonda and Lylou are having a playful wrestle. Neither has noticed me yet, so I stand and watch while a tingle blooms in the center of my chest and gradually spreads through my torso, then limbs, then to toenails and fingertips. This is it. Everything, everything depends on the next few seconds.

"Hey, Danny," Rhonda calls. I want to hear those lips speak my name every day for the rest of my life. "Lylou, run over there and give Daddy a wet one right on the mouth."

I drop to my knees, then convulse in laughter when our little girl does exactly that.

Rhonda steps over and says, "Good dog. Now go fetch." She tosses a raggedy half-stuffed gorilla across the yard and Lylou gallops after it.

I open my helpless, hopeful arms and Rhonda falls into them, instantly erasing every doubt, every fear, every disappointment of a lifetime. We pull each other in for a deep, lingering kiss, two bodies pressed together till they seem to melt into one.

When we finally, reluctantly, break for a breath, I whisper in her ear, "I cannot live one more day without you. Will you marry me?"

"No," Rhonda says.

"No?"

"No, as in, I won't marry you."

"But we just share the most wonderful—"

"How about," she says through the sweetest smile, "we start out as best friends—who get it on once in a while."

"Yes, my dear. That's perfect."

"But I can't spend the rest of my life in St. George, Utah."

I break into a laugh. "There's nothing keeping me here."

"Your job?"

"I threw it out the window. Literally. Got room for me in Timmalook?"

"I'm afraid," she says, wrinkling her forehead, "we'd have to share a bedroom. And you might get tired of the walks with a certain little dog." The W word sends Lylou into happy circles, and Rhonda says to her, "We'll take you to the park, sweet baby. But for the next hour or two, you'll have to entertain yourself. Mommy and Daddy have urgent unfinished business inside."

§

"Lose the shorts, LeBron. "

Rhonda is in my bed. She lies beneath a thin white sheet that reveals every voluptuous curve. A sweet smile crinkles her face next to her eyes, those amazing gold and green orbs that stare into mine without blinking.

She rolls onto her side, and as I slide in next to her, I slip an arm around her waist. She wriggles her body till she's pressed against mine, back to chest, rump to junk, and knees to knees.

"A friendly cuddle?" I ask.

"Oh, hell no." Rhonda extricates herself and turns, that perfect face inches from mine. We kiss…and kiss…and kiss, not with desperation, but in a slow, lingering way that seems to acknowledge that a lifetime of kisses lies before us.

"What do you think, Danny? Time to live out our little fantasy of spending the night riding like a rodeo queen?"

"In that scenario," I say, "are you the rodeo queen—or am I?"

"We'll take turns. Me first."

I roll onto my back and say, "Hop into the saddle, Missie. Best find somethin' to hold on to, 'cause this ain't no eight-second ride."

§

Quite a while later, Rhonda says, "Is this the part where we light up cigarettes?"

I begin to extricate myself from a glorious tangle of arms and legs.

"That stuff is only in the movies." I make it out of bed and lean over for another kiss. "This is not a movie, it's real. And it's forever."

I step out of the bedroom and return with our dog at my heels. When Lylou spies Mommy, she takes a running leap…and makes it all the way onto the bed for the very first time. "We made it, girl," I mutter.

"What's that?"

"Nothing." I join my family—what a wonderful ring that has—and the three of us make a happy pile of tussling and teasing among the joyfully disheveled sheets.

Chapter 35

A few minutes ago, I'd exited I-84 and parked our Subaru—thank God it had only been impounded—in the Memaloose Rest Area just outside tiny Mosier, Oregon. We'd driven through heavy rains since Boise, but the sun is finally out, sending wisps of steam up from the fenced Pet Relief Zone where our brown baby zigzags across the squelchy grass. With no apparent thought to toileting, she seems determined to make the most of the time outside her travel crate. Wish I could help her understand we're less than three hours from Tillamook—and all that that means.

I take Rhonda's hand as we gaze down from the bluff to the sun-crinkled surface of the Columbia River, a vast horseshoe a full mile across.

She moves closer, and I put my arm around her shoulder. "In all the confusion and rush to get out of town," she says, "I never got to ask you—why the sudden change of heart?"

"Thank God, the universe, or whatever—you're not my sister!"

"Sister? What the hell are you—?" Then her expression changes as quickly as a flipped light switch. "Aunt Martha told you about her and my dad."

"You knew about it?"

"The day after I got back to Tillamook, I drove down to see my father; he's in an Alzheimer's facility in Gresham."

"Rhonda, I'm so sorry."

"Actually, I lucked out, found him in a rare moment of lucidity. I knew I might not have much time, so I got right to it, confronted him with the report and, confession being good for the soul, he spilled his guts."

"About the affair?"

"Affairs. Three, as best he could recall."

"Wow. But how does that explain—"

"The rest of the Deloy and Belinda story," Rhonda says, "is that somehow my mother caught him out. Can you imagine how furious she must have been?"

"Aunt Belinda knew about him and my mom?"

"She never knew the women's names, thank God. But she was certain he'd been unfaithful—and decided to exact her vengeance."

I do a quick visual check—Lylou is finally squatting. "Vengeance?" I say, turning back to Rhonda. "What did she—"

"She had herself a one-night stand and rubbed it in his face."

"Oh, my God," I gulp. "She literally—?"

"Figuratively," Rhonda says, rolling her eyes to the Oregon sky. The word is accompanied by an elbow to my ribs. "I asked if he knew the man's name, but before he could answer, Dad slipped back into a parallel dimension. Whoever the adulterous asshole was, that man has to be my biological father."

"Adulterous assholes," I muse. "That could be the name of our family tree."

Rhonda turns to face me. "No, Danny," she says. "Our family tree begins now, just you, me, and Lylou." We seal it with a full-body embrace and long, soul-satisfying kiss. "Best friends," she whispers in my ear, "who get it on—a lot."

AUTHOR'S NOTE

My wife Nancy devours romantic comedies one after the other. So I paid close attention the day she surprised me with, "What this world needs is a rom-com about people who may—or may not—be cousins. And if the story were to be told from the point of view of a male doctor who swears like a longshoreman, so much the better."

"And his cheating wife dies on the first page?" I prompted.

"Of course, dear. Now go lock yourself in your office and make it so."

ACKNOWLEDGEMENTS

Many thanks to talented friends and family without whom you, dear reader, would not hold this book in your hand—or ebook reader.

First and foremost is my wife. Thank you, Nancy, for tolerating untold hours alone while your husband was in the next room alternately cursing and laughing like an idiot.

I am also deeply indebted to Brenda Lowder, Karla M. Jay, Brent Blaisdell, and Brad Lowder for reading and critiquing early drafts. Your input made the finished product better.

I am fortunate to meet regularly with a critique group of brilliant—and nonjudgmental—writers. Thank you, David Tippets, Ericka Prechtel, Sherri Curtis, Linda Orvis, Richard Casper, and Karla Jay.

Special thanks to the crazy talented Scott Perry for the cover design, and to editors Ann Riza and Ann Suhs, aka the Happily Editing Anns.

www.ingramcontent.com/pod-product-compliance
Lightning Source LLC
Chambersburg PA
CBHW030602180626
46816CB00005B/1637